SKIN HOUSE

Skin House

a novel by
Michael Blouin

[ANVIL PRESS • VANCOUVER]

Anvil Press Publishers Inc.
P.O. Box 3008, Main Post Office
Vancouver, B.C. V6B 3X5 CANADA
www.anvilpress.com

Library and Archives Canada Cataloguing in Publication

Title: Skin house / a novel by Michael Blouin.
Names: Blouin, Michael, 1960- author.
Identifiers: Canadiana 20190088923 | ISBN 9781772141184 (softcover)
Classification: LCC PS8603.L69 S55 2019 | DDC C813/.6—dc23

Cover design by Derek von Essen
Interior by HeimatHouse
Author photo by Michaela Rutherford-Blouin
Represented in Canada by Publishers Group Canada
Distributed by Raincoast Books

The publisher gratefully acknowledges the financial assistance of
the Canada Council for the Arts, the Canada Book Fund, and
the Province of British Columbia through the B.C. Arts Council
and the Book Publishing Tax Credit.

The author would like to acknowledge a grant from the Ontario
Arts Council to assist with the writing of this book.

PRINTED AND BOUND IN CANADA

Everything is based on a true story.

Did the world break your heart, son? Well, that's what the world does.

This book's for Gerry. The real one.

INTRODUCTION

Bukowski says: "You're buying my book to cheer yourself up? Christ, you must be some down."

Bukowski says: "Well, good luck with that shit."

Bukowski says: "Fucker."

I turn down Bukowski's volume in my head and take one step closer to the cashier with her round framed glasses and her hair as straight as if she has ironed it. And maybe she has. Some women do things like that, maybe she's one of them. My friend Gerry currently has a broken nose, which is about the ugliest thing you can do to your face, other than setting it on fire or having it torn off with pliers.

"Do you have our rewards card?" the cashier asks.

"No," I say. "No, I do not."

And I decide to write a book. This one.

When the water's at the door, you'd best get paddling.

i.

SKIN

Skin flick. I'm watching porn again, which I should not be doing because it's bad, but it's not as bad as killing people, but it is bad. In life sometimes it is hard to tell the good things from the bad things. Sometimes it is easy though and this is what we call innocence and what we call knowledge. So porn and killing people are bad but baking things is good, unless you bake things that kill people. And there is no pornography in baking so you don't have to worry about that at all. There is some dirty sexy baking like private parts made out of bread or a couple fucking on top of a cake, but it doesn't make use of real people so it's okay I guess. In real life it can seem hard to tell who the bad people are but really it is so easy — they're the ones who aren't like you.

In porn it's much harder to tell, mostly because everyone is so busy all of the time.

And they pretend a lot. We are made up of almost nothing but also out of everything.

We are good.

We are bad.

ii.

HOUSE

My hair on the couch. You can see through it to the green pimply fabric but you can't see my bald head through my hair or my skull through the skin or my brain through the bone. Ghost in an old black-and-white movie on the late show. Curtain in the breeze. Book falling from the table. Finger taps on the table. I'm here. I'm here. Please hear me. Invisible. Uncertain. On the edge of everything. Moon on snow. Dead star shining. Feeling of falling asleep but never quite there. TV on with the sound off and light silver black jumping on the wall. I will never be able to move from this couch. It will not happen. There's a piece from a Monopoly game under the couch. A small green hotel shining green in the silver television glow. I'm the only one who knows. Between the cushions there's a Raisinette withered shrivelled grape perfectly smoothed in chocolate. Gum wrapper and a quarter. I will never remove them. If I was small enough I could move into the small green hotel, my small green room, shining floor, small green window, small green curtains, small green table where I'd sit my small green hands clasped, take the small green elevator down to the small green dining room, small green waiter, and everything smooth clean plastic. He'd serve me a slice of the Raisinette on a small green plate and I'd pay with my improbably large quarter. I'd never leave the hotel because of the thick coating of dust covering everything. My smooth green plastic eyes watching. Alone. I could stay there forever until I am dead finally and never have to leave or get off this couch. No map to where I am now. Always late and getting later. Where I am. Now. This must still be me. I don't know how to be anyone else. And. I am not happy. I am not happy.

(I am not. I am angry. That or something very like it. Yes, I am angry.)

There is a photograph of my parents and in it my father holds my mother from behind and his sleeve — the sleeve of his work shirt — it is pulled to his fingers as if they might wither, as if he was loathe to touch her or because he revered her so that he would not allow his skin to touch hers, at least not publicly. Their lovemaking stopped the house and it rattled the cupboards shaking cans and doors. Even too much is sometimes not enough in the end.

I do still like my house. I am at home here. And I have these dreams. I will never get up off this couch. It will not happen. I don't see how that...will ever happen. My head feels like it's been boiled. Eventually I'm up and staring into the bathroom mirror. My hair could be black. Could be brown. That's up to you.

Once I met this guy at the bar and we got to drinking and talking. He told me he was at peace with himself. That he'd come to accept himself just the way that he was and the world too, the way it was, and he was just gently at peace with everything.

I wanted to punch him right in his fucking throat.

1.

THE DEATH OF MUAMMAR MUHAMMAD ABU MINYAR AL-GADDAFI

The beginning will be a chapter about me and Gerry and it will be the one where I decide to definitely write a book called *Skin House*. This book. My life has mostly come out to shit. And I think it may soon be done. I'll get something down first anyway.

It was me killed Tom Thomson. **Mystery solved.** *I went after him with a machete and it wasn't pretty. Then I sent the canoe out on its own. They can dredge that lake all they want, they'll never find those bones because they're not there. Do you want to see them? They're right here in this bag. He smiles.*

I am really fucking awake in the middle of the night now. Awake. I have dreams like that all the time now. I don't know why but it's ever since my son died. He was young. I try to stay awake as long as I can but eventually there's nothing you can do about it. Which is true about a lot of things. Gerry says if I stopped sleeping in my Jeep I'd probably sleep better and not have so many dreams and he's probably right, he is about a lot of things. He was right about that guy in the bar, and about his wife, but that just got his nose broken for him, so being right isn't always the best thing is it Gerry? It may not sound too

13 •

scary, that dream the way that I wrote it out there, but in the dream that guy is actually standing in a cold cellar in the mushroom black and he's got one lonely light bulb swinging slow over his head like a cleaver and he's leering and he's got this burlap bag in his hands and he raises it up and it stinks of mould and wet cardboard and the guy, that guy, well, he's me.

So it was scarier than it sounds.

"Gaddafi's dead," Gerry says. He's looking in through the open window of the Jeep, squinting and grinning. What time is it?

"That guy from the shawarma place?"

It's morning.

"No, Libya, the dictator, Moo-mar... people are complaining that he got shot, that it wasn't right to just shoot him."

"Those'd be the people who don't live in Libya?"

"Right."

"Right."

This wakes me up and gets me sitting as opposed to curled up in the back seat with my legs sticking out into the front. This is not good for my back at all. I am so hung over that the air is white. Like a soft French cheese you could cut with a knife. It's hot already and you can tell it's just going to keep getting hotter. I squint out at the street. The sky is green grey and hovering low like it's about to have all the houses for lunch. The sun is pissed off and trying to hurt people.

"Well, I feel like a boiled shit," I tell him.

"Yeah," he says.

There's an empty bottle of vodka on the floor of the passenger side, a shot glass on the dash.

"Why a shot glass?" Gerry asks.

"Only bums drink from the bottle, and I'm not a bum."

"You're sleeping in your Jeep."

"That's a choice, I am choosing to sleep in my Jeep, I have a bed that I choose not to use. Bums don't have choices."

I want to get back at him.

"How's your wife?" I ask. She's gone again so he doesn't like that question. Gone with a sixteen-year-old to boot.

"Fuck you."

Bingo. I start to pull myself out of the Jeep. My mouth is a toilet. Not in a figurative or a metaphorical sense. More like in the sense that a toilet brush would be more effective at this point than a toothbrush. Literal. That's the word. My mouth is actually a toilet. Somebody shit in my mouth.

"You oughta get that snoring checked out."

"I was snoring?"

"Not really. Snoring is breathing really loud when you're sleeping. This sounded more like someone chain-sawing sheet metal."

"No wonder your nose gets broken a lot."

"Not a lot. Twice."

And so it goes. After I get out of the Jeep I'm still feeling a little faded and we walk slow up to the house.

"You end up getting that bandsaw working?" I ask him.

That's how last night had started, his bandsaw was jammed somehow and we drank a lot of homemade hooch while we were trying to fix it.

"I did. And I still got all my fingers and toes. I can still count to twenty-one," Gerry says.

The screen door is coming off the hinges. Since when? How do things like that happen and not get noticed? Or ever fixed?

I'll tell you the story of how Gerry's nose got broken. In case you were wondering.

They were trying to close the bar. They wanted the bar closed. There was too much light in the bar and they wanted it dark again. And they wanted to clean it. As if you could ever really clean a bar.

"No hard feelings," said Gerry.

"Hell no Buddy," the guy said, putting down his glass on the bar.

"Name's Gerry," Gerry said, "What's yours?"

"My name? It's a funny name. It's pronounced Fuck You."

Then he tore off a right straight into Gerry's gut. Gerry folded right up like an accordion and the guy brought his knee up into Gerry's nose. There was a crunch. Nothing else crunches like that. Squishy wet and crisp at the same time. He held Gerry's head there and kind of turned it in his hands. Gerry dropped to his knees his shirt flowering with red.

"Need a hand?" I asked, "I mean there's still a chance to talk this whole thing over."

Gerry got back up and moved toward the guy, blocking his jab, catching his right fist on his elbow as it came across and unleashing one that broke the guy's nose clean. There was a lot of blood then. You couldn't tell whose was whose. And that's when the guy pulled a knife.

Enough shit, I remember thinking that. Enough shit I thought and I rushed the guy then and we were all just swinging blindly, we slipped in the blood and we all went down, Gerry and I just hoping that the blade wouldn't connect with anything. I took someone's knee to the belly and then I heard the guy saying:

"Okay, okay..."

And then we all had a little drink.

"I still say your wife's a slut," Gerry said, "Her skirt's so short I can see her ovaries."

Which might not have been the smartest thing he's ever done, the guy being close to three hundred pounds and still kind of pissed off about his nose being broken. But you end up laughing about these things usually. We did. All because of that girl's messed up tattoo and how she didn't like people talking about it, especially drunk guys in bars, especially Gerry. And her husband didn't like it much either. But I don't know why you'd get a pack of Skittles permanently inked between your breasts and that's pretty much the sentiment Gerry was expressing though he was doing it a little more crudely and he probably didn't mean to insult her. But things happen in spite of our best, or our worst, intentions. Anyway, she didn't like it.

So that's how Gerry's nose got broken. But he doesn't like talking about it. That's why I keep bringing it up. And I don't think the girl was a slut anyway. A slut is just someone who sleeps with someone you don't want them to.

I come downstairs after starting my shave upstairs. I don't know why. I have this bowl that I use when I'm shaving. I've always done it this way. I put my bathrobe on over my clothes. Morning is easier to deal with in a bathrobe. And I feel better when I shave.

"You got any peanut butter?" Gerry asks.

"How'd the goddam door get busted again?"

"Everything's busted, you got any peanut butter or not?"

"Not everything. Not everything's busted. You mean your nose, you mean your nose is busted, but not everything. The TV still works, and the toaster works…"

"If I use it to make toast will there be any fucking peanut butter to put on it?"

"Let's make some toast first and then we'll worry about the next step. Stop bein' a root canal."

Toast with nothing on it is good really. It's simple. Gerry doesn't appreciate simple things usually. His mind doesn't have the subtlety for them. It's not his fault, it's the way that he is. There isn't even anything really wrong with the lack of a subtle appreciation of simple things. Eating dry toast just takes some faith. Faith that things will look up eventually. That things aren't as bad as they sometimes seem. Only I don't seem to have much of that faith right now. It also takes some water to choke down the fucking ball of dry dough that you end up with. And that takes a tap that's not broken. Or the ability to swallow a lot of shit. I finish shaving, kind of, and I put the bowl of soap and beard stubble in the sink.

"Why do you always go to mass?" Gerry asks.

"I don't always go," I say.

It seems very bright in the kitchen. I want to make some eggs. There are no eggs. I'm cranky. I need sunglasses. Is it Sunday?

"I mean when you do go, how come?"

"I like the story."

"But it's always the same story; guy gets killed, guy comes back, guy leaves, always the same thing."

"That's why I like it," I tell him. I put another piece of bread into the toaster. "Wouldn't like it if it came out different. I guess I don't like surprises," I say, but I'm thinking mass is something that I can still hold onto. So I do, I hold onto it.

"Me neither, but I don't like things always coming out the same."

"What about the casino?" I ask him.

"What about it?"

"Well, things always come out the same at the casino, but you keep going back."

"I guess I'm a betting man."

"So, me too."

"So you wanna go to the casino?"

"I don't like going there. Bad things happen there."

"Bad things happen everywhere."

I consider this.

"Yeah. But they happen there more often."

The toast pops up but I don't want it anymore. I need coffee.

"You think Tim's is open yet?"

"It's fucking ten-thirty. I think they've probably got a pot on, yeah."

I was spinning off to the side taking empty swings into the night air going down with no one there to fight me. My shirt was wet. The pavement, when it hit, felt gentle, either it had pocketed itself to receive me, or my face had flattened out to meet it. I am shaped by my surroundings. No one left to swing at now. If there was, it wouldn't matter, there'd be some easy kicks in it for them now. I'm down for the count. I'm fighting just toward morning, just for the chance to get up again. It's snowing. And someone laughs. I am cold. I don't care, it is nice here now. I'll stay down here. Nobody wants to lose anything. Can't be helped. There's a lot of blood here, and most of it is mine.

This wasn't last night, I don't think. But this happened. Sure it happened. I can't remember when. I do not suggest this way of living for anyone. This blur. I would really like that coffee now. Mr. Coffee I need plenty of you. I can take you on right now. And maybe a donut. Anyway, something sweet. She couldn't handle it. The long trail of whiskey out of the shit maze. Neither can I maybe so maybe I can't blame her. Maybe it doesn't lead out at all. Maybe that's why I'm on it. It just leads in further. Maybe that's why she left. I remember her naked, leaning over something. I never meant to hurt her. Her or anyone else either. I never meant to get this hurt myself. Why would you? Anyone? I'm getting a maple glaze. One large coffee with one milk and two sugars. That's what I'm getting. Baby. And old, I'm getting old. There's not that much left of me, I'm whittling down to nothing now. And I'll feel better after I vomit.

Which I do.

I don't like the shaking. I've never liked the shaking and the cold fingers. Who would? Old water stains etch the mirror. Like milk. Someone walks in. I don't move. I can't. Move.

"Do you find it hard to make new friends?" I ask Gerry when I finally make it back to the table. The Tim Horton's is crowded and he's holding onto the little plastic table like a lifeboat.

"Fuck off."

"I mean I would understand, what with your conversational skills. And your face."

The bruises around his eyes and the spread of his nose give him the look of Mike Tyson on his worst night.

"You probably frightened the counter staff," I say.

"I got you a chocolate dip."

"I wanted a maple."

"I know."

I try the coffee. Two kids come through the door and stand looking up at the menu. One of them keeps looking at Gerry and his Tyson face.

"Something came out of my nose this morning," Gerry says.

"Yeah. What?"

"I'm not sure. Looked a bit like wet cornflakes. I might take it to the hospital just to get it checked. Not sure if it was supposed to come out."

"You kept it?"

"Yeah, I got it in the car. You want to see it?"

"Fuck no. Maybe later. Jesus, that's just like that time you had crabs and took an envelope full of them to the doctor."

"I wanted to get an official opinion. What's wrong with those kids?"

"You. They're looking over here because you look like shit."

"I look like George fucking Clooney on a good day. You look like shit. Day old shit, that's what you look like."

"Did Ray talk to you about looking like that at the store?"

"Can't fire a man for getting sucker-punched."

"Nobody wants to buy meat from a man whose face looks like two pounds of ground beef."

"Fuck 'em. I'm a butcher not a priest. I think people want to know their butcher can handle himself in a bar fight."

"You think that's the message your face is sending out?"

"Fuck off."

"You said that already."

"So do it then."

"Make me."

"Fuckdonkey."

When I do write the book about this I'll add these lines in:

"You gonna eat that chocolate dip or not?"

"Yeah buddy."

But I'll leave out that part about going to mass. It would be good, but I don't go to mass anymore. I'll put in a part where Gerry talks about his parents:

Gerry says: "I woulda come out better if my parents hadn't been in the iron and steel industry."

I'll say: "They were?"

And he'll say: "Yeah, she'd take in the ironing and he'd steal shit."

And I'll take out that part about Bukowski. Or maybe I'll leave it in. I don't know. It might confuse people. Fuck Bukowski anyway. No. Fuck the confused people. "We're all going to die, all of us, what a circus!" He said that once.

He had a point.

God likes everyone.

Just not me.

Just not now.

2.

THERE WAS A RESTAURANT AT THE BUS STATION IN 1952

This dream starts in the store. I'm stocking shelves. Which is pretty much my real life, only now I'm dreaming it instead. This seems like a real waste of the little time that I have available in my life to not stock shelves. Surely there is something else I could be doing in my dreams. But. What can you do? So there I am as usual, stacking things one on top of the other or side by each. This time it's toilet paper. I line up the circles at the top of each stacked package with the circles at the bottom of each new package and front face the labels evenly. Nothing much else happens. Which is often the case in my real life now. I like my job because it has no surprises.

Except today. I'm stocking milk bottles. In real life I mean. This is what I'm doing. Ray has started stocking some organic food and stuff from local producers to try and give the store an edge over the Wal-Mart they're saying might be coming to town, as if grain fed chickens are going to do well in a fight against brightly coloured tubes of very red meat from Mexico at a dollar a pound. Those meat tubes will kick the chickens' scrawny asses. So now the toilet paper is done and I'm loading these little glass bottles of organic milk from Johnson's Dairy into the cooler and—

"Hey."

—it's Melanie standing there as if she's just material-ized. Which, really, she has. She's supposed to be in Toronto and now all of a sudden she's not. She's here. All of her. It certainly looks just like her.

"What the fuck's wrong with you?" she wants to know.

It sounds just like her.

"Lots Mel. You want a list?" I ask.

"I want you to send that stuff you said you were going to send to me, my books and CDs and shit."

"You just asked for them last week. I'm packing them up."

"Asked for them last month you mean. What's the matter you can't find a box?"

She's beautiful like always of course and I want to take her right there in the dairy case, pushing her into the waxy cartons, her hands holding onto the wire shelves. Those days are gone. No way to count how much has gone the wrong way since then. But she really is something to look at. I'd show you a picture but the only one I have is a Polaroid and she's in bed and it's not that good. It kind of looks like a picture a serial killer would take as a souvenir.

"I'll find a box. What are you doing back here?"

"What am I doing here? What are you doing here? This is your job now?" She looks around the dairy aisle, scans the yogurts, the strawberry milk (on special at a dollar seventy-nine today). "This is what you do now?"

I set the last milk bottle in, break down the empty card-board box and set it on the cart.

"This is what I do. I put the stuff on the shelves and I clean up stuff when it breaks. I have a mop. This is what I do."

"You clean up stuff?"

I push the cart past her and head for the back of the store. I don't want any more of this.

"When it breaks, yeah. I'll have your shit packed up tonight. Come by and get it or I'll just leave it on the porch. I don't care."

The truth is a conversation stopper. I pass through the green plastic strips that mark the line between staff and customers insofar as who is allowed and who is not allowed to pass through the wall of green plastic strips. I am allowed. I have a green cloth apron with "Food City" written in white script. I have a box cutter. I have two bottles of rye in the closet with the mops and the buckets. I have three cigarettes. As a rule I do not bring a lunch. As a rule I do not eat lunch. I lean back against the concrete wall and feel the cold sweat on my forehead break out like dough being pushed through a sieve. That's when I hear the crashes one by one. There's the first one and I hear that and I think well, someone's dropped something and I need the mop. Then another. Then there's a regular pattern. I pull back the green plastic strips and there's Mel in the centre of the dairy aisle calmly reaching into the case, taking out one bottle after another and dropping them. Milk is everywhere. Some of the glass has cut her leg just above her ankle. Another bottle drops.

She's really pretty though. Like I said, she's beautiful. Did I mention that?

I wait for her to go and then I clean up the mess. Ray maybe isn't in the store right now, or he hasn't noticed at least. Or no one's told him. "Ray, hurry, some crazy bitch is having a milk rave in the dairy aisle." This is a lot of milk. It looks like the store is lactating. I have to block off the aisle to traffic while I clean it. Set up the little signs. Make sure all the glass is mopped up. I can see Mel naked. I remember how it was. But I try not to. When I'm done I go over to the meat department. Gerry has news.

"They're sending me to Montreal on a course to learn how to make sausages. Takin' the bus down Tuesday."

"To Quebec?"

"That's where they keep Montreal."

"All the way to Montreal? To learn how to make sausages?"

"What?"

"Well, I mean, nothing, what's to know?"

"Not much that I don't already know, but this'll make me an expert."

"You stuff the ground meat into the skin, right?"

"Expertly. I'll do it expertly. That's what will make me an expert. I'm having breakfast at the bus station before I leave, it's all covered."

"There's no restaurant at the bus station."

"Sure there is."

"In 1952 there was. Now there's a vending machine. Anyway, you mean if there was a restaurant at the bus station you'd actually eat there?"

"Why not?"

"Same reason you wouldn't pay for a hooker behind the car wash, a certain lack of cleanliness in spite of appearances and some serious degree of regret later on."

"Nothin' wrong with car wash hookers. They're clean. Maybe I'll just get some Timmy's on the way then. Hey, Mel was here, you saw her?"

"Yeah. I saw her. Yeah."

"She looked mad. I'd be careful."

"Great. Got any other pointers?"

"Pace yourself. Drink lots of fluids. Don't cramp up. You sure there's no restaurant there?"

"Positive."

Mel is like a lot of people. She's pissed off.

She's like me. But she doesn't actually like me, not anymore. Feels like... you know that feeling when you wake up in the middle of the night and you've shit yourself?

Maybe you don't. Sometimes there's nothing to say but the wrong thing. I've learned just to accept things that other people would not. I've learned to make do. The ocean could dry up and not leave a trace and I wouldn't care. I'm on the way out anyway. What's she doing back in town? Looking for her husband. Well he isn't here, and I'm not him.

I do what I often do when there are too many people in the store and I need some time to myself. I set up the "Wet Floor" signs and front-face the cans of green peas. They don't need to be front-faced usually but I don't let that stop me. It's amazing how people don't really argue with a "Wet Floor" sign even when they can see that the floor is perfectly dry.

"Excuse me I need some green peas."

"I'm sorry, the floor is wet."

I point to the signs. How are you going to argue with that? You're not. That's how. I'm pointing to fucking yellow plastic signs that have a picture of a stick man falling on his ass and the words "DANGER WET FLOOR". You can't argue with all caps or graphic illustrations. Or with danger. Or with yellow. You can't argue with yellow. People don't even try.

Sometimes I feel two-dimensional. I'm a drawing. A photograph held to the wall with masking tape. Old masking tape with not too much sticky left on it. I'm cold coffee. I'm station drift. The end of the film when it loops out of the projector. I'm the broken helmet. I'm a message from God written on a bathroom stall. A car in the ditch. This is how I would describe myself to try and give you a picture of what I am like right now. I'm ineffective. I do what I can do. No. That was before. Now I do nothing.

I do as little as possible now. I do nothing at all.

I'm every last motherfucking bit of doing nothing at all. The glass left empty at the break of the day. The sweater left on the beach. The "Wet Floor" sign with no wet. Finished. Done.

Back when I was still trying to write things I wrote this down when I overheard it in Montreal, two guys coming out of an alley: *Man, I just totally pissed all over myself.* The other guy: *Want to stop and wash your hands, man?* The first guy: *Nah, it's not a hand-washing night if you know what I mean.* I mean I thought I could use it in a book I might write. At the time I wasn't expecting to just live it instead.

I never got back up. You get knocked down you're supposed to get back up. But I couldn't.

How do you turn yourself into something you like?

I'm a reasonable man about things. I just don't give a shit.

3.

YOUR GIRLFRIEND LOOKS LIKE A CIGARETTE MACHINE

In this dream I'm working on the Jeep. This is not an easy one to dream or to write down and for some reason I keep dreaming this one over and over. I'm not really sure what I'm doing with the Jeep. Trying to fix it obviously but I don't know what's wrong with it. Maybe in the dream I do. But I'm not saying in the dream and in the dream it's never important what's wrong with it, it just has to be fixed fast and outside of the dream I can't tell why. There's white paint flaking off the back porch steps in the sun. Sometimes it's fall and sometimes it's winter. Maybe it's a filter wrench in my hand. Maybe I'm changing the filter. Maybe it's more than that. I don't know. But there's oil everywhere. More and more and more oil, and it won't stop. I don't know what I'm doing. Why did I think I knew what I was doing?

So we're in the bar again. It's better than sleeping these days. It's more like getting away than sleeping ever is now. Getting away for sure. Because we're laughing, and we laugh a lot in the bar. And no one ever laughs in my dreams. Or anywhere else. People laugh a lot in bars.

"I'm going to get us some shots, if I don't come back…"

"If you don't come back you're stuck in that?" I point to a girl at the bar.

"Yeah," he says, "Stuck in that, or I'm dead."

"But, dead, that would be a worst case scenario?"

"Yeah. Worst case."

Tomorrow morning's going to happen. There's no getting around that. But it's not happening yet. You gotta be calm about things, and not let them get to you, is the thing. 'Cause they want to. It's what they do. They're born to do it. It's what they're all about. Things. It's how they survive. In our minds. Fucking things. Fucking us up. And this is what's stoppin' 'em right now so THIS is what we need to do now. More beer. Okay? Okay then. And in the morning they're not going to mess you up either 'cause you'll be too messed up to mess with in the morning. Not going to mess with you in the morning either.

"You talk to her?"

"Yeah I talked to her."

"So what'd you say?"

"I said sorry."

"That's what you said to her?"

"That's what I said. I said sorry."

"Why'd you say that?"

"I told her I was sorry that I spilled your drink all over her top."

"My drink?"

"Yeah, yours was in my right hand, that's the one that hit her boob."

"Was she pissed?"

"Not as pissed as her boyfriend, here, drink up, we may not have very long in here. I don't think he likes you."

"Me?"

"I told him you said his girlfriend looked like a cigarette machine."

"Why'd you say that?"

Gerry shrugged.

"Well she does. And to distract him too. To take the focus off me, otherwise I might not have got these drinks over here."

"He's coming over. Shit, he's a big man."

"Where'd you get those shoes?" Gerry asks.

"He's a big man. What?"

"Those shoes."

"Why?"

"I always liked 'em. Just thought I'd tell you now. You know, in case."

"You're gonna like 'em when they're buried up your ass."

"Don't be hasty. You're gonna need them when you're running. Which probably you should be doing, right now."

The thing about running top speed in the dark when you're drunk is that you don't care so much about tripping and falling, which makes you better at the running, unless you trip and fall. Which you probably will because you're drunk and it's dark. Hopefully when you do fall the guy who's all sensitive about his girlfriend looking like a cigarette machine has given up chasing you. Which he has, as it turns out. By the time I hit the ground I don't hear him coming anymore.

"That man moved real quick for a big man." Gerry is on the ground next to me breathing hard.

"Yeah," I agree, "He had all the unexpected grace of the large man, you know, like when you see a fat man dance," I wipe the little pieces of gravel off my face, " . . . and it's not really that great, the dancing, but . . . because he's a fat man . . ."

"Yeah, yeah, like when they dress monkeys up in cowboy suits..."

"Well, no, it's not like that..."

"Yeah, they give 'em those little cowboy hats and the little six guns and little vests and all that shit..."

"Yeah, okay, it's just like that."

There's no point in arguing with Gerry when he starts in on monkeys — logic and reason have no effect.

"Hey," he says quick, "...weren't you supposed to leave Mel's stuff out for her tonight?"

"Yeah."

"Well did you?"

It only takes a few minutes to walk the five blocks to the house. From three blocks away we start running because it's obvious there's a problem. There's that glow in the sky.

"Shit."

We stop up short a few houses away and watch the fire on the little porch get bigger.

"She's pissed."

"That's my fucking porch gone."

"House is still there," Gerry says. "Get the garden hose and maybe we can save the house."

But we're still standing there watching the fire.

"Never kick a gift horse in the cunt," Gerry says. "C'mon."

But I'm thinking. I'm not moving. I'm thinking.

I'm thinking once a bitch always a bitch. But that doesn't stop me wanting her. No, not at all. Even standing there watching my porch burn down and listening to the sound of the metal eavestrough warping and popping, like the tinny sound of a kid's piano. Tink, tink, tink. Like red twisting pine needles in a campfire. I remember when my son asked me:

"You ever done any needle drugs?"

No. But I married your mother.

"C'mon," Gerry says, "C'mon. C'mon."

I don't know why the fire department never showed up. Probably none of the neighbours ever called. They don't like me much these days, the neighbours I mean. They'll like me even less now that the front of the house looks like a scorched marshmallow. The white vinyl siding around where the porch used to be drips grey and charred black shit, like icicles pissing shingle stones. I don't mind the look really but I imagine there's those in the neighbourhood who might.

Never kick a gift horse in the cunt? What the hell does that even have to do with my porch burning down? I don't know what the hell he's talking about half the time.

"Your mother has a boyfriend," my ninety-year-old father tells me, looking up from his bed.

She's been dead six years now.

"How do you know?"

"Because she never comes around."

"Well. She's pretty far away," I say. "It's hard for her."

He looks back at the Humphrey Bogart movie and drifts away for a minute.

"What?" he says, turning back.

"Nothing."

"I thought you said something."

"It was the nurse in the hall."

"Oh."

All the things that have happened in our lives sit there

in the room with us. But he does not remember most of them.

"What did she say?"

"Who?"

"Who. The damned nurse in the hall."

"I don't know."

"What?"

"She has a speech impediment, Otis."

I've called my dad Otis for a few years now. Since he had to be reminded a lot of the time he was my dad. It's easier than saying Dad and have him look at me all confused. But it's always hard to tell with him. Sometimes he remembers nothing and sometimes he pretends to remember nothing because it's easier that way.

"Got a what?"

"A speech impediment. It's hard to understand her." It's either that or make up something and say that she said it. Again, it's just easier this way.

He wipes at his mouth with his hand as if there's ketchup or mustard there.

"That's true of everyone," he says, starting to cough, "That's true of you."

He sits and thinks for a moment, gazing off.

"Bunch of crap wagons walking around."

He wipes at his mouth again and looks at his hand.

"Liver sacks. Hands in their pockets. Slack-jawed cock wipes."

"Some of them are okay."

"Nope."

"What about Mother Teresa?"

"Cunt."

"A saint now? You're saying saints are bad people?"

"No such thing as a good person. Don't teach you that in school, do they? Sittin' there with your dick in your hand."

"I am not sitting here with my dick in my hand."

"Metaphorically."

"Why are you so lucid today? I like you better when you have a flat effect and can't remember shit."

I do. When he gets all conscious like this he gets much harder to deal with and you can't just slip out on him when he's not looking. When he knows what's going on he gets all pissed off about it. This, I think, is why a lot of people prefer not to know what's going on. It saves a lot of effort.

"Listen, let me tell you what. Fuck you. That's what."

"Listen…"

"Fuck you fuck you fuck you…"

"Okay."

"…and fuck you."

"I think Mother Teresa did some good things."

"I never liked her pancakes."

"That's Aunt Jemima and you know the fucking difference today."

"Cum wad."

"Shit rag."

So we sit and watch the Bogart movie some more.

"Humphrey Bogart did some good things," he says.

"He slept with Lauren Bacall."

"Damn skippy."

When the nurse comes in with his dinner he doesn't want it. Chopped up Salisbury steak and whipped carrots.

"Rather eat the ass end out of a dead owl," he tells her.

I could give up. But I don't. Instead I eat the dinner and finish watching the movie with him. Whipped carrots. Peel the thin skin from the chocolate pudding. Lay the plastic fork and spoon on the tray. Nothing that could cut him. Nothing that could hurt him. I don't give up on him. No.

"I'd rather be dead."

It's hard to sleep with the smell of burnt porch wood and nylon and something that smells like wet hair. I lie staring at the ceiling. There was a moment or two when it looked like what we were doing with the garden hose wasn't going to be enough to save the house but we managed okay. We had to tear the carpet out of the front hall the next day, no way it would ever dry and lose that dead mouse smell. Anyway. I'm awake and not wanting to get up and not being able to stop these thoughts that I don't particularly want though some part of me must because there they are. There were times we'd have sex and I'd lose track of time and then I'd realize it had been over an hour and I'd won the bet that I'd usually place with myself. I mean a straight hour of, well, you know what I mean a straight hour of. I'm not counting any lead-up activities or post-game cool downs either. I lie here and I think to see if I can recreate one of those sessions from scratch actual minute to minute in my head and make it last a whole hour again. It's just a blur though and after the first few minutes, you just can't do it. Positions change too quickly. There are jump cuts. Everything's over too quick. And then you think about how you're never going to have that again. And then you think about how you might as well get up and make yourself some coffee. I'm saying an hour is nice too but after a while your mind wanders. After a while there's chafing. Knew a guy once, his wife wants to have sex and he says "Game's almost over, you go ahead and get started without me, I'll be in soon…" To each their own.

"She's an attractive woman," Gerry said once.

"Yeah, as long as you don't put your hand in the cage."

Once she asked me how big my cock was.

"What do you mean?" I asked "I mean, you've seen it. You're seeing it right now."

"Yeah," she said as she closed both hands around it, gripping it like a golf club, "but it changes. I don't have the head for these things, measurements and things, numbers…"

Then she started moving her hands up and down slowly and I forgot about the question. Until now. I just remembered the question now.

I get up and put some coffee into the machine. There's something wrong with the tap still, which there will be until I get around to taking it apart I suppose. That might be some time from now. It takes a while to get enough water and I'm just standing here in my bathrobe. There's a tape measure around here somewhere. While I'm waiting I search the drawers. It should be in the shed though. Do I want to take my bath-robed self out to the shed for the sake of a measurement? The neighbours hate me already so why not? It's colder out than I thought though and so by the time I get into the shed and find the measuring tape, which isn't easy because it ends up being in the tackle box, it's also not as easy as it might be to get it hard. I think about Mel, think about bending her over in back of the shed on a fine summer day and taking her pants down, her kicking one leg to get her panties off her foot so she can spread her legs for me and she does and I …there it is. There it is so I grab the tape measure and slide it out. It's blue plastic and I got it at Canadian Tire. The tape I mean, not my cock, the metal tape is yellow and it's rusted a bit at the edges because I always used to leave it on the ground when I was finished working on something and it would get rained on. I get my cock out and line up the tape next to it, worried that the procedure and the cold will have an effect on the results which seem to be, wait a minute, seven and a half. Seven and a half. Okay. That's enough I guess. And I let go of the tape and let it slip back into itself and I see it before I feel it, snagging metal and a sudden red expanding line, because of course there's so much blood just waiting there, just surging with nowhere really to go and now all of a sudden there is and it does. The door's wide open. And then the pain which is sharp like a razor paper cut, a long thin line, a slit, a dammit, dammit, dammit. Maybe the neighbours are right. They're right. I'm not a fit man. I double over quick but I've opened myself up in my own shed and I'm bleeding through my fingers and there's no way to take this to the hospital and dammit. I remember that day I had her behind the shed. Who wouldn't? Her red sneakers in the sun. That was very different than this day. That was fine.

We'll all die soon. Every one of us.

But if this streak keeps up I'll be among the first.

The painter Jackson Pollock, there was a woman with him in the car when he died. A crash. Then there wasn't. Neither of them made it, they went straight into a tree. I think there were two women, one of whom, no doubt, he thought he loved. He thought of himself as second rate most of his life, I read that.

Seven and a half.

It'll do. It did. It does.

Seems she was beheaded on impact. Him too. There would have been a lot of blood. There is a lot of blood. There's always a lot of blood. Until there isn't any more. Then it's too late. It's not too late yet. Gotta find a towel, or something. Save what there is to be saved. Learn what there is to be learned. Though I have learned that it's seven and a half inches this morning and at least that's something I didn't know before.

Eight would be better.

I might go to California. But I'll get that towel first.

Eight would be nice.

I'm sure it's not that bad, but it is a slice down the side of my cock so it's not that good either. There is no chance of stitches and the bleeding isn't slowing down so I lurch to the kitchen and look for the Band-Aids but things like Band-Aids and batteries, pots, and bottle-openers, they're hard to track down these days. Whatever it is I'm looking for is not where I'm looking. Just like measuring tapes. I use twelve Band-Aids because there's twelve in the box, it's a travel pack. I wreck a couple with the blood at first and they slip right off but I get the hang of it and tape myself up pretty good, like a hockey stick. So I'm standing in the bloodied bathroom now with my vinyl latex dick and I try not to look in the mirror. I never liked a clown act.

I bet Mel has a voodoo doll of me. I'll bet there's a sharp pin stuck through its cock right now. I have to get over to the store and pick up my cheque. It's Sunday. Dad needs his Cutty Sark. And I need more Band-Aids. And I should have slept in the Jeep. I sleep better there. I might pick up a bucket of chicken.

"Why did you say she looked like a cigarette machine?" I asked Gerry.

"Didn't you see her? She looked like a fridge. All she needed to be a cigarette machine was a row of buttons on her tits and a tray down near her crotch."

"Yeah, but why'd you say it though?"

"Oh," he said, it looked like he was thinking about it, "I don't know."

"Not everything has to be out loud."

"Too late now. You gonna put that in your book too?"

4.

THE BEST GROUND CHUCK MONEY CAN BUY

It's not that I'm really uncomfortable thinking about it. I think about it all the time.

It's that I would rather be dead than think about it anymore than I do. Or at all. Really I would rather just be dead. There is a sound that comes through tall grass in late summer and I might miss that. But that's all I would miss. Most of the time that's all I would miss if I was gone. And of course if I was gone I wouldn't really miss it would I? The night is cold and freezing and I am the same. I'm the same as the night I mean. Not the same as I've always been because I'm not sure that I've always been just one way. I don't think being one way for a long time would be any good anyway. Hitler was probably like that. Stalin was probably like that. These men are not recommendations for ways to be. I'm definitely not the way I used to be. So it's not that I want things to just stay one way forever I know things have to change I just don't want them to suck so much. There are parts of me that are very different from how they used to be and I don't think there's any way to change them back. There are parts of me that are just not here anymore. Parts of me that are just gone for good. Not for good, gone for bad. So I don't think things are going to change for the better anytime soon, that's what I'm saying. Might as well just get used to it. These little parts at the beginning of each section are supposed to be about dreams that I have, but I haven't had any good ones lately to tell you. What is it when we hurt the people who love us? What is that?

The Jeep doesn't want to play today. I could walk to the store but if I keep turning the key the engine will eventually turn over. *Turn over. Turn over.* What kind of motherfuckery is this? I tightened the battery terminals yesterday. There. There. I don't like that, when it doesn't start up. It makes me uneasy.

Mel once spent four days watching the shopping network. I don't mean she watched it for a while and then did some laundry and then watched it some more and then painted her nails and read the newspaper or had lunch, I mean she watched that motherfucker for four days solid. She looked away to go to the bathroom. She bought a plastic dish set. She bought a doll with real hair. Real human hair. Scariest fucking thing you ever saw. She bought a motherfucking golf cart. The breakup wasn't all my fault, that's all I'm saying.

There's nothing like being in the store on your day off. It's a pain in the ass to go in but at the same time it's kind of nice because everyone is working or making it look like they are and you don't have to do either, you're just there to pick up your cheque and shoot the shit a bit. Ray is in so I'll have to talk to him which it would be better if I didn't have to but I do, I need the cheque. Hopefully he won't ask about the broken milk bottles.

"What do I know about broken milk bottles Ray? She's a fuckin' biiiiiiiiiiiiiiiiiiiiiiiiiiiiiiiiiiiiiiiiiiiiiiiiiiiiiiiiiiitch. That's all I know."

Ray gets rattled when you talk a bit crazy because I

think it unnerves him to realize that he has hired some crazy people or potentially crazy people anyway and that he could conceivably walk in the store and find them fucking in the aisles or swinging from the lights or trying to kill each other with axes in the frozen food section. Not that any of that's going to happen. Well some of it has. This is a fact that Gerry and I like to use to our advantage when necessary. If I have to I will pull out the word: biiiiiiiiiiiiiiiiiiiiiiiiiiiiiiiiiiiiiiiiiiiiiiiiiiiiiiiiiiiiiiiiiiitch.

If I have to. And I'll bug out my eyes a bit and sweat. Or break some bags of Oreos over my head. Whatever it takes to maintain job security.

But Ray doesn't ask about the broken bottles. Guess he didn't hear about them. He doesn't seem much interested as he writes the cheque. His little office is up a flight of stairs and hangs over the top of Gerry's butcher section and he has this mirrored window he can look out of over all the aisles but I don't think he ever does. There's always a lot of cash in his office unless he's just done a bank run. Whenever I'm in there I always feel like I'm doing a drug deal.

"You can work next weekend?"

"Yeah, sure."

"Yeah?"

"Yeah, I mean I'd prefer not to, but I prefer to eat than not eat you know?"

"You can work next weekend sober?"

"Yeah. If I haven't been drinking."

"Yeah?"

"Theoretically."

Fuckbucket. He's got a six foot by six foot office and a

shirt with mustard stains on it and a sixteen-year-old son who's about twenty-four cents short of a quarter in the Harvard department and a plastic radio playing Celine Dion and he's sweating me about my rye and vodka hobby. He hands me over the cheque.

"Thanks."

"Yeah."

And Gerry's bald, did I mention that? The fluorescent lights bounce back off his head as he leans over the meat.

"Hey."

"Hey."

"You goin' to see Otis?"

"Yeah."

"Just give him this for me."

Gerry tears off a big sheet of red-brown paper from the roller and wraps up a wad of ground beef. Tapes it up with that brown paper tape. He hands it over the counter to me with a smile.

"From me, for Otis," he says.

"What's the man going to do with two pounds of ground beef?"

"That's the best ground chuck money can buy," Gerry says like he's offended, "...he can fucking frame it if he wants."

"Okay."

"Okay?"

"Okay."

"I'm off in an hour, what are you doing after?"

"I don't know. Bar I guess."

Some people, the only reason they have to be alive is because their parents had intercourse. Not Gerry. He's a certified butcher. He's got a certificate. He's got meat. He's got a reason. A direction. Maybe he's a few clowns short of a circus but he's a good man. Holy Mother, jugs and speed, my dick hurts now. I double over a bit. Gerry's wiping blood onto the white canvas of his butcher coat. Normally this would have no effect on me but right now I think I may throw up on the meat case. Ray would not be a fan of that. It's...

Fuckbox. Now I'm sinking down to my knees onto the linoleum. I don't really want to be doing this in front of the young mothers and their children looking for some nice pork chops or chicken cutlets at a reasonable price, especially with my hands curled into fists trying not to ground themselves into my crotch but I really don't feel like I have much to say about it right now because I'm a complete slave to the icicle of pain that is rocketing up my dick and into my lungs. Fuck on a cracker.

"You okay?" Gerry asks.

There's a kid with a yellow sucker in a shopping cart looking at me like I'm something on television. This ain't SpongeBob kid. You wait. You'll be here someday kid, you wait. I can't breathe.

I stand up.

"Never better." I tell Gerry.

I pick up the ground chuck and I go. It's hard to drive anything while you've got a sliced up penis but driving a standard like this is even harder than an automatic, at least that's the theory I develop on my way to Piney Manor where Otis lives now. No one knows why it's called Piney Manor other than the fact that it's got to be called something and Piney Manor sounds a bit better than "A Reasonably Clean and Convenient Place To Die." There's some pine panelling in the dining room. Maybe there were some pine trees here once that they ripped down to put up the building back in the seventies. There are no trees now. Just a view of the strip mall down the little hill. By the time I get the Jeep parked and pull on the handbrake I've stopped sweating so much because the pain is a little less. The focus of having to drive helps, I guess. Now if only Otis is awake enough to keep my mind off things a little while longer. Then I'll stop by the mall to pick up a bottle of Extra Strength Tylenol and I'll go home for some vodka. Nothing like the promise a day off holds.

"Everybody lies," Otis says as I come through the door of his room.

"That right?"

"In this place it is. Listen, I need you to keep your brain at least half-cocked for a minute. These people are trying to kill me."

"What now?"

"Just listen to me for a minute you vagina," he says, turning off the television with the remote, his long, old fingers fumbling. "I need some help here."

"I'm pretty sure I'm adopted, so I don't know. And I'm not helping you go to the bathroom again. Last time you pissed all over my hands."

I put the wrapped up chuck down on the nightstand then think better of it and sit down in the only chair and I rest the chuck in my lap.

"What's with the meat?" Otis asks.

"How do you know it's meat?"

"'Cause it's bleeding like shit all over your pants idiot, who wrapped that?"

Fuck.

"You look like you been shot."

Fuck.

"You don't look so good to me."

Fuck.

And Lisa walks in. Which probably is not going to make things go any better. If I was going to be putting my penis inside of anyone these days it would be Lisa and I've been thinking about this quite a bit lately in fact but the fact is I'm not going to be putting my dick inside of anyone for a while, especially now that everything's all unraveling and shredded like flaked tuna. My life I mean, not my dick, though I guess it's true of both things now. But I crave her and this would take another man down and make him think of the inevitable losses in life and everything that you don't get to do before you die but not me. Because I'm a fuck-eyed optimist. And then Lisa sees the blood and because she's a nurse everything that happens next, well, happens. And she gets all nursey and takes me by the hand quick into this little room down the hall that's filled with hospital supplies: cardboard boxes with elastic bandages and plastic boxes of latex gloves, crutches, toilet brushes, and folded-up walkers.

"What the shit happened to you?" she asks, with her hands on my belt, which doesn't sound all that medically professional to me really and that's how the next problem starts.

"Let's get these pants right off you quick."

And that doesn't make it any better. If she'd just talk like a nurse I'd be fine. If she'd say "What seems to be the problem?" or "What's the nature of your injury?" but her fingers are undoing my belt and she's crouched down there and the way her too-white skirt stretches into fine crinkles at her hips, by the time, I know this is probably not normal when there's a seven-inch slice down the side of it, but by the time she has the belt undone and the zipper down it's right up and ready. It kind of pops up like it does anytime it's angry and pants get pulled down over it and she says:

"Oh, um...fuuuck..."

But it's not like it looks good or anything, there's blood everywhere on it, dried and new, although the new blood is not as much as I was expecting, not as much as the hurt would suggest, especially with it mostly hard; I guess I pictured it kind of pumping out, maybe the cut is closing up so that's good. Plus all of the Band-Aids have worked free which I guess was the problem, and the ones that are left are just kind of hanging from it like feathers off a buzzard or kind of like a snake getting rid of its skin I guess.

"Hmm."

It looks like the little flags hanging over a used car lot. Only covered in blood. She looks up at the shelving unit with all the stuff on it like she can't think what to do next and she looks back and puts her hand around the base like a tourniquet and I'm trying not to let it, but it gets really fully hard then.

"I, um..." I say.

"Yeah," she says. "Just a sec."

Nurses must get this all the time I think, though maybe not so much at Piney Manor. It must still happen though. Nothing new. She reaches up into the box of latex gloves and pulls one on using her teeth. This also does nothing to help the problem. At all. It seems kind of preparatory to something non-medical. So I get even harder, the skin at the top is really stretched and shiny now, which hurts more, and I'm pointing at the ceiling now and it's looking like the seven-and-a-half measurement may have been a little off. But then she gets all businesslike.

"Don't worry," she says, and she tightens her one hand back around the base and starts taking the crusty Band-Aids off really delicately. This is helping a bit. Pain helps. Then she washes it down with something on a cloth and dries it and then she takes some antiseptic cream and rubs it along the cut and it stings a bit and now I'm looking at a poster on the wall about the proper disposal of material contaminated with human waste and trying to sort of calm things down which is working a bit.

"Can you keep it down like that?" She asks.

And I'm thinking, *Lisa I think I can pretty much keep it any way that you want it,* but I just say, "sure."

Because the tone of her voice is all starchy white now not warm stretchy and panties slipping down over soft hips anymore. This also helps.

She takes some stretchy gauze bandage and wraps it up pretty tight and then tapes it in place.

"There," she says, still eye level with it and looking at what she's done with a smile like she's finished a Christmas handicraft and it's come out the way she planned.

"You can put your pants back on now," she adds, in a

way that suggests nothing but medical efficiency. "I'll give you some more of this to take home, you should change it twice a day."

So I put my pants back on. There's still blood stains, but there's nothing I can do about that. She stands there looking at me.

"I might be able to find you some other pants," she says.

Her cheeks are flushed. I notice that. She has a way of standing there that really makes me want to see her naked. There's probably not much chance of that now though. Plus, I've pretty much decided it's not a good time in my life for that right now, so it's probably best that it works out this way, is what I'm thinking. Funny how what you're thinking usually has nothing to do with what's really going on. With me that's the way it is anyway. And she must be wondering how I got a cut like this — I hadn't even thought of that. So I'm thinking that any potential that there might have been for anything happening with Lisa is shot now anyway and she nods her head like she's reading my mind and she's decided she can go now and she says, "That's a really nice one though, you should really take better care of it."

And she opens the door and leaves me alone in the little room in my bloody pants.

So.

Pretty good first date.

When I get back to the room my dad is still in his wheelchair looking out of the window at the roof of the mall down the hill as the sun goes down and everything gets grey. There's an old movie on but the sound is off. John Wayne and Dean Martin walking slow down a Western street. Dad looks up at me and says, "Who are you? Why do you have blood on you?"

He is scared. Nothing stays good around here for very long. Around here it's like a bar at the end of the night with all the lights turned on. All the time.

"Oh it's you. I want to die in Montreal," he says. And then: "Promise me."

So I do. What the hell. I like a road trip. But all my promises have had a way of bitching on me and leaving me sitting by the side of the road like a pickup truck live bait sale. Lisa comes back with a box of bandages and a pair of charcoal grey pants that have a belt sewn right in. I thank her but she's back in full nurse mode again like she's handing over a prescription or something. It's alright. She needs someone less hopeless than me. So I go over to Gerry's place to see if he's home from his shift. He's watching *Dr. Phil*. He's been doing that since his wife left him. He says it's just to check if she shows up there talking about him.

"If I have to watch one more sad-ass pathetic little motherfucker tell another broken-down story about his dime-store drug addiction I'm going to start using up some crack myself, and at a furious rate, you know what I mean?"

"Why don't you just stop watching?"

"'Cause *Judge Judy*'s not on till three. You want a Caesar?"

"Sure."

I do.

"Where'd you get the slacks?" he asks on his way to the fridge.

"Lisa."

"Ah. Lisa."

"Fuck off."

And he doesn't ask anything more about the fact that I'm wearing charcoal polyester slacks with a sewn-in belt that a young girl gave me. That's what I like about Gerry. He has simple needs. He wants for nothing.

"Otis wants to die in Montreal," I tell him.

He hands me a Caesar.

"Who doesn't?" he says. "... who doesn't?"

"Why do you watch *Judge Judy*?" I ask, removing the celery from my glass and laying it on the coffee table. Gerry likes garnish.

"Eat that, it's good for you, when's the last time you ate something?" He sits down using his celery to stir his drink. "Lisa's back in now? What's the ups with that?"

"What do you mean *back* in? She was never in."

"Neither were you. In her I mean. You back to trying?"

"I was never trying either... I was thinking."

"There is no thinking, there is only fucking."

"What about Judy the Waitress? What happened with her?"

"Nothing."

"Well?"

"That's different. She's inexperienced."

"I thought you liked that."

"Not her. She had a menthol hymen."

"A what now?"

"You know, all cold and minty."

My glass is empty. I chime the glass at him.

"Shit, Clamato's not cheap you know, d'you just want the vodka?"

"And bacon, I would like some vodka straight up and some bacon."

"I don't have time to cook bacon, *Judge Judy*'s on sooner than that."

Gerry likes to fry bacon really slowly and lay it out flat on paper towels to drain away the fat.

"So you going to do something or just look at her from afar with dreamy eyes and sweaty hands?" He asks.

"You know how I feel about it."

"Oh Jesus don't fuck this up with your feelings."

"Well."

"She wants to dance on *that* pole and that's pretty clear and for some reason you're just walking around with it in your hand."

"I don't know."

"You know."

"I don't."

"Fuck yes, you do. Look deep in yourself. You want some bacon in this?"

"Yeah."

He drops a slice of raw bacon into the vodka. You don't eat the bacon. It gives the vodka a smoky flavour. It's best not to look at it though. Just let it sit there like, well, like a slice of raw bacon. Gerry sits back down.

"I watch *Judge Judy*," he says, "you know this, I told you … because it's the same as all great stories — reminds us how we're all doomed to come to nothing in the end."

"And be judged."

"That too."

It's not the first time we've had the conversation.

"I could use some corn chips."

So *Judge Judy* comes on and we follow the long trail of the late afternoon and then the evening, which eventually leads us nowhere. I fall asleep on the couch. When I wake up Gerry's not there which is weird because it's his place. The television's still on. For breakfast I have a cigarette. There's no coffee. The problem is time's not a straight line, sometimes it doubles back on itself. You can't depend on it to do what you think it should do. It'll do what it wants. Or maybe that's just memory. And here I am again, looking for coffee where there isn't any. Wife gone. Son dead. Father dying. I'm using an empty can of Beefaroni for an ashtray. That doesn't seem like a good thing does it? Or maybe it's all right. Is it all right? It's all right.

It'll be all right. What I had with Mel. By the end. That was a swamp.

5.

THE BASEMENT BAR
BURNED DOWN

Dream. Sometimes I don't. I didn't last night so I'll tell you this one because even though it's an old one I've had it more than once, so it counts. I'll probably have it again, though I'd pay as much as fifteen dollars not to. I'm in Cuba or somewhere like that, somewhere warm and cheap. I've been walking on the beach through the washed up seaweed and drinking beer. In the middle of the night I wake up in a motel and I know that something is wrong. There's a fan and a screen window and the light from a sign. There's a tightness in my chest and something moves slow inside of me and I know without knowing how and with the certainty you find only in dreams that there's a pelican inside of me, a live pelican. And I know that if I move too much it will wake up and want out and that will be the end of me. But I have to get up anyway, I have to get to the bathroom and deal with this pelican and I know if I do get up that it will stretch its wings inside me and tear the walls of my lungs and there'll be no way to fix the damage it will do and my breath is sardines and stale crap and salt water and blood and I just want out of this situation and I stumble into the bathroom holding my chest and I turn on the light and its huge head is just pushing its way out of my mouth and there's a lot of blood coming up and the bird is trying to flap its wings now, trying to take off up out of me. It couldn't care less that it'll kill me in the process. In the morning somehow I have survived and my

throat is bandaged and I'm checking out and the motel owner be-
hind the counter is smiling wryly and rubbing the back of his neck,
"No matter how many times we tell you people not to touch the
pelicans..."

It's not a symbol of anything. It's a fucking live pelican inside
my chest.

"That's the thing, I know, I'm just in a good mood tonight
for some reason."

"Why?"

We're at Zamboni's which is the only real bar in town.
The other places are all restaurants where you can drink
with your food. Here you can have food with your drinks.
If you want to. But not many do. Maybe it's the blood and
hair on the walls, which isn't always there, but sometimes
it is. That can put you off your burger if you're a certain
type. It's been the only bar ever since the Basement Bar
burned down. Its real name wasn't the Basement Bar
that's just what everyone calls it, or called it, since they
don't call it anything since it burned down. Technically, it
burned up. Because it was in the basement. No one calls
it anything anymore.

"That's the thing too. I don't know why I'm in a good
mood. There's no reason for it. But there it is. An arrow
to the knee wouldn't kill it."

"Might."

"Nope, fucking wouldn't, and I would know."

"I forgot. You good for another?"

"You mean payin' or drinkin'?"

"Both. Either."

"Yup."

After we get the drinks set up I want to talk about something serious with Gerry but he leads off with, "And her name was Cotton."

"Yeah?"

"I was fifteen and I met this girl..."

"Yeah?"

"Her name was Cotton. Wild name, right? She said that when she was little her parents called her that because she was so soft."

"Yeah?"

"And that as soon as she was old enough she was going to move to Calgary and change her last name to Candy because Cotton Candy would be such a great stripper name."

"So she had it all worked out."

"Oh, she was ahead of us all. She saw it all clear."

"I used to tell Mel she should be a stripper, she had everything she needed for it."

"Including a suitcase full of bitch. What'd she say?"

"Told me to fuck off, we were always like that."

"You mean with you making smartass comments about her and her telling you to take your fucks to the off department? Yeah, you two were like Charles and fuckin' Diana..."

"I don't know."

"You don't know what?"

"I've just gotta get myself unfucked."

"Cotton, she just used to want me to fuck her on top of her parent's television."

"Yeah?"

"She liked to think about us doing that every time they made her sit and watch *Dallas*, they loved that bastard J.R."

"That's tricky."

"What?"

"Fucking on a TV."

"Not really, this wasn't some new plasma flat-screen, this was a good old piece of furniture, good solid legs on her..."

"Cotton?"

"On the TV. Big box of a thing."

"Cotton?"

"The TV. They could've buried Elvis in it. Made of that old plastic wood you know? It wiped right clean."

"Yeah."

"So did Cotton. Who was also a big box of a thing come to think of it. Fuckin' cold in Calgary in the winter though. That's a three sock town."

"Yeah."

"Lived there in a basement apartment January and February one year, boy that was all I could take. Only time I was warm was when I was doing hot knives on the gas stove."

"And when you were fucking Cotton."

"No, that was earlier, she'd left me for an accountant by then."

"An accountant?"

"Steady income, warm house, all the cocaine she could blow and apparently a nine-inch dick too, which she was also welcome to blow."

"Nine inches?"

"Yeah. He told her she could count on him, that's right, he said that, the ass bone, and she repeated it. To me. Accountant with a nine-inch dick said she could count on him. I'm not making this shit up. He left her for one of those girls that sells things on the Home Shopping Channel though. Pots and pans and beauty aids and such. A pretty girl."

"She ever become a stripper?"

"Cotton? Last I heard she was working at Arby's. Funny world."

"Arby's?"

"Net revenue over a billion dollars last year, pal. Smart position for a self-starter."

"I wanted to ask you something."

I wait a moment. Gerry waits.

"It's about Otis. He's not happy."

"The creamed chicken?"

"Yeah it's the creamed chicken and it's the Jell-O and the white bread, it's no sex in over ten years and I think it's the thin blankets and the cold white ankles. It's pulling the sheets around himself the same way every night and every morning waking up in the same spot and opening his eyes and finding a teenager washing his pecker for him with a cold facecloth. Every morning waking up and all you've got to look forward to is a teenager washing your pecker and orange Jell-O and the fucking grilled cheese milkshake."

Everything at The Manor goes into the blender, doesn't matter what it is, putting it into the blender makes it easier to serve, easier to swallow, easier to digest, and easier to clean up. But it sure makes it harder to look at and harder to stomach. And if you've never seen creamed asparagus I suggest putting it off for as long as possible. Dinner comes in a bland painter's palette of orange and green and red and brown, all mixed with grey. Otis wants to grab a hot pastrami at Schwartz's in Montreal before he dies. Order it up with fries with extra salt. A pickle. A cold cream soda and maybe a smoke after. Nothing blended.

Gerry wants to change the subject. He likes Otis but he doesn't like old people. Or young people.

Or people.

Most of them bother him.

"After Cotton it was Gertie. An unfortunate name. Called her BFG. Big Fat Gertie. She didn't like that much."

"Probably not."

"But she was an axe-and-a-half wide."

"He's a good man."

"Otis? Sure he's a good man. The best. Shit, what does it matter what you say about people...everybody dies."

"Nice."

"Sorry, was that a spoiler for you? Want me to say that again in a way that they don't? Sure. Everybody lives forever. That better?"

"Cheer the fuck up."

"I was perfectly happy thinking about Gertie's big ass. You're the one who brought up sad. You want sad? My father died of slow cancer."

Gerry empties his drink. Looks up as someone new comes in.

"At the end you could hold his stomach in your hand like a roasted walnut."

He cracks an ice cube between his teeth and holds his clenched hand up in front of his face. Squeezes it.

"Like that."

We sit in silence looking at his fist.

"What the fuck does that even mean?"

Gerry starts to laugh.

"I don't know. Sounded good though right? He's not even dead. Cocksucker lives in Winnipeg now."

"Same thing."

"I'll tell you a story, I call him every Christmas, he tells me how he can't find good shoes anymore. Every Christmas. Same thing."

"And?"

"And what? Nothing. That's it."

"Really? Christ that's not even an anecdote. You can't just say shit like that like it's going to be an anecdote or something. People expect a story when you start off that way. 'He can't find good shoes anymore and...' You shouldn't tell stories like that unless you carry a drool cup around. Then people don't expect any more than that from you."

"Don't have to be a cunt about it."

"Fuck. Why don't you sit on the corner in a folding chair and sell pencils out of a cup. Then you can tell stories like that all you want."

"Fuck."

I want to cheer him back up though so I ask him about his lawsuit. He loves his lawsuit. Gerry used to work for Domtar and got his hand stuck in a machine. Still can't feel one of the fingers on his left hand.

"It's great. I got them comin' and I got them goin'..."

He stands up and grabs his head with both hands.

"They don't know whether to protect themselves here."

Grabs his crotch.

"Or here."

His head.

"Here."

His crotch.

"Or here."

He leans over.

"But it don't matter 'cuz by the time I'm done they're gonna be bleedin' everywhere."

He does a little dance like a leprechaun.

"They'll be fuckin' BLEEDIN'...EVERYWHERE..." he yells like a song, in time to his steps. It's beautiful when Gerry dances.

But not everyone thinks so.

The waitress comes up. "The manager has asked me to ask you if you'd care to leave now?"

"If I kiss you can we stay?" Gerry asks her, still dancing.

"If you touch me I'll break your arms."

"Okay."

Gerry sits. We have another beer.

"Every man's life is a piece of magic, you know?" I ask Gerry.

"I like it when they saw the ladies in half."

"Yeah."

"Yeah. That's good. I wouldn't want to be a magician though."

"No?"

"Not for all the little plastic toys in China."

"They make them in the Philippines now."

"They do?"

"Yeah."

"Fuck the Philippines."

Jesus, I just remembered. Nobody wants all this cuntin' dialogue in a book. Nobody cares about Gerry's lawsuit. Forget that.

Sorry.

Sorry. I'll wrap this up. Won't mention it again.

Well that's all really. We close down the bar. We stand outside in the street and I have a smoke. And it takes a while to find the lighter. There's not much to tell. Gerry pisses on the wall.

Somewhere a dog goes insane in the night.

"Jesus, d'ya think he's laughin' at us?"

"Who? The dog?"

"No. Jesus."

"Christ, probably he is, someone must be."

I want to look up at the sky. But I never look up at the sky.

Here is a movie about her leaving.

First, you have to know this: she was probably right to do it. When a house is on fire you get the hell out. Even if there's someone else in the house at the time. Especially if they're pushing you out the front door. It's easy to say she was a bitch for doing it because she is a bitch. Well she is. But that's got nothing to do with it really.

I wouldn't have stayed either.

Here's the movie: It's June. It's a hot day. I've got this old turntable going that I found at a garage sale. I'm playing "Wichita Lineman" by Glen Campbell. I've probably played it fifty times in the last two hours. A little while ago she poured the rest of the vodka into the toilet. I didn't care. The liquor store's open. Hell, I'll drink it out of the bowl with a straw. She's naked in the kitchen except for her panties. Light green. And she's holding her head. Okay. Okay, she's saying. Okay. Yes, and she's crying too. You can hear kids playing outside. It's hot. She's out and across the front lawn. In this movie of it the light is really bright like everything's faded in the sun and about to float away. It's all in slow motion. She's got a bag with her. "I can't," is a line she might be saying, "I can't, not anymore." And she's gone with the car. Guess she had clothes in the bag because she left in just those panties, I remember that. Marching across the lawn in green panties. And I get up off the couch and I start the record again. *I am a lineman for the county. And I drive the main road.* I lie back down on the couch. It's not a promising start to a movie. You might think about going out for popcorn. Except for that part about her being naked. Mel does look great naked. You don't want to miss that.

You ever kissed a drag queen? I'm just asking. Mel is no drag queen, she's...well she's great in the bedroom. And in the kitchen. The bathroom. The foyer. I mean. I still love just about everything about her. Except for that part about her wanting me to die. Except for that. That's the unfortunate part. Even the bitchy parts I liked. I still do. If I'm going to be honest about it. Mel is always the most interesting thing in any room she's in and that's true whether she's half naked and beautiful or half drunk and angry and spitting nails.

I kissed a drag queen once. It was in Florida. It was part

of the show, you went up on stage, you slipped a buck. Gave her a kiss. I was drunk. She was crying. Gerry doesn't know this. Don't tell him. Jesus don't tell him, we'd never hear the end of that would we? You can't take the piss out of a guy anymore if he finds out you've kissed a drag queen. Doesn't matter how many times you've been in knife fights or almost died or been shot at. Drag queen kissing is trump.

The M1911 is a single-action, semi-automatic, magazine-fed, and recoil-operated handgun chambered for the .45 ACP cartridge. It's cold in your hand unless you hold it for a while. It warms up to match your body temperature which is nice but also a little creepy I think. Otis brought it home from the war. That's not quite right, he bought it here after coming home I think. He got it somehow and he said it was to, "shoot the heads off those fuck-booted bastards if they ever come over here," which made me a bit nervous because I assumed he was talking about the Germans and there was a German family down the street and I didn't know if he knew that or not but I imagined him taking each one of them out, one at a time, into the backyard. Blood exploding onto the fence and picnic table. Grandma and Grandpa German tied to the tetherball pole with piano wire.

In spite of this Otis, as Gerry knows, is a good man. He taught me everything I know about being a good man. It just hasn't taken hold yet.

Anyway, the gun. Oh yeah, the gun. I'm wondering how it will feel if I shoot a bullet through my left hand. I'm sitting here on the bed in the afternoon and I can see myself in the mirror on the closet door. I'm wearing boxers and a bathrobe. Socks. I haven't had a shower in a while. Can't bring myself to do it. The shower I mean, not the shooting, but I'm seriously considering shooting my hand, it might happen. This is an improvement over last week when I couldn't get up off the couch. I don't mean that I was too lazy to get up. I mean I didn't think I would ever move. I didn't see how it would happen. Still don't see how it did happen. But it must have because here I am with this gun.

Don't do it, don't do it, don't do it is what you're saying. Aren't you? Are you? It would be a stupid thing to do, you're saying. I won't. Do it. I guess. They wouldn't let Otis bring a gun into Piney Manor so I have it now. Nobody likes an old, cranky, screaming bastard but they particularly don't like him when he's well-armed.

There's a hole down which, lately, I cannot help but fall. The shit and the dark and everything else down there. I got some bad advice somewhere down the line. Just do your best. That's all that counts.

Who said that? Some shit-fuck-cunt-lick bastard who'd never won anything in his entire life.

It's like that song from the eighties or from the seventies. *Loving yourself is the greatest love of all* or something. What a load of ripe horseshit.

Really.

You believe in that shit you're an asshole.

And the last asshole out can turn off the lights.

6.

THERE'S A MAN CRYING OVER THERE

"What's brown and sticky?"
"I don't know. What?"
"A stick."

You're either someone who thinks that's funny or you're not. He did. In this dream we're driving in the Jeep. I'm driving because he's eight and you can't drive on the main roads when you're eight. People get upset and call the Children's Aid about it. I know this from experience. And your feet don't reach the pedals right when you're eight but he manages. The wind blows through his hair.

I can tell this is a dream because he's dead now and since he's alive I must be dreaming. Half of me wants it to stop and half wants it to keep going. Now you're thinking: Oh, I get it you're like this because your son's dead and maybe you think it's your fault and your wife left you and you lost your job and your dad's dying. No. It's not that simple, bitch. Maybe.

So...

The paint on the walls in the room where they kept his body was dirty white. I don't mean it was a particular shade of white I mean it was white paint that had gotten dirty over the years. It wasn't the room he died in. I guess that was in emergency or in the place they take you right after emergency. It was a special small room that they put people in after they die. If you compared the white on the walls to the white of the sheet they were very different. The sheet was very white. A little while ago I looked up the colour white, this is what it said: *White is a colour, the perception of which is evoked by light that stimulates all three types of colour sensitive cone cells in the human eye in equal amounts and with high brightness compared to the surroundings. A white visual stimulation will be void of hue and greyness. White is the lightest possible colour.* That was the colour of the sheet. It looked brand new. I thought they should paint the walls or at least clean them, especially because of what the room was for. I also found out there's a colour called Ghost White: *The colour ghost white is a tint of white associated with what it is imagined the colour of a ghost might be.* It's a true colour, you can look it up. That was the colour of the walls. They ought to clean them. The sheet was held up by his nose in a point like a mountain under snow. He looked smaller than normal. The window was open.

Okay, look, there's other things to talk about here. Armed robbery for one. And I think my dick might be infected so let's just move this along okay? Fuck off. It started to snow today. There's a reason birds fly south in the fall; they're not stupid like we are. They don't let themselves get attached to things. The shit starts falling and they get the message and they get the fuck out, simple as that. So when Gerry suddenly starts talking about robbing the store, I'm surprised a bit, but I listen. I've gotta get my dick looked at again soon, but I listen.

"Ten thousand dollars, that's all I'm sayin'. To twenty. Ten to twenty."

"Which?"

"Thereabouts. But on a Saturday or a Sunday? Could be even more."

"Be a shitty thing to do though."

"You'd get over it."

"Yeah."

"That's . . . ten thousand, that'd be, three hundred two-fours . . ."

"Is it?"

"I think so. Give or take."

"Doesn't seem like much, when you put it that way."

"'S two hundred and ninety-nine more than you've got now."

"Be really stupid to do though."

"So?"

"I thought you liked your job?"

"I do. I'm not quitting it. I'm taking an employee benefit package. I mean we'd have to be at work the next day same as usual. Nothing out of the ordinary. Nothing suspicious."

"Yeah."

"What?"

"I think my dick's infected."

"Well I'm not a doctor, you sort that shit out yourself."

I miss cigarettes. That's why I'm starting up again. He's right of course, he's not a doctor. He's a butcher. I need to get this looked at. The last cigarette I had put me on the ground. That's the way it goes if I don't smoke enough, if I go too long between smokes and then I have one my body says what the fuck is this shit and puts me on my ass and spins the room around and then I promise someone big and in charge of things that I'll never have another, which is true, until I do. Then usually the second one I'm okay. But I'm always afraid to have the second one because I really don't like that feeling so I haven't had one in a while and I miss them but I might be done for good this time. I don't know. Some people know the names of the constellations. Or the names of different kinds of trees. There's a maple tree and a pine tree. That's all I know. I think there's a larch. A larch tree. Maybe not. Birch. I don't think it matters if I don't know the names of the stars. I know they don't care. The stars I mean. I've gotta get someone to look at my dick. I smell like a Band-Aid. I'm tired. Ten thousand dollars is a lot of money. So's twenty.

So I'm on my way to see Lisa about having a look at my dick. She's the only medical professional I know. I'm on my way to see if she's working and it starts to snow. I'm on my way to see Lisa about having a look at my dick. That's a weird ass thing. Lisa do you think you could have a look at my dick? Lisa, ah, remember my dick? Big flakes drifting. It's the first real snow of the season. Lisa, want to see my dick?

"Why don't you just talk to Ray about getting some more money, like a raise I mean?" I ask Gerry.

"'Cause if I do it'll come out all crooked and probably mean."

"You give Ray too hard a time, he's just trying to run a business."

"He can't button the bottom button on his shirt. I don't want to ask him for a raise."

"So stealing it is better?"

"Hey Ray, could I have a ten-grand raise? No Gerry, you can't. There. Done."

There's a kid trying to catch the flakes on his tongue

standing in a front yard with his face up to the sky. There are two garbage cans lying sideways behind him and a thin dog on the porch. The door's a big, black rectangle behind him. Nice looking kid. I'm trying to get this down just the way I see it. Sometimes I think this shit ain't cocky enough. I'll try to do it better.

The kid's got his head shaved but somebody did it wrong and it's all patchy. He probably eats alone at lunch. It's only October and he's already got mitts on. Poor bastard. Then he stops trying to catch the snow and looks at me walking past like I'm the loser. Then he runs up the steps and into the house. And the dog stands up and barks. Fuckers.

There.

"What's wrong with that fuck ache?" Gerry nods at this guy nursing a beer sitting alone at a table by the window.

"What makes you think something's wrong with him?"

"Well, first, he's crying."

"He is?"

"Fucker's crying, watch, every once in a while he'll wipe his eye. Watch."

He does.

"Maybe he's got a cold."

"You don't cry in a bar. That's just wrong."

"Maybe his wife left him."

"Your wife left you, and she kicked you in the nut sack and set fire to your house. I don't see you getting all Oprah about that. My wife left me, I'm right as fuck."

"The day Mel left she was wearing lime-green panties."

"You remember that?"

"Wouldn't you?"

"I guess so."

It's eleven forty-five on a Saturday morning. Late enough for a beer but too late for breakfast and fifteen minutes before we can order lunch so we just get another beer.

Nobody says anything.

"Well, holy crap, I just don't give a fucking bitch shit about anything anymore," Gerry says.

"I guess that's a good way to go."

"Good as any... but if that bastard doesn't stop crying soon I'm going to lay him out. I can't enjoy my club sandwich with extra bacon if there's a crying man in the room. I just can't."

When they rolled my son out of the little room all covered up I reached out and touched that blanket on its way by. It was the best I could do. It was just a blanket. A grey, felt blanket. They'd left the window open. I didn't know where to go. I still don't.

Except I do have to see Lisa. It's not really somewhere to go, it's just that I have to get this checked out. It's not like I'm using it lately, but I don't want to see it infected and falling off either. And I'm not trying to chat her up or anything. *Hey, wanna check and see if my dick's infected?* I don't think I have a winter coat. Just occurred to me. Maybe somewhere I do. Walking along the road to The Manor I think about Mel. I don't mean to, I never do mean to, it just comes over me like a seizure or like the flu. I think about the first time I met her. It was at the bar and there were people playing charades. I'd never seen people playing charades in public before. Never have since either. At Zamboni's there's this place in the back, it's like a big table that's attached to the floor, and this couch that goes around three sides of it. I think it's called a banquette. Anyway, they're all sitting around it and they're trying to guess what Mel is doing and I know from across the room what she's doing and then somebody yells out, *"Multiple orgasms!"* and she yells, *"Yes! Yes! Yes!"* and she's pointing at the other people and screaming and, well, that was it. I knew I'd get married. Later on we passed each other in the little hallway to the bathrooms and I thought I was pretty smooth having my number already written down on a scrap of paper in my pocket and I said, "Here." And I slipped it into her hand. She took it and looked at it with eyes that looked like they were squinting through razor blades.

"That's my number," I said.

"Oh yeah?" she said focussing on it, then on me, and then she grabbed herself. "This is my vagina," she said.

And that was it. One thing you can say about Mel, and there are a lot of things you can say about Mel — she's direct. It's one of her things. *Razor sharp trailer trash.* Things like that just pop into my head, words all in a line like that. *Razor sharp trailer trash.* I feel like I should keep them, but I always forget to write them down and then I can't remember them after a while and what would I do with them if I did? I'm in a mess, right? Oh well. I'm used to my dick being sore after a busy night, but I haven't had a busy night for a while and my dick is really sore. Sore enough that walking is starting to feel a little rambunctious, but I keep going. When you need bandaging you need bandaging, cheerful optimism won't do it. I'll see Lisa for a minute or two in the supply room and get wrapped up right again.

So I walk.

I must have a winter coat somewhere, I had one last year.

But Lisa is not working because she called in sick so I guess I'll go to see Otis because, well, I'll go because I'll look like a dick to the lady at the desk if I don't go see him now that I'm here. A badly bandaged and slightly swollen dick.

"Going to see your dad?" she asks.

You know sometimes I feel like I'm wrapped up in a shower curtain. You know? Like one of those heavy plastic shower curtains that you can see through but it's kind of misty. If you wrapped one double or triple that's what I feel like. Layers of minty-green plastic. Of course I'm going to see my dad you Nazi, what kind of son would come to see a young girl about his dick and then just leave his old man alone in his room with a blanket around his knees and his TV on static because the young girl isn't around? This is what I'm thinking of saying and, like I say, I'm feeling this separation like we are just two different kinds of people and there's layers of damp, minty-green nylon between us. I can barely see her through them. I'm in considerable pain and yes, I am going to see my dad in spite of that. You bitch.

"Of course."

"Just remind him to drink his supplement," she looks up smiling, "...he tends to forget."

Oh.

"And if you could make sure he takes these," she hands up a little plastic cup with three pills rattling in it.

"Okay."

"Thank you."

Otis is sitting in his wheelchair looking out the window at nothing. He turns when I walk in.

"What the fuck is wrong with you?" he asks.

"What?"

"Lisa said you're not feeling well, what the fuck is that, the clap? You got the clap?"

"'Course I don't have the clap, what makes you think I have the clap? What did Lisa say?"

"You pokin' her?"

"No, I'm not poking her."

"You seem damned concerned about what she says for someone who isn't dippin' into her."

"I'm not dippin' into anyone."

"That's a first."

I put the cup down on the table next to him.

"Yeah, it is. I'm in a slump."

There's a movie on. No sound. *The Dirty Dozen.*

I sit down and we watch the screen for a while in silence. Otis turns and looks at me.

"I think I'm going to die."

"Well..."

Conversation stopper really.

"Happens to the best of us." I say.

"Eh?"

"I say it's going to happen to all of us."

"Sooner for me."

"Maybe."

"What do you mean maybe? Think you're goin' first?"

"I could get hit by a bus."

"Where?"

"What?"

"Where would you get hit by a bus? There's no buses in this town."

"I might travel to a larger metropolitan area. One with buses. You never know. I'm just saying you never know."

"I know what I know. I'm goin' soon. You better just get in line."

When I was packing up my mother's things after she died I found all of the photo albums she kept on a bottom shelf in the basement. Most of the pictures were special events. The camera usually came out at these times and then went back into the box it came in from Sears until the next birthday, Christmas, or vacation. There's a picture of me somewhere in those albums at Easter. I look about ten. Wearing a shirt with a dickey. They were big then. I'm smiling for the camera but behind me on a bookcase is a foil-wrapped egg peeking out purple from between two books. I wonder how much longer it lasted in there. In the picture it's mocking me. *Hey, asshole,* it's saying, ... *turn around.*

I know I've got a winter coat somewhere.

I fuckin' had one last year.

It was brown, I know that.

7.

EVERYTHING IS WET AND RED

Getting a tattoo. And it hurts like a bitch. Because he's doing it right direct onto my heart. We're behind the curtain in the little room and somehow in the dream it makes sense that he's opened up my chest and is poking the needle directly onto the beating surface of my heart. It's for keeps this way. *There's quite a lot of blood. All I can think is how's he going to clean all this up, not how will I survive, why aren't I dead yet? The blood is pooling onto the floor and thickening like black ink. He's saying that it's harder to get the image right onto the surface mostly because everything is wet and red but that at least this way once it's on,* "There's no fucking way it's coming off," he says.

So I end up meeting Gerry back at Zamboni's for a drink. Just one or two.

"You didn't make it out last night?"

"Wasn't feeling up to it. Was it busy?"

"Busy as free carwash night at the whorehouse... that guy Weller was in... your lawyer..."

"I hate that bastard."

"Why?"

"No reason... yeah, there is actually, it's because he wears a suit."

"So? Lots of bastards wear suits."

"Yeah. So. It's just that no suit-wearing bastard ever good news-ed me, that's all."

"This about Mel?"

"Nothing's about Mel."

I found my winter coat. It was underneath the couch. What the fuck is that about?

And what's this shit he's throwing around about Mel now? Not everything's about Mel. It's not.

"Not everything's about Mel," I say.

"Lots of things are about Mel...it's about her leaving then, you still pissed because she fucked your divorce lawyer? He probably wasn't wearing his suit at the time."

"Fuck off."

"Pretty sure he wouldn't have been. Maybe. So. Why don't you start over? Why don't you rebuild yourself?"

"Saying what?"

"Turn the page."

"New page. Same book."

We order more drinks.

"Is it wrong that I think of vodka as a friend?" That's me talking.

"Probably, yeah."

"Probably?"

"Yeah."

"I told Mel this dream I had once."

"Yeah?"

"That we were driving, well she was driving, lost control and we went over this cliff and it was really clear, you know, like one of those really clear dreams, and the ground's coming up fast, it's like a ravine we're diving into and I take her hand and just keep telling her I love her, you know, so it's the last thing she'll hear..."

"And you told her this?"

"Yeah."

"You told her about this dream?"

"Yeah."

"How'd she take it?"

"Well, how...as a woman I mean...how would you take it, as a woman?"

"If I was a woman?"

"Yeah."

"I'd be in front of a mirror checking out my tits."

"But when you were done with that, I mean when you thought about it a bit..."

"I'd never be done with that. As a man I'd say you were pretty much a pussy, but as a woman..."

"It's romantic, right?"

"It's pretty sweet I guess."

"Yeah?"

"Yeah, I guess, so what'd she think?"

"She said: But we're dead right? We end up dead anyway so what the fuck does it matter?"

"She's got a point."

"Yeah, but...fuck."

"Did you point out that since she was driving it was her fault?"

"No."

"Well you should have."

"Yeah, I guess."

"What a bitch."

"She is, you're right."

We sit and drink for a while.

"What's the best thing you ever said in a fight?"

"Not much time for discussion in a fight."

"Still."

"Ass corn, I guess."

"Ass corn?"

"Called this guy some ass corn, you're nothin' but stinkin' ass corn I said."

"What is that?"

"You know, when you eat corn and it gets stuck in your ass on the way out."

"He understand that?"

"No, and while I was explaining it to him he busted my lip wide open."

"Fucker."

"Ass corn..."

"Right."

"So. We still taking Otis to Montreal?"

"Yeah."

"Well, we should get going on that, he's not getting any younger."

"That's the best advice you've got?"

"Never kick a gift horse in the cunt."

"I heard you say that before. What the fuck does that have to do with anything?"

"Nothing. That's the best advice I've got, that's all."

"Never kick a gift horse in the cunt?"

"They don't like it. Much."

Only it's going to take a while for us to get going. Things always get in the way. Armed robbery for example. That. Lisa pulling her sweater up and off and over her head. That too. All kinds of things. We'll overcome them. That's what makes us such high-octane, fructose, full of testosterone motherfuckers. We can't be dealt with. So don't even try.

Lisa. Right. She finds me. Next morning. At the house. She drops by. Things happen. Well.

She heard I'd dropped by looking for her. I'm looking at this envelope on the table by the door, a speeding ticket I forgot about. And her clothes are off very quick. Door's hardly closed. She's pushing it closed and she's climbing me, one leg up and looking for traction and both hands holding onto my head like my ears are handles. These things happen quickly when they do. Back against the wall. White cotton panties with black edges. Warm and damp. Then they're gone too, pulled off with my left while my right holds her tight at the small of the back and then I'm into her real quick. Hardly ever see it coming when it happens like that. They surprise you with everything and suddenly it's all there all at once. Right there for the having and the taking.

Her hands on the wall at the head of the bed, then blood-drained knuckles, dry skin and her full-on hard pushes back and her hard-laughing grind. And a sudden catch of her breath.

So there's that.

And she has a tattoo of Olive Oyl from *Popeye* on her shoulder. Not sexy. But she makes it work. And one on her inner thigh right next to her jay-jay. A skull with a dagger through it and two roses. Well sir, that one works better. Her parents are on disability and welfare, which seems to bother her. I don't know why. She's at college part-time and almost done. They give her a hard time though, you can tell it's been rough. Why's she here? You'd have to ask her.

I'm sitting on the corner of the bed listening to her in the bathroom.

"You have a towel?" she yells.

"Yeah, there's one on the door there."

"Um, you have a different towel?"

Oh.

"Clean one under the sink. Maybe."

Anyway. Looks like the healing's pretty much done now. There is nothing like the services of a health care professional. It still hurts a bit.

"There are no fucking clean towels in here anywhere."

That's probably very true.

When I go out it's going to be big. I refuse to go in my sleep or lying down. There'll either be a hail of bullets or a ball of fire and it will not be pretty. But I don't think it will happen today.

"Hey."

"What?"

"Come here."

Anyway, I looked it up. Average Canadian penis size is 5.1 inches. It was worth measuring after all, I think. In spite of all the trouble. Some wad has actually found out the average penis sizes for every country in the world. Somehow he does that for a living. Hopefully, for him, this is work he does over the phone and not in person with a ruler.

Have you ever been to hell? The service sucks. Just saying. And if he does this work over the phone then why isn't the average Canadian penis size 9.5 inches, I mean, if no one's actually checking.

Careful this book doesn't rip you up. I mean these are just things that happened. Don't take it all too serious. We'll all get through this if we all just stick together and keep a clear head. Okay. Here we go. I'm talking around the fact that we're having sex again right now, right here on this bed corner. Mind? I'm not going to tell you all the details. I'm busy. Got my hands full. Do you mind?

Okay.

"I don't know, she's not the sharpest beer in the box," Gerry says.

I wait for a minute.

"You mean in the fridge."

"What?"

"You said 'in the box,' you mean in the fridge."

"What?"

"The fridge."

"Yeah, the fridge."

"And you mean the coldest."

"What?"

"The coldest. You mean. Not the sharpest."

"Yeah. I guess."

He doesn't think Lisa is too smart. Probably because she's fucking me. And there's something to be said for his thinking on that. Also once she said, *Who's Ray Charles?* Gerry didn't like that and he hasn't quite forgotten it.

"Amazing ass though," Gerry says, "and she's smarter than most of those ratchets you usually notch up for yourself."

"Like who?"

"Like Donna."

"What's wrong with Donna?"

"Donna? I wouldn't go near her if my cock was on fire and her vulva was a bucket of cold water."

"I don't know."

But I do. He's right about Donna. That was an ill-advised interlude. And he's right about Lisa too. She is smart. Her fucking of me notwithstanding. She's kind of kick ass in a few different ways.

My spirit rises when she's in the room, or when I think about her, so I order another round. She smiles when she looks at me. I don't know why. It doesn't matter. Maybe she'll show up. We can explain to her again who Ray Charles is. It's not that she's not smart, she's just young. Ray Charles. "I Got a Woman," "Mess Around," shit.

So when I was a kid. Let me tell...when I was a kid...I remember my dad before he went to work he'd grind up these two little pills for my mother. She'd still be in bed. He wore a grey suit. It was many mornings, it was each morning. But I remember one morning. It was early July, at least that's what it feels like on my skin when I remember it. His grey suit turns to me like a wall and it says, *Keep an eye on her son.* So I do. What else do I have to do? And eventually she gets up, this is after he's gone off to work some place where they wear grey suits every day even in July, I don't know where the hell he was working but he couldn't have had that job long. Mostly I remember him leaving in jeans and a T-shirt with a blue shirt over it that said "Otis" on the chest. Life goes down, not up. Anyway, she gets up and she stumbles to the bathroom and she crouches there throwing up the pills, her fingernails red and on the rim of the bowl. Pink ceramic tile walls. Two round yellow pills sitting in the scratchy glass in my father's hand.

The pills are to keep her from drinking while he's gone and they're supposed to make her throw up if she drinks any alcohol at all and even back then I'm old enough to understand that if she throws them up in time they won't work. But usually she doesn't manage to throw up in time and I watch her in the late morning sun sitting in her bathrobe at the metal kitchen table drinking and retching, drinking and retching. Her spit on the floor. At noon I make us bologna and mustard sandwiches. The bright yellow stripes of mustard on the Wonder Bread. We sit and eat them on the porch.

Anyway — the fact that he once wore a suit to work just shows my dad once had a better job than the one that he ended up with. Well, so did I. Like father like son.

I remember in the evenings sitting on the concrete front steps with my father, and we wait for the thunderstorm, which always starts from behind the houses across the street, and we can watch it come over the houses and toward us and we wait for the last possible moment before running in, the bang of the screen door, the smell of the metal and electricity in the air and the new heavy drama of the rain. We sit on the stairs inside then, watching the heavy sheets of water like it's never rained before.

"Oh well," my father says. "Oh well."

The cooler air after.

That's when I learned gentleness. Sometime after that we both forgot it I guess.

And once at night when she sat looking out the window into the dark like she was watching television. Staring at her own stricken face in the bare kitchen light. I remember that. I remember too that my father stopped trying to help her.

I remember once Mel arrived home late at night and she was drunk. It was raining and she stood in the bulb-lit hallway reflected twice in the black glass of the door. Her white T-shirt clung to her and she was silent and she was crying. She'd hit a dog and she just kept going, too scared to go back and check it, but she thought maybe it had been okay and kept running and did I think maybe it was okay and I told her probably so, probably it was. She was shaking with the back of her hand to her face in the bare hallway light. We went to bed. I left the hall light on. I'm not sure why.

Early in the morning, I walked out to the highway with a shovel. There were no houses anywhere near. The light was cold. I buried the dog next to the ditch.

Went home and had a drink to take the edge off. Edge of what?

I don't know.

8.

GOD AND I WILL NEVER GET ALONG

In this one I'm sitting by the side of the road right there in the gravel on the shoulder and I've got my head on my arms and I'm weeping, and I mean really crying. I don't know if it's about the accident because there's no wreck and nobody's around. And then I hear footsteps coming in the crunching gravel and I look up and it's Johnny Cash. Fucking Johnny Cash. And he looks down at me and he says: "What is it, son?"

And I say: "I'm tired, John. And I'm sore. And I don't want to keep going like this anymore."

Johnny looks up into the sun and he wipes his hand down both sides of his mouth like he's thinking.

"Shit," he says, "Whyntchu just get up off your ass and get on with it?"

So I do. I get up and brush off my pants. I'm wearing a slick black suit and it takes a while to get it clear of the dust.

"Thanks, John," I say. "You've always helped me to do the right thing."

He looks at me with his face pulled to a point.

"I thank you for that," I say.

"Do me a kindness," he says, and he spits, ". . . don't piss on my leg and tell me it's raining."

And I'm not sure what he means, but I keep walking. I walk as if there's somewhere to go. I remember singing "Happy Birthday" in a bowling alley once. When was that? I wake up.

We're back at the bar. It's late.

"I ordered us some coffee," Gerry says.

"By accident?"

"On purpose. I've got to drive home."

"And?"

"It's the responsible thing to do."

"And?"

"And if we're going to, you know..."

"What?"

Gerry lowers his voice.

"Well if you're going to burn down a convent it's best to not walk around with your pockets full of matches mumbling that you hate nuns, you know what I mean? I mean, about robbing the store. Not the best time to get tagged for drunk driving. People notice things."

"Not most people."

"Cops notice things."

"Most people wouldn't notice their own ass if it was right in front of them, and it was on fire."

"Not cops. They notice stuff. They're trained for it. They take notes."

"Bleeding and on fire."

"It just wouldn't be a good time to draw any attention. Not if we're going to rob the store."

"Most people couldn't find their own ass with two hands, a compass, and a book titled *How To Find Your Own Ass With Two Hands, and a Compass*. Most people are just stupid..."

"Time to lay low."

"What?"

"You know, not do anything too flashy."

"Here's your coffee, boys."

"Thanks."

But I'm going to be walking home, and I don't want any coffee.

"I don't know what you're talking about," I tell Gerry.

"That's because you're self-absorbed. And you don't care about other people."

"And you do?"

"No," Gerry admits, "But I accept that about myself. I know exactly why it is that I don't know what other people are talking about half the time."

"Because you're self-absorbed?"

"No. Because I just don't fucking care. Listening to the points of view of other people is like sticking your hand into a fat woman."

"And what's wrong with that?"

"A dead fat woman or a sloppy, unconscious fat woman with corn chips on her breath."

"And?"

I know he's got more.

"She's lying in her own vomit."

"I see what you mean, but why, I mean, how is it the same?"

"As what?"

"As listening to the points of view of other people?"

"Oh. That. Intimate connection. Feeling of. But not really."

"No real connection."

"Exactly."

"What about the corn chips?"

"Eh? Oh. That was just for the detail. Like the vomit. You know."

My washing machine got broken. Twice. This is how. The first time it just broke down. Water all over the concrete floor and my clothes wrapped like a dead cat around the bottom of the drum. I swept the water to the drain and took my clothes out to the porch and draped them on the railing. Dead cat porch.

After that I started using the coin-operated machine place across from the Mac's Milk. Hauling your clothes in garbage bags makes you feel younger. But not in a good way.

The way it got broken again was I was already mad and then for some reason I just got a lot madder that this broken washing machine was still in my house. This was about, I don't know, maybe six months later. I was thinking how I was never going to get to Paris this way. Of course the only way to get to Paris is to go to Paris but this was before I knew that so I thought I'd just never get to go because I was stuck in Kemptville with a broken washing machine. I was twenty-seven and I didn't know anything. So by myself I hauled this machine out of the basement, up the stairs, and out into the backyard. I got a baseball bat out of the shed and I just went off on it. I remember neighbours looking pale out of their windows but I didn't care. I remember the grass was pretty long and I didn't care about that either. I'd never been less interested in the length of the grass than I was at that point. Not that things are much better now though because I still sit around in front of the closet mirror with an M1911 in my hand sometimes and I'm still not much for lawn maintenance. I'm the picture of health. Anyway at one point I think I was growling and the bat split and the end of it went flipping up into the air. I thought it was going to land on me and knock me out. I went back to the shed and got the sledge hammer. I remember how the plastic knobs shot right off the machine like flying saucers lifting off. I kept at it until my shoulders ached and a cold spit was draining from me and the machine just kind of melted into the ground but with a lot of noise. It was like time lapse photography. The sixties had Woodstock. The seventies had the moon landing. The eighties had the Berlin Wall, or maybe that was the nineties. Doesn't matter. Then there was 9/11. I'm not comparing my washing machine Holocaust to any of these things. I just felt better when it was done, like something had changed. It was what you call cathartic. Maybe the moon landing was in the sixties, I don't know.

There's nothing like going down on a girl, you know? Guy I knew in high school called it "dining at the Y." I think because he thought that made it seem more like he'd actually done it. We were fifteen. We read our brother's *Playboys*. Maybe he had, I don't know. I doubt it. He died in a bar fire two years after graduation. There was a band and they packed too many people into the bar. It was a metal band and there were fireworks or something. Set fire to the ceiling. Exits were blocked. About a hundred people gone in only a few minutes. Maybe you read about it. Somewhere...Orillia, I think. Anyway. I never liked metal.

Women always want more than we have to give them.
Why don't you talk to me?
I am talking to you...right now.
But not the way I want you to.

I mean. Fuck.

I don't know. At the end I just couldn't give Mel what she deserved I guess. Not that she's a great person or anything. Ask anyone. They'll tell you she's not. They don't like her either.

God and I will never get along.

There was a guy at the bar the other night. He was wearing a wife beater and these big pants, I think they call them cargo pants. He was giving the bar girls a hard time, complaining about his beer, saying it was skunky. Talking about how the service sucked.

"Hey, Gumby," Gerry yelled, "...this is not the only bar in town you know."

It is though really. The only bar.

"Why don't you try and find the other one? It's fun. Like *Where's Waldo?* Where's that other fucking goddam bar?"

And this is the thing about Gerry, this guy was bigger than him by a yard but Gerry gets this look in his eye that makes him seem more like a pirate or some shit. Like he'd slice into you just to see it. Which he wouldn't do. Sure he'd get into a fight but he wouldn't pull a knife or kill anyone. But you can't tell that when he's yelling across the bar with that shiny right eye that he gets. Plus he sometimes wears his work clothes to the bar and, being a butcher, well, they're spattered with blood. This puts people off.

"I mean," eyes glaring, "...it's gotta be around here somewhere, right? Where is it Gumby? Where?"

The guy folded.

"Fuck," Gerry says. "This beer is skunky though... what the hell?"

I don't know. Maybe I was just a cheap version of what she needed. But then so was she. Of what I needed I mean. Then there's all of that other shit. But never mind about that now.

"Whatever happened to that big fucking guard dog they had out back of the bar here?"

"Stolen."

"Fuck, what?"

"Yeah, stolen."

"Who the fuck steals a huge fucking guard dog?"

"Pros."

"Pros?"

"People who know the dog's worth more than the money inside the bar. People with fucking leathery nut sacks too — that was one mean son of a whore that dog."

"When did that happen?"

"I believe it was during that same period of time you were experimenting with the vodka breakfast. Therefore you can't be held responsible for not having noticed."

"Stealing a fucking stolen guard dog..."

"Stolen?"

"Jack stole it in the first place. He told me. Couple of years ago. But it wasn't a guard dog then. He meaned it up a lot."

"I did not know that."

"Well now you do."

"It's a wide and wonderful world."

Are we having the time of our lives? Bet your little ass. Bet it. Break and enter and possession of stolen goods and plea bargaining and serving time are the farthest things from our minds. For the moment.

The darkness can be on you sometimes, every time really, just like the dark cold lying smug emptying bitch that it is. You have some time without it and then it's back all over you again. I'd say it's like a heavy cold wet thick black blanket that gets between you and every other fucking thing that there is in the world except that it's not like that and it is like that but that doesn't say the half of it. I guess it's like being dead and still being alive I guess it's like that. And blind. Or wanting to be blind instead of seeing things clear, instead of seeing at all. Blind drunk. You're okay for a bit and then not. People look at you strange. And they have every right to. Suddenly you're not where you are anymore and you don't want to be anywhere and you're back to sitting in front of the shitty bedroom door shitty mirror with the M1911 sweaty and palm cold and never playing the good guy again. Not that you ever really did anyway, not in a way that would convince anyone. Sitting in front of the shitty bedroom door mirror with the M1911 sweaty and palm cold and shaking and head down and never never coming up again ever. Blind dark dead and no way out. Lying on the carpet and then the grey sun but you can't feel it on you and there is no way you are ever going to get up off of that nasty shitty floor again. Because

there

is

no

fucking

reason.

To.

When it's really bad it's like that. Just like that. Maybe you don't know. I hope that you don't.

You do get up though finally because there's nowhere else to go but up, there being no further way to go down. Pull yourself up with the bedspread. Little fucking clear plastic clips that hold the cheap-ass mirror to the cheap-ass plywood door.

You got a smoke?

"What?"

"I said, do you have a fucking smoke?"

"What the fuck would I be doing with a smoke? I haven't had a smoke in years."

There's lots more people in the bar all of a sudden. Or what feels like all of a sudden, we've been here a while. The band's starting up. I have to get out but I have nowhere to go.

"Just thought I'd ask. C'mon, I gotta get a smoke."

"I just got my coffee."

"Bring it the fuck with you, it's just coffee. Look, I need a smoke right fucking now and I'm going."

There are things in this world you don't get over. You have to keep them with you. And sometimes you need a smoke to make it okay for a minute and just to clear your head out. And when those ads come on TV about smoking and dying you just laugh and you say yeah, bring it on. You say we're going all the way with this, we're all going to go some time anyway.

I have to stop fucking Lisa. No one else needs a tearing down the way I can do it. Why she's around in the first place is one question, some women want to be life rafts. Why I'm letting her, well, that's not a question at all. But it should end. It would be better for her if it ended now.

Not enough room in this world for everything that I

don't need to be a part of anymore or all of the people who have no need to be a part of me. This is no longer a winning proposition for anyone. No trifecta. Not even any leaving of the paddock.

I don't want to bring you down.

"You gotta smoke?"

"Yeah, here."

Some guy out on the curb with his girl.

"Thanks."

"Yeah."

"You happy now?"

I'd tell him to fuck off, but this is Gerry, not the guy with the girl and the smokes. Out with his fucking coffee on the street when he could be inside where it's warm. Oh well. Fuck him.

But not really.

"Happy with your smoke?"

"How's the coffee?"

"Fuck you. That's how it is. It's cold now."

And so we're laughing. And it's better with the smoke and with Gerry bitching in his coat and his toque.

I take a long drag and spit it out slowly over the street.

"So we're really going to do it," he says.

"It?"

"We're going to knock over the store."

"Knock it over, who are you, Edward G. Robinson?"

"Fuck you. So we're doing it though?"

"Yeah. Why not."

She's not going home with him. Sometimes you can just tell. Maybe he's got another smoke on him I could bum before he goes back in.

"Yeah," I say, "Yeah, we're doing it."

And Gerry seems very pleased all of a sudden for a man who's got no fucking idea how to break into a store.

Lisa's got these little dark marks on the undersides of her arms. Both arms. Like she was burned once or something. I'm going to ask her about them I think.

I feel better now. Yes, I do. Better like I did in the hospital with the heavy rubber curtains shut tight against the day and all those drugs, just like always quiet and just always like night. And all those drugs.

It feels like snow coming soon.

It's not that I need another drink, just that I'd enjoy the fuck out of one if it was offered. But it's gone past last call already.

"I'm going home..." I say, "...now."

The moon was bigger when I was a kid. Bigger in size but also a bigger deal. But I guess it's not the moon that's changed. Look at it, it's all watery-silver smooth. Hanging. There.

9.

BLOW JOBS AND
ICE CREAM

*Three guys. I don't know them. They're sitting on some run down
torn out couch in this mediocre room somewhere bad. Smoking in
the cold. Detroit in the winter maybe. There's no heat in this building. Plywood over the windows. They look up when I come in. I
can see my breath. They have a mickey of something brown and
oily that they're passing back and forth. It's dark. One of them offers me the bottle. He smiles at me and his teeth shine in the hanging light. Something is smoking. Something's really really bad in
that room and I want out. If you ever have the misfortune to run
across the Devil for real he probably won't look too bad, is what I
think. In fact he'll probably be the smilingest good-lookingest bastard you ever saw.*

But in heaven it will be all blow jobs and ice cream. Not
that there will be. You know. Heaven. But maybe. Lisa
slept over. So, well, so much for ending that. There is
nothing as interesting as a good girl gone bad. Or as dull
as a bad girl gone good. She's both. I don't know. Maybe
she's neither. I can't quite nail her down. But I keep trying. There's no ice cream. But otherwise things are pretty
good. Here's a picture of her naked in the morning. Only
I don't have a camera. But trust me, you'd want to see this

one. The sheets and her skin patchworked in the sun. She has another tattoo. It's a Ferris wheel. Top of her ass, on the left side. Right there. Pink fingerprint now.

I feel like some scrambled eggs.

There's this saying a famous Quebecois chef said once, I saw it in the paper: *Food — it's all just the shit and the waiting*. And what he meant was, what I think he meant was, a great meal, it's mostly about waiting for it, the anticipation of how it will taste, the work involved in making it, and that it takes a long time, and then there's the eating of it, that takes a second, and then there's the waiting for the shit, and then there's the shit. And then it's over. And that's life.

When I tell people that my dead son is living in the metal of my 1998 Jeep Wrangler they take it funny. So I don't tell them that. Knowledge of something like that changes the way that people look at you. That's why I don't tell them. I just sleep in it sometimes and I make sure the oil changes get done. I'm not going to tell Lisa this. I'm going to watch her ass a while longer and then I'm going to make some fried eggs. Or I could wake her up. And show her this, what I have here. I just want to lie here. Like this. For a while.

A Ferris wheel is perfect. Best ride in the park. All thrills and view. No danger. No feeling like you're going to throw up after. You're alive and you'll stay that way; illusion.

I was going to wake her up and show her what I've got here now but I don't know, I'm hungry and it's fading fast anyway, like a snow cone in early July. Eggs it is. If I have any. Wondering if I have eggs makes me feel old because it's the kind of thing you wonder when you're twenty. And I'm not twenty. By my age either you're married and there are eggs in the fridge or you're still single and by now you're so set in your ways and habits that you know if there are eggs there or not. I'm neither now.

Shit though. Lisa might be. Might not even be. I don't know. And I don't want to know and I don't need to know. No, she's twenty-one. She told me. I think.

Those three guys in my dream though, they wanted to get me drunk on that oily shit and then they were going to roll me. Greasy bastards.

Oh. Eggs. Look at that.

While I'm breaking the eggs this happens:

You know how memories of some things will get stuck in place and you can always return to them? Others get lost and they might as well have never have happened. This is a sticky one. We rented this place in Mexico once. It was cheap. Down the strip from the resorts in a little beach town run by drug gangs and patrolled by soldiers and police that you could tell weren't anything like real soldiers or real police. Cesspools in uniforms. Or maybe not. Maybe they were regular guys who enjoyed barbecue and went home to their wives. But I doubt it. It was called a villa but really it was a concrete box with some storm damage and a palm tree knocked down into the empty pool. There were shots at night and broken glass in the streets. It was three hundred Canadian for a week. How else were we going to get to Mexico? Jake was sleeping well then and there was a lot of sex. A lot of sex. Mel was wearing almost nothing most of the time and whenever Jake was asleep or distracted with a movie we'd be at it.

In the afternoon standing by the open bedroom window, Mel with her head resting on her folded arms on the concrete window sill looking out over the street, me taking her from behind, the sun everywhere, her head bowed down then when she was coming, pushing back against me and I remember her fingers gripped onto the concrete, her knuckles stretched white and red. Dark hair covering her neck. Half an hour later we were fighting again. The bananas I'd bought were rotten in the heat, and somehow that was my fault.

We went for a walk in the afternoon the three of us and I remember out of the corner of my eye something quick like a flurry of birds rising or a newspaper in the wind. It was a guy with an Uzi moving at a trot about eight feet away, out the front door of this little white bungalow and down the sunbaked driveway to the door of a silver SUV. Slow motion sharp blur. Another guy with one of those machine guns, I don't know what they call them, the ones with skeleton stalks, no big rifle butt, just like a wooden crutch. My hand reaching down and pulling Jake closer to myself as if my hand could stop the bullet before it split his skull. The sun on the short, blond hair at the back of his neck. Mel, unaware, walking ahead of us in the middle of the street, wearing a towel over her bikini, the flower print stretched by her ass, her ass swaying in the hard sun. She was eating fresh fruit she'd just bought. Then the SUV swung past her spraying dust.

"Motherfucker!"

Lisa and I eat the eggs and have some coffee then we go back to bed. I push into her from behind, my hands full of her hips, Ferris wheel tattoo moving under me, under my thumb, watching myself slide in and out of her really slowly, pulling her back and forth onto me, the smell of morning ass and sex rising up into my head.

Mel kicking the gravel down the street after the pearl-silver shine of the SUV. That short hair at the base of Jake's neck, lit by the sun, warm and damp.

The truck pausing at the corner, turning and speeding off. Some things, they stick with you. The way those guys walked with purpose as if what would happen when they got where they were going was already a done deal.

"You look so good like that," I tell Lisa. Hoarse voice. She does.

Later that day Jake and I went out walking in the dusty afternoon sun and in the white, baked street he stepped on the cut bottom of a Coke bottle, the green glass etching into the sole of his foot. It was deep enough that the blood refused to stop and kept coming electric red through my fingers as I carried him back to the villa/bunker. Washing and wrapping it with a clean towel, the bright red fold in the dried river beds of his summery paper skin.

"Will I die?"

"Not today."

What you say sometimes is so important, when you say it, and then, after.

Of course it was my fault for not making him wear his sandals. Of course Mel pointed that out. And of course I said it wasn't my fault. We were only going to the beach, a two-block walk. What if it had been a rusty can, she screamed, a syringe? Him lying there in the sun like a small dark line on a piece of paper, jaw slowly clenching permanently shut, body slowly filling up with AIDS. Or like he actually was now, staring up into the sun, a little dizzy from seeing all the blood, slowly rising up into the air like a balloon. Some things are not our fault. Some things just happen and then you can't unhappen them.

Now that we've had sex a few times is there anything left for me and Lisa? There either is, or there isn't. There will be. Or there won't. I don't know right now. I remind myself that I don't have to. Know right now I mean. I don't really have to know anything right now. There's nothing I really have to do.

"When did you first notice me?"

Damn.

Damn.

Damn it.

Is this the time of my life? Fifty-three minutes by the bedside clock. That's not bad. She came three times, maybe four. Am I having the time of my life? Fucked if I can tell and probably not if I can't even tell. Not now. Maybe I loved Mel the wrong way. Maybe there's a right way to do that. To do these things. All of a sudden I feel weary and I feel lost. Lisa wants me to tell her all of the things I cannot think of to tell her right now. Her hand wanders over me.

"The first time I saw you I..."

I start, and then I get stuck.

"You thought well now, there's a girl I'd like to ass end up after some eggs and some coffee," she suggests.

"The food wasn't really a part of it."

"Ah."

"I wasn't hungry at the time."

"How does the rest of the experience stack up?"

My hand is on her breast.

"Well, I knew you'd be multi-orgasmic."

"How did you know that Mister?"

"You might as well have been wearing a T-shirt."

"I didn't know they made those."

"They should. It would make things a lot simpler."

"Yeah?"

"Well, you'd know going in, what to expect."

"It's not always best," she says, her hand backing its way onto my cock, "...to know...what to expect...when you're..."

She shifts position and her mouth is on it now.

"...going...in..."

"Maybe not."

"Besides," she says, taking a moment to stop and observe what she's achieved, "I'm not always...multi...orgasmic...Mister..."

"No?"

Her hand working. Now. Small white hand. Sliding.

"Takes something...

fairly special...

to get...

my trigger...

stuck..."

Two hands. Faster now.

"Yes, Mister...I can tell you..."

My hips rising off the bed, here we go.

"it...

sure...

does..."

And I'm coming

she's biting her lip, her breath in her throat
eyes shining, smiling
and everything's
all right. Everything's
better.
Now.

We fall asleep again. She falls asleep. I lie with my head tilted up against the wall, my eyes open open.

Everything's not better. Everything's not all right. Voices outside. Passing.

Sometimes I feel like a jukebox all filled up with quarters. Other times I feel like this. Most of the time I feel like this. Like an emptied out pie plate. I'm unhappy most of the time. I'm a confident lover, I can go for over an hour, if need be. But I am no lover of needless activity. And I lie. A lot. Small things can make me cry. Not big ones though. Not big ones, ever, which maybe is a problem, I don't know. Some days I just want to get behind the couch and stay there. Most days. Today. I can get things wrong. I do. Sometimes it's all I can do not to pray. Most times I'm just all eaten up with the dumbass. And I know it. I am...generally not well. I'm a man who's come home in a pine box and been left on a winter train station platform. No one there to pick him up. That's how I feel sometimes. Wind kicking up the snow off the tracks. Plastic bag stuck at the top of a tree, the wind at it. Won't let it go. That's how I feel now. She shifts and drags her arm across me. Warm breath now at my neck. Soft skin of a freckled shoulder. Maybe.

"I gotta cut back the drinking," Gerry says, "I'm gonna wake up some morning and find my liver in my sock."

"Yeah."

"You know what this beer tastes like?"

"What?"

"More. It tastes like more. You know what it says to me, this beer?"

"What?"

"It says drink me, it says, drink me Gerry, drink me."

"Yeah."

"It says drink me and then drink all of my friends too. That's what it says. Listen."

He holds the bottle up to the side of my head.

"Yeah."

"Yeah? What the fuck's wrong with you?"

If I were going to commit suicide I wouldn't get it right. I know this about myself now. It's not that I get everything wrong. I get the big things wrong. I got Mel wrong. I got. Well. I don't do well with the big stuff. I'd either take too many pills or not enough. I guess you can't take too many. Maybe you'd throw them up before they took hold. I'd be on the side of the cliff and I'd place the note under a rock and somehow the wind would take it anyway. *Fuck*, I'd be heard to say in a resigned and diminishing voice as I fell. Typical. The power would go out just as I dropped the radio into the tub. At first I'd believe that the darkness was death. Then I'd realize I was still up to my nipples in water and that the tap was dripping. I'd sit there till the water got cold. It takes, I imagine, a great deal of resolve to rise up out of a bath gone cold and reach in the total darkness for a towel when what you had hoped for was death. I don't know that I'd be up to that. Funny thing about darkness. It's never on your side. Anyway, the rope would break. I'd be lying on the basement floor with rope coiled on my chest. I'd misjudge the angle in the subway station and end up a paraplegic. There's not a surgeon on the planet who wouldn't resent having to do that surgery. Fucker should have aimed better. That's what they'd be thinking. I didn't spend ten years in med school just to scrape this fucker off the tracks like an omelette. Maybe they don't think like that, I don't know. I would if I were them. Maybe that's why I stock shelves. I'd take a stutter-step run into traffic that would miraculously miss every car. I'd win the Heisman. Alcohol's obviously not working out as a solution, that's a long-term project. But I get home most days and I keep at it. The alcohol I mean, not the suicide. The bottles are on the counter and the phone is crouching on the table like it's getting ready to ring. I hate answering the phone so I never do. I'll never have a cell phone. Ticking bomb in your pocket. The neighbours talk about me on recycling day, I know that. Particularly in the stern air of nearly winter when you can hear the bottle clinks clear down the street. And I think the furnace is broken. True story: guy in Australia shot himself in the stomach with a shotgun. Didn't die. Had to go out to his truck to get more shells. Then he shot himself in the throat. Missed. Probably the loss of blood affected his aim. Took the side of his neck off though. Then he walked around a bit, they could tell later by the blood trail. Finally he shot himself in the chest. That one took. A handgun's better than almost anything else for the job I think. I'd chicken out with the razor blades. I've already seen most of the blood come out of my body once and I have no interest in watching that show again.

But there'd be no stopping the M1911. It's a machine built for ending things. Life is too long to live like this.

I don't mean to be so dark. I just am.

"What in the name of God is wrong with you?" Gerry asks.

"I don't know."

"No?"

"Let's leave God out of it for now."

"Why?"

"I don't think he's too pleased with either of us at the moment."

"Speak for yourself."

"You think you're doing well with him?"

"I don't think about it at all. Best to leave all that up to him. That's what I think. Why don't you have a drink?"

"I don't want one."

"Why are you so crunchy?"

"How come you never go to church?"

"Church?"

"Yeah."

"Those bald-kneed bastards."

Everything's not better. Everything's not alright. Voices outside.

Passing.

I don't know.

But there's a Ferris wheel turning in the night. Slow.

And all lit.

I gotta buck up.

"What makes you so damned optimistic today?" I ask Gerry.

"I don't know, I just feel good, I'm like a buzzard on a gut truck."

"Yeah? How many beers have you had?"

"Not enough of 'em. Not yet and not nearly."

"I was thinking..."

"Is that a good idea?"

"We should call Johnny. Get him in on this."

"What? Why? Guy got suspended for trying to have sexual congress with a Coke machine. Nobody could ever use that machine again. Big win for Pepsi. He's the stupidest fucker in the history of stupid fuckers."

"If we're going to do this thing we should call him. That's what we need, we need a stupid fucker."

"Why would we call Johnny Socks in on this? Socks could put two and two together and get an egg salad sandwich."

That's not his real name. We've forgotten what his real name is. Gerry and I have both known Johnny Socks for a long time which is about how long we've been calling him Johnny Socks. Knowing Johnny a long time is nothing to boast about really, but he's not the kind of guy who goes away unless you tell him to. Though you've got to like him. Though most people don't. I don't mind him.

"Johnny Socks is dumb as a cob," Gerry says.

"That's why we need him in."

"He's a tool bag. You want some wings?"

"We need somebody in this operation who doesn't know anything."

"Thought that was you. I think I'm gonna get some wings. We need somebody who knows less than we do?"

"That's right."

"Why?"

"What?"

"Why?"

"It gives us the edge. I just always feel smarter when Johnny's around."

"That's because he sucks all the stupid out of the room and uses it all up for himself. He should just end himself. Johnny's like a pubic hair in a biscuit. Hard to get rid of."

"And we need someone to drive."

"Johnny can drive?"

"Not legally no, but he's got two hands and two feet."

"Shouldn't we have someone with, I don't know, a license?"

"What for, so he can produce it when the cops stop us in a car filled with money and crowbars and shit?"

"I think the legal term is break-and-enter tools. You want hot and spicy?"

"I want Johnny outside with the car running, too stupid to know that that's a stupid place to be."

"And cut him in for how much?"

"I don't want hot and spicy."

"Then we'll just get regular."

"Doesn't matter how much. He'll do it just to do it. He's got nothing else to do. Curling doesn't start for a month."

"I don't know, once you get him into this you're not going to get him out, and he's the kind of guy who could surprise you."

"He's too dumb to talk, if that's what you're worried about."

"He's too dumb to remember to breathe. How do you know what he'll do? Maybe we come out looking for the car and he's off getting fries at the chip wagon. I don't like surprises."

"No surprises."

"Never liked surprises since my fourth birthday."

"What happened?"

"When?"

"On your fourth birthday?"

"Nothing. Cake and shit. I think there was a clown."

"That's it?"

"Clowns don't come free you know."

"I mean you said you never liked surprises ever since your fourth birthday."

"Oh. Yeah. Well I walk through the door and everybody jumps up and screams like their jewels are on fire—I get scared as shit."

"You do?"

"Damn right. There's my Uncle Jack jumpin' up from behind the couch like someone shoved an umbrella up his ass and opened it. Screaming like a woman. And he was not a small man."

"And?"

"So I turn around and I blow lunch onto some little girl in a party dress standing there."

"Seriously?"

"I told you, I don't like surprises."

"And that's when you found out."

"That's when she found out, I'll tell you that for fuckin' nothin'. Never saw that dress again."

"See her again?"

"I believe our relationship became strained. I couldn't say for sure."

"You want sour cream or blue cheese?"

"Both."

I know it was my idea to get Johnny to drive but now that we agree to do it I do get this bad feeling about it. Not really really bad though so I drink just enough vodka to kill it. He got his nickname in high school because he always went around the locker room calling condoms sex socks.

"Stock up on the sex socks you womb weasels it's gonna be a big weekend. Gonna be tossing semen around like pizza dough."

Gerry's nickname in high school was Grrr. Obvious reasons.

I never had one.

This afternoon Lisa said, "How come you're always drunk when we fuck?"

Which isn't fair because I wasn't actually drunk at the time but I said, "'Cause I'm drunk all the time?"

Apparently that was not the answer she was looking for. Which, when you really think about the question there's no really good answer to it so I don't know what she was looking for. It's a trick question really. That's pretty much the best answer you could expect under the circumstances.

But she didn't like it.

We will run afoul of the law maybe, Gerry and Socks and I. Maybe not. It seems pretty simple. If it wasn't against the law it would be simpler. But I guess we need laws. I was thinking about that. If there were no laws people would be fucking everywhere, and I don't mean just good-looking people, I mean people you really just don't want to see fucking. There'd be nothing to stop them. Cars, park benches, alleyways, fields, sidewalks. Maybe not everyone. I guess nobody would if there were kids around. Or if it was really cold. But if you think of the number of people doing all that now when there's laws against it how many more would there be if there weren't? People don't get sent to jail for breaking the law Gerry says, they get sent to jail for getting caught.

I change my mind about the wings. What I really want is a big fucking steak and a baked potato.

But people in hell they want a glass of ice water now don't they? So whattya gonna do?

Q: Where were you when the towers went down?
A: Drunk.

If somebody gave me the keys. I'd be gone.
"I need a big bottle of drop dead," Gerry says.
"Let's order some more drinks."

10.

WE ARE SOMETHING UP WITH WHICH THEY WILL NOT PUT

Everything is going wrong. I'm missing something important I think. I don't know. I'm sitting at a folding table at an outdoor shopping mall. A galleria I think it would be called. It feels like 1962. There's a shoe store. Each letter of the name in the sign is on a coloured diamond of its own. The diamonds have long tails hanging down. Black glass in the window. A line of leather shoes behind the glass. The sun is blinding off the concrete where I sit at my table in my black plastic sunglasses with dark circles growing under each arm. I'm handing out pieces of paper to people who pass by. They take the pieces of paper in the bright sun. I smile up at them in my sunglasses. I know that they are throwing out these pieces of paper, my pieces of paper, many without even reading them. I keep smiling. My mind is not right. In my head. You understand that this is a nightmare. Scientists do not really understand why we dream. Synapses firing. We have no idea. I'm handing out pamphlets. Maybe they are maps. These sons of bitches aren't buying them. You understand that this is a nightmare. I can't wake up. These people don't want maps. Don't want to be told where the treasure is. No X marks the spot for them. I don't know what to do. That's the most frightening part. You know? And when I pick them out of the garbage all of the little pieces of paper just say "Fuck You." There's a new study that says we sleep and we dream to clean our minds, get rid of the residue of thinking all day. Like brushing your teeth. I don't think it's working.

I don't remember at what point it became a good idea to sneak a bottle into Otis's room or whose good idea it was. It may have been mine. It turned out to be kind of a bad idea though.

"I heard that if you drink every day that makes you an alcoholic."

"Where the hell'd you hear that shit?" Otis asks.

"It was on television."

"Well I'll tell you one thing for nothing."

"What's that?"

"You watch too much goddamn television."

"I guess."

"Whyntchu turn the hockey game on the radio and let *Dr. Phil* fuck himself up the ass on his own time?"

"You might have a point there."

"Might have a point? Ferchrisake, what the hell would you listen to anything that bastard had to say for? Might as well get yerself a colostomy bag."

"What?"

"It's a bag you shit into when you can't crap out your own hole."

"Shitsake I know what it is Otis, what the hell's it got to do with *Dr. Phil?*"

"What?"

"I said whatthehell's it got to do with *Dr. Phil?*"

"Oh. Nothing, I guess. Just a hell of a thing is all, shitting into a plastic bag. Bastard down the hall has one. A year of shittin' through his belly button from the cancer

BLOUIN

and now he has this bag for the rest of his life. Brings it to breakfast, lunch, and dinner and it sits there in his lap like a cat. I believe someday he's going to start petting it. The bastard."

"You do spin a colourful anecdote."

"I should be on television."

"You could take *Dr. Phil*'s spot."

"Fuckin' right and you know what I'd say? I'd say fuck you and fuck you and fuck you and you all get the fuck off the television and get a fuckin' job and stop fuckin' complaining that's what."

"That's what."

"What?"

"I mean that's what you'd say."

"That's what I'd fuckin' say."

"You're right."

"Fuckin' right I'm right. Fuck."

My heart's on fire. I think it was the wings.

"You got any Tums?"

"Any what?"

"You know, antacid, heartburn."

"I got more pills'n China's got Chinamen, just look in that drawer there..."

The top drawer of Otis's cabinet is filled with pill bottles.

"They let you keep all these in your room?"

"Those aren't mine, mine they bring me one at a time in those little paper cups."

"So?"

"So everybody in this fuckin' place is dying or so strung out they don't know where the fuck they are so you don't think there's a chance now and then to pick up an extra bottle if you still got the brains to tie your own shoes?"

"This one's Percocet."

"Nothin' but the best sonny. Don't use any of those, I'm savin' those. The day they put me in Velcro shoes izza day I'm gonna swallow that whole bottle. They take away yer laces yer as good as dead I'm tellin' you that right now. But one or two of those'll take away your pain quicker'n a two-by-four deftly applied to the forehead."

"Valium. Morphine. Tylenol three. OxyContin. For fuck sake are you on all of these?"

"Sometimes. Collecting them's more of a hobby. If I was you I could sit here and watch *Dr. Fucking Phil* all day but I need more than that from my life. I need the challenge of the hunt. You think it's easy scrappin' all that medication together?"

"In a building filled with pills?"

"Fuck you. Yer the one asked for the fucking pills."

"You two always get along this well?"

I forgot Gerry was here.

"He started it," I say.

"Fuck you," Otis says.

"Fuck you and your pills then," I say closing the drawer.

"Are you fucking my nurse? Are you fucking Lisa?"

"Maybe I am and maybe I'm not."

"That means you are. I wouldn't give you any of my pills if you were the fucking Pope."

"You got any Viagra in there?"

"You need some?"

I was going to say something about using it to fuck his

nurse but, something about his nurse being Lisa, I found the whole sentence just stuck in my throat like a peanut.

"You know the Chinamen don't like it when you call them Chinamen," I say instead.

"Fuck 'em then. Should'na been born that way if they don't like it."

"You know, how, when kids sleep, they look, you know, like angels, and there comes this point, in the aging process, where when you're asleep you don't look like a kid anymore, you look like a corpse."

"You saying I look like a corpse?"

"I'm saying you look like fucking Lon Chaney."

"You boys aren't playing nice," Gerry says, "Let's us have us another little drink."

Well it's true. His face is deep treaded like a winter tire. Gerry starts pouring more shots into the little paper cups.

"C'mere and take my pulse," Otis says.

"What? Why?"

"Whaddya mean why? I'm an old man and I might be dying. You and your fucking foul mouth have got me all wound up. My heart gets going too fast, it's gonna bust up like a hot tomato. Just do what I tell you."

I edge up on him and reach for his wrist. Before I get to it he's grabbed my nuts and he's twisting them like they're in a food processor.

"What the fuck d'you have to fuck my little nurse for you little fuck? There's no one else out there you could fuck, you gotta come here and sort through my trash?"

Spit's coming out of his mouth like ice.

He won't let go of my nuts. Jesus Christ he won't let go of my nuts.

"Gerry…"

"Hey," Gerry says casually.

That's helping.

"Hey," he says again.

I'm going down to the floor. Otis has me like a vice. He's pretty sure I won't hit him. I'm pretty sure I won't either but *Jesus Christ he won't let go of my nuts*. I've gotta move my nuts beyond arm's reach then he'll have to let them go.

"Drinks are ready boys," Gerry says. I'm kicking against the wheelchair.

And he lets go.

"Why didn'tya pour 'em up to the top Gerry? These are pretty small cups," Otis says.

I hear this sideways from my spot on the floor.

"More where that came from. Drink up Oty."

"Pick yer nuts up and have a drink," Otis calls down to the floor.

My heartburn hasn't got any better.

"You got anything to eat?" I ask.

Gerry says I'm grabbing onto Lisa in desperation. But isn't that what we always do? We always grab onto women out of desperation like they're life rafts. Most of them aren't though. I'm okay with that. That's not their fault. We put that on them. It's not their job. Besides, she's great in bed. Not every girl is going to shove her thumb up your ass when you're coming. Not on a second date anyway. She knows what I want. Women always know what we want because it's so fucking simple: we want them. And we know what they want. They want a world where they don't have to put up with us.

"I got some saltines, the unsalted ones..."

"You do live on the edge."

"Look, fuck you again Sonny Boy. You want the Nut Scrambler again? Floor hasn't seen a mop like you in a while. Look, it's shining."

"It does look nice and smooth where your legs were kicking there," Gerry adds.

"Fuck your saltines, I'm hungry."

"Have some nuts."

"Funny."

"Where I come from you ask a man for food, you take the food he offers, you don't tell him his cupboard's full of shit. I didn't ask you to come over here tonight so's you could critique my snack foods you know."

"I didn't ask to be born."

"Couldn't be helped. I came inside your mother."

"Where're the crackers?"

"Second drawer down. Pour us out some more Gerry."

I move towards the dresser.

I look Otis in the eye.

"You touch me again I'll kill you old man."

"Big words."

"Fuck off."

"Big words...little nuts."

"I thought you were going to die soon. Didn't some doctor say you were going to die soon?"

"They don't know nothin' around here. You just want your hands on my will."

"Yeah. I'm here waiting to inherit your bathrobe and your unsalted saltines. What the hell do they call them saltines for if they ain't got no salt?"

That shuts him up for a while. While he's thinking about it I open up a sleeve of crackers.

"Time for more drinks Gerry," I remind him.

"Oh, yeah…"

We eat the crackers while Gerry pours out more shots.

"Anything on TV?"

"There hasn't been anything on TV since Johnny Carson signed off. What the helld' this Kim Kardashian broad do to get famous for besides getting her ass fucked in a home movie? That's what I want to know. You know what you got in my day when you got your ass fucked in a home movie? Crabs. That's what you got. You got crabs. You got piss like yoghurt."

"You speaking from experience?"

"You never mind that little nuts."

"FUCK YOU — you're an asshole!"

That isn't now. I'm remembering this time that Gerry starts yelling at me from nowhere. Just shows up at my door in the middle of the night under the lightbulb and he's screaming this shit at me.

"What?"

"I SAID FUCK YOU — YOU'RE AN ASSHOLE!"

"What the fuck's wrong with you Gerry? It's…it's four o'clock in the damn morning."

"FUCK YOU ASSHOLE I DON'T CARE WHAT FUCKING TIME IT IS!"

"What the hell? Gerry get in here, I don't need any more shit with the neighbours…"

"FUCK THE NEIGHBOURS! FUCK ALL OF YOUR NEIGHBOURS, YOU HEAR ME NEIGHBOURS? FUCK YOU! ASSHOLE! ASSHOLE!"

"Fuck you. I'm going to bed."

I start to close the door but Gerry grabs it and pushes it against me.

"ASSHOLE! ASSHOLE! ASSHOLE!"

Every time he yells it he's banging the door against me.

"Fuck off!"

"MAKE ME YOU PUSSY! WHY DON'T YOU? WHY DON'T YOU? PUSSY!"

His face is all red and he's spitting the words and I'm banging the door back at him now. It's like we're wrestling with the door. I've had enough of whatever this is, friend or not.

"JUST FUCK OFF GERRY OR I'LL PUT YOU DOWN!"

"DO IT THEN, EH? JUST DO IT! TRY IT!"

So I do. My right hand's jammed up with the door so I give him a left undercut, I've seen that one put him down before. He doesn't go down though, he bounces off the porch railing and feels his jaw. He looks at me.

"NO YOU FUCK. THAT'S NOT A HIT! THAT'S NOT A HIT! YOU CALL THAT A HIT? YOU CAN'T HIT SHIT!"

So I hit him again. This time right to the jaw. I remember thinking it was funny he didn't counter. It put him down backwards off the porch and onto his ass on the lawn.

I stepped down and helped him back up to his feet.

He started feeling his jaw again. Then his tongue lolled out all like red liver and like it was looking for something.

"YES!"

He's laughing now and doing that little dance he does when he's happy. Which is funny because blood's just pouring from his mouth now like he's tried to set the record for eating catsup. The blood is streaming. That's what it's doing. Like a garden hose.

"What's wrong with you?"

"Nothing! Nothing, not anymore...that infected tooth I had, it was killing me. You just knocked it out!"

"That's what this was about?"

"Bitch was killing me."

He's looking around on the lawn for the tooth.

"There she is!"

He picks up the white gleaming red smeared tooth like it's a Kinder Surprise Egg and holds it up between us.

"Thanks man! You got any beer?"

That's Gerry and dentists. He doesn't like 'em.

So we watch the TV for a while. Me and Otis and Gerry I mean. This is now again. There isn't too much on TV. Otis doesn't get many channels. After a few more drinks Otis is slack jawed in his chair, his head drawn back. I take a close look to see if he's breathing.

"Are you dead or are you dying?" I ask him.

His eyelids flicker.

"Fuck off."

His breath smells like plastic wrap.

That night I told you about, when I put Gerry down on the front lawn, we just had one beer and said that was enough of that. We had to work in a few hours.

My hand bruised up really bad that day. The skin was stretched tight over the purple.

"Wow," Gerry said, "That looks like a blueberry pie mashed up in a plastic bag. Sorry man."

I couldn't move my fingers for three days.

Walking home is a bit of a challenge, but not too bad. Ahead of me by about a block I see something in the dark and I'm not sure what it is at first. It looks like flashing red lights going around and around and down close to the ground like a small circus midway. Then I realize it's a kid in a pair of those shoes that light up on the bottoms. The kid's out late.

I get home. No Lisa. But at least there's nothing on fire.

"Why'd you fuck my nurse?" I remember Otis saying.

Because she's pretty.

Because she let me.

And by God, if she lets me I'll do it again.

And why's that kid with the shoes out so late? What the hell are his parents thinking? What the hell is it with those light-up shoes anyway? *Hey look at me!* That's what those shoes are saying. That's what light-up shoes are for, to draw attention. Look at me! Look at me! Like a spotlight. Like a burning bush. Who the hell needs that? I'd rather walk in the dark. I'm nobody's fucking burning bush.

Jakey's joke:

Question: What do you call a lady with marmalade on her head?

Answer: Margaret.

Makes no sense right? That's what's so funny.

Like life.

11.

WHEN GOOD THINGS HAPPEN TO BAD PEOPLE

It's a dream where I'm skateboarding and I'm doing all kinds of tricks. I'm so good it looks like I'm moving in slow motion. Only I don't skateboard when I'm awake. That's it. That's the whole dream. That not enough for you? Fuck you. I don't have to make some kind of shit up just to impress you. No. I won't do it.

"What do you think about that new kid on cash?"

"The one with the glasses?"

"Yeah."

"Kid smells like a Band-Aid."

"Is that what that smell is?"

"That's what it smells like. I don't know what it is."

Some girls like to be treated rough. They like it that way. I mean treated that way all the time. That's not for me. I like it when they're just like that in bed. Not in the rest of their lives. And not all the time in bed either. Just sometimes. And not really rough there either, I mean...a little. Otis's advice on sex: *Whatever she wants, give her some of that, as much of that as she wants, much as she can take, but no more than she wants, 'cause there's some other yokel in the wings who'll do her better, give her just the right amount of whatever it is she wants, you betcha.* That's what I was thinking when I was front-facing the Fruit Loops. Then I was wondering what kind of a bird Toucan Sam is. I had moved on to the Corn Pops before I realized: Jesus Christ. He's a toucan.

Johnny Socks comes in. Which seems as unlikely as hell since we were just talking about him and now here he is. That's the universe at work, trying to give you what you think you need. He's sorting through the cans of tuna. I haven't seen him in months, maybe in a year.

"Socks is in the store," I tell Gerry.

"What?"

"Socks. Johnny Socks. Aisle Three."

"What the hell's he doing here?"

"He's fucking up my tuna cans, that's what he's doing."

"He's a fuck up, I told you. He's as irritating as a fucking mime. Except that he talks."

Gerry wipes the blood from his hands.

"That's the worst kind of mime. Fucking talking mime."

Of course he's whispering this. People do not appreciate profanity from their grocery staff. Ray has made this clear to us more than once. Mostly he's made it clear to me. Nobody cuts meat like Gerry so he has built-in job security, like I said, he's not getting fired. Ray still doesn't like it when he says "shitfuck" in front of the customers though. Which he does more than most other butchers do I think. Butchers, on the whole, are a pretty quiet group. Not likely to speak unless spoken to. They stay mostly in the back room drenched in blood. Do you have any nice pork chops? *Yes Sir, I do.* Sirloin tips? *Yes Ma'am.* Is this beef fresh? *Shitfuck what the fuck do you think? You think I'm selling fucking tainted beef here? What the fuck's wrong with you? Who climbed up your fucking jamhole?* That last one was just Gerry. Other butchers don't talk like that. Ray was quite unhappy that day. Gerry says what the fuck do I care? Gerry says until there's an employee of the month program I'll talk however the fuck I want. But mostly he keeps it low.

"That's weird, you talk about him and he just shows up like this."

"It's like the Bermuda Triangle."

"Some Area 51 shit."

A woman in a jean jacket asks Gerry for some ground round. I don't know what that is. I think it's like fancy hamburger. He wraps some up in brown paper and hands it to her.

"What is ground round?" I ask him.

"Hamburger."

Not even fancy then.

"Not fancy hamburger?"

"No. That's sirloin chuck."

"So it's just hamburger then."

"Pretty much."

"Why doesn't she just buy the hamburger in a tube then?"

"Because she enjoys dealing with an artist, how the fuck do I know? That meat they sell in tube's been a long time away from a cow."

"How long?"

"These days? May not have ever seen a cow. Probably grown in a test tube in China."

"Really?"

"Enough ketchup and you'll never know the difference."

"Really?"

"Until you grow a third testicle. Look, there he is."

Johnny Socks is walking by with his arms full of salt and vinegar potato chip bags and a large ham. He looks happy all the time. Like I said, he's not very smart.

"Johnny," I call out.

He doesn't hear me.

"Socks!" Gerry yells.

Johnny turns quickly, as if someone is trying to steal his ham. Then he sees us and smiles.

"Hey fellas."

This is what I mean about Johnny, well, it's one of the things that I mean. Nobody has used the word "fellas" since 1966. But it fits him like a glove.

"Neither one of you been arrested yet?" He asks.

And this is what else I mean about him. Or maybe about us, because even though what we're looking for is someone who can be relied on to drive a quick getaway car and keep his mouth shut about it and even though he starts talking about getting arrested right after saying hello, we hire him anyway. We hire him based on his smile and his name and his armful of canned, cooked ham. We are not a gang people will write books about. We are the kind of gang that goes down in a hail of bullets and nobody cares about it when they see it in the paper. *Serves 'em right,* they say…*what were they thinking?*

We're the gang that says:

"I thought you brought the gun."

"I thought you brought the gun."

We are that kind of gang.

But Johnny's the kind of guy who thinks we should get T-shirts printed up.

"T-shirts?" Gerry asks.

"You know, gang shirts, so people'll know we're in a gang."

"But we don't want people to know that Socks, and I think it's important that you understand me on this point, we will require a degree of deception and a certain amount of subtlety that will not be augmented by T-shirts."

"Sure. But it would look cool, that's all."

"You know what else would look cool?"

"What?"

"Your face curled up around my fist. That."

"Why?"

"I just think it would widen your perspective."

"I think what Gerry is trying to say..."

"I'm trying to say that if you even mention this to anyone I'll plow my fist into your face up to my elbow. You'll need a pry bar to get it out again."

"...is that it's important to stay quiet about this."

"Quiet as the dead." Gerry is nodding his head and staring at Johnny as if he is going to grasp his head on either side and start nodding it too, or smash it into the table.

"Quiet as the dead," he says again.

"Quiet," I emphasize, putting my fingers to my lips.

"As the dead," Gerry adds.

"Got it," Johnny says.

This will all work out fine.

"We're not using any guns," I say to Gerry quickly as if it's suddenly the most important thing, which it is kind of.

"Why would we use guns?" Gerry asks.

"Okay."

"We're not going after the Nazis here, it's a simple job."

"Right."

"A crowbar. Maybe some bolt cutters. Just stuff like that."

"Just the stuff we need."

"Right. It's the difference between months and years, if you get caught, a gun."

Gerry finishes his beer.

"If you get caught," he adds.

"But we won't get caught," I point out to Johnny.

"Because we're not getting any fucking T-shirts, so you can stop acting like an itchy hillbilly at a crack barbecue," Gerry adds, the red coming back to his eyes.

"And we're not bringing any guns," I add.

I like all of this because it makes my head stop thinking about anything else. I just think about this. Being inside Lisa makes my head stop too. I just think about Lisa and it's like taking some kind of pill. I'm drinking less this week too. I think.

An hour and fifteen. That's my limit. I mean not counting warm-ups or any of that other stuff before. Just the main action. An hour and fifteen. Much more than that and there's a lot of sore to be had the next day and to be honest, good as it is, after that long you do start to wander a bit, think about what's on television, get hungry, want sleep. It's not like that every time, I don't think you'd even want it to be. It's different every time. We're pretty good at it, that's what I'm saying. Lisa gets pissed if she catches me checking the clock though.

"You got somewhere else you have to be right now Sailor?"

"Nope. Just...right...here."

"Oh. Mm. Yuh."

But my eyes wander back to the clock from time to time.

"I ain't billin' you by the hour you know."

"Good, 'cause I can't afford it."

"Get your head in the game, boy."

"Good. Yeah."

"Right…in…there…"

Anyway. I try not to look at the clock because it does piss her off. Of course sometimes it's all about the quick. I mean when it's all over real quick, but in a good way. And sometimes it's just, well, like I say, it's different every time pretty much. So I'm kind of hoping she doesn't go anywhere soon. Wander off somewhere. Forget where my house is. Want me dead. But I'm realistic about it too. Bad happens.

But it looks like not right now. She'll want me dead eventually.

In bed I'm a sure bet. Other places. I'm not. This is what it looks like from here anyway. I'm in a house and it's on fire.

"You really think Johnny's too stupid to drive the car?"

"Well, let me tell you this: if it sucks cock like a sheep and it takes it up the ass like a sheep then it's a sheep."

Gerry has a way with an expression.

"You know what I mean?" he asks.

"Yeah."

Stop drop and roll.

Here's a story I heard, some guy was in New York once, eating French fries somewhere, some crowded restaurant. And this hand reaches in and takes one, dips it in the ketchup. And it's Bill Murray. He whispers, *No one will ever believe you.*

Probably not a true story but a great story. You can get a lot of what you need in this world with a smile and a good line. You can get a lot of other stuff you want with money.

"I think there's something wrong with your vagina," I tell Lisa.

"What? It's four in the morning."

"I said...I think there's something wrong with your vagina."

"Like, what?"

"I think it's asleep."

"Well..."

"I think it's sleeping."

"Try poking it..."

"Yeah?"

"With a stick. Might wake it up."

Twenty-six minutes later she says, "Oh no. I don't think I can do that again..."

And then she does.

Okay. Enough of all this wandering around. What happens in the next part of the book is that we rob the store. So you know what's coming. Me and Gerry and Johnny Socks. On Christmas Eve. That's Gerry's idea. "Nobody's around," he says. "I don't even think the cops are out. And it's not like any of us have anywhere else to be right?" He has us there. Otis isn't going to be trimming the fucking tree. Lisa is going to be with her family which is as good a reason as any to be out robbing a store. I didn't think I'd ever rob a store, but once we start, everything about it seems pretty normal. That's the way it is with most things I guess. I read this thing once on the computer about a guy who got caught having sex with horses. He said that after the first few times it just felt normal. Like he forgot that nobody else was doing it and the horse probably wasn't a big fan of it and it was just plain crazy. Poor bastard. There's a lot more snow than I'd like on Christmas Eve. Socks doesn't have real snow tires and we spin out twice on the way to the store.

"Socks why don't you have snow tires or chains or some shit for winter?" I ask, just out of interest, "This is Canada."

We should have used some other car. Not mine or Gerry's but some car. Socks has agreed to ditch his car after the job in case it's spotted and neither of us can beat that. We could have stolen one. In for a penny, in for a pound, and all. But why multiply the crime when Johnny's being so accommodating? The car's on its last legs anyway, you can see through the floor to the road in spots. And nobody wants to wake up and find their car gone.

"Slows me down. I'm a hundred per cent go," Socks says.

Gerry shoots me a look.

"Hundred per cent stuck you mean."

"What do you say that for?" Socks asks.

"I mean you lack a certain suppleness and agility of mind. You really do."

Gerry is now reaching into a bag at his feet and taking out three fluorescent-orange balaclavas.

"Merry Christmas. Put these on," he says.

"Shouldn't these be black?"

"Yeah, but black is harder to find than you'd think. They just make the orange ones for hunting. Tried Canadian Tire, Giant Tiger, everywhere. Think about it, black is for bank robberies and terrorists. Limited market."

"Well..."

Johnny decides to put his vote in.

"Gerry's right," he says, "they're not to make us unvisible, just hide our faces."

"Socks," Gerry says.

"Yeah?"

"Just drive. And there's no such word as unvisible. Jesus."

Johnny drives. It's taking a while now because the snow is really coming down hard and only one of the wipers is working.

"Oh," he says, "Look at that. That is butter."

Johnny's looking at some girls walking down the sidewalk holding scarves in front of their faces.

"Socks, how can you even tell, they're wrapped up like Subway sandwiches. Hell, Socks, those could be guys..."

"Nope, that is some creamy butter, I bet they'd like a ride, especially with guys with guns and shit..."

"Eyes on the fucking road Johnny, and we don't even have guns."

"They don't know that. We got crowbars."

"Yeah. Nothing gets a teenaged girl more interested in random sex with a stranger in a ski mask than a crowbar. You're an idiot."

"I'm just sayin'."

"No, you're just drivin'. You just focus on the driving. Do you actually know how to drive?"

"Shit you shoulda seen me last night spinning out doughnuts in the beer store parking lot, you wouldn't even ask that question."

It's two o'clock in the morning so there's no other cars around and it still takes half an hour to get from Johnny's place to the store. It occurs to me that I should ask why he's wearing a cowboy hat.

And why are people so goddamned goddamned goddamned stupid?

I'm just asking. It's been on my mind. It's one of the shitty things I end up thinking and then I end up drinking and watching lesbian porn and crying. Sometimes. It's snowing out and I'm sweating like a Mexican drug mule. I'm not excluding myself from the question above, about the stupid people. Obviously.

We pull up at a stop sign and there's some guy standing there on the corner in a parka and a hood looking into the car with a face like an angry vagina. This whole thing might be a bad idea.

He's tapping on the window now. His breath is steam and snow is banking up on his hood. Maybe he's pissed off that he has nowhere to go on Christmas Eve.

"What do we do now?" Johnny wants to know.

"Well, I don't know," Gerry says, "We're wearing facemasks, I gotta bag of break-and-enter tools here, and you forgot to take the license plates off your car, so, I don't know Socks, drive?"

But Johnny's already got his window halfway down.

"Good, you?" he's saying to the guy.

Guy's giving us the spit eye.

"You boys goin' huntin'?" he wants to know.

"Just drive, Socks," Gerry's saying, on the quiet.

"Early start, you know? Catch 'em before they're up."

"On Christmas?"

"Drive, Socks."

"They'll still be in their pajamas. They won't know what hit 'em."

"Drive now or I'm going to use this pry bar to pop your right eye out of your head like a fucking cocktail olive."

"Better watch yer toes, Mister."

And we're off fishtailing down the street like we're leaving the pits at Talladega.

"You know, Socks, if that plug catches your plate number and puts it together with the store getting robbed tonight the only course of action will be one that takes hours to clean up."

"You see I…"

"Hours."

"Yeah."

"I will put you down."

"But…"

"I'd explain it to you in a way you'd understand but I don't speak moron."

I guess until we've all gone home to Jesus, I guess we're free to make as many mistakes as we want. That's the way I think it is. I wish I was home. I wish I was inside Lisa and coming like a fistful of amphetamines. I wish.

If wishes were horses we'd all be up to our curled hairs in horse shit. You know what I mean? That's some snow out there. It's really fucking snowing now.

Guy had sex with horses. You can't make that shit up even.

12.

IF A NAKED WOMAN COMES TO YOUR WINDOW

It's like everybody in my life is just squeezing past me to get out the back door. Okay, I'm out of dreams again so this isn't one. This happened just like this. Just like I say.

We're sitting in the Jeep and we're waiting for Mel. We're going to her father's funeral. It's the hottest day of the decade and she can't figure out what to wear. It's taking a long time. Kind of day where you're sweating before you get your clothes on. I keep fiddling with the keys because I'm a little nervous that the Jeep isn't even going to start.

"Lucky looks like he's going to piss," Jakey says. He's holding the beagle up in the air. We have to take the damned dog with us because he'll eat everything in the house and shit it out everywhere if we don't. Jakey's twelve, he'll be dead before he's thirteen. He'll die in this Jeep. Neither of us know this. We're just living.

"Just drop him out the window," I say. "If a dog's gonna piss on your seats you toss him out of the window. Unless you're driving ... unless you're driving fast."

Jake's just holding him.

"Drop 'im out there."

"I am."

Mel's taking a long time. We have to get all the way across the river over to Gatineau. For ten. I feel myself sticking to my shirt. Then she's coming out the door swinging her keys.

"Here she comes. Get the dog," I tell Jake.

She has her sunglasses on. She opens the door and gets in.

"Lucky, c'mere boy," she says and she pats her lap. She has a short black skirt on. Black stockings. The dog jumps up like we're going to a dog party.

"Did he piss?" she asks Jakey.

"I think so . . ." he answers from the back seat.

And then of course comes the scream and the hot piss on her lap and then she throws the dog into the back seat and slaps at her legs trying to get rid of the wet.

"Damnit damnit damnit," and she looks at me like I can do something about a skirt covered with dog piss. Which I can't. She looks at me like I can never do anything and that's not true, sometimes I do. And then she's out of the Jeep and slamming the door and she's crying all the way back into the house.

"Are you going in there?" Jakey asks.

"Of course . . ." I say, "Yeah, I'm goin'' in there."

I open my door and get out. I'm still looking at the door of the house. Her sunglasses are on the grass. It's fucking hot.

"Dad."

"What?"

"Go."

"Yeah."

And she's sitting on the floor next to the washing machine crying. She has her face in her hands. She's in her underwear, her skirt's in a ball on the floor. She looks just like a little kid. I sit down on the floor next to her and put my hand on her leg. I have no idea what to do. People die. Then you're sad. If I could be sad instead of her I would. Maybe I should tell her that. I don't. She puts her hand on mine and then she gets up.

"Let's go," she says.

"You sure?"

"Let's go," she says again, nodding her head. She pulls another skirt from somewhere. I can tell it isn't as good of a skirt. It's not the one she wants to wear. I think about Jakey in the car. Probably wondering what's going on in here. Hottest day in ten years and he's sitting in the back seat of a car with a tie on.

I loved to watch her pulling on a skirt. Sliding her legs in one at a time and then hiking it up over her ass with little tugs. Smooth and soft.

So then we're driving a while and she turns and says in a very small voice that's turning to tears, "I don't want to go," and her voice is so much like a little girl who's afraid to go somewhere, to school or to the dentist, that I want to hold her and tell her it's going to be okay. But I'm driving. And I know it isn't. It isn't going to be okay. No one knew then how much worse it was going to get.

"I know," I say.

"It's okay," I add.

But I know that it isn't. And her head is shaking slowly back and forth and she puts the back of her hand to her mouth. She looks out the window. She just keeps shaking her head as everything goes by.

I want to help her.

And I can't. And I'm sweating like a whore with two beds.

Actually, Socks does a pretty good job of driving up behind the store, nice and slow and the lights off at the right time, and you can hear the crunch of the snow under the wheels and not much else. Then the crunch gets slower and slower and then we stop.

"Good," Gerry says, "Good. That's good Socks."

The snow is ticking against the windshield. The one wiper is doing its best.

"That's good. Okay."

We wait for Gerry to do something.

"What do we do first?" I ask.

"Right. First we get out of the car."

So we get out of the car. All three of us get out and we're standing there looking at each other over the roof in our headgear like three thermometers with eyes.

"Get back in the car Socks," Gerry says.

"Why?"

"Because this isn't a fucking cocktail party, do you see any bastards walking around here with shrimp on a stick? No. You stay in the car. You're the driver. You never fucking get out of the fucking car Socks. If aliens land here you stay in the fucking car. If a naked woman comes to your window and asks you to get out and pleasure her you stay-in-the-fucking-fucking-fucking-fucking car. Right? Fuck."

"What next?" I say after Johnny gets back into the car. This is the point at which it occurs to me that I might have thought this out more in advance. This is not the first time in my life I've had this thought. I do have to unfuck some things in my life. I really have to get some things unfucked.

"What's that?"

Gerry has opened the trunk and he is sorting through a gym bag.

"What?"

"Fucking that, that fucking gun, what the fuck is that? Is that a fucking gun? That's a fucking gun. That's a... that's a fucking gun."

"Yeah."

"Fucking yeah? Fucking *yeah*?"

"It's a gun. You never know."

"Never know? You never know what it's like to get shivved in the exercise yard until you get shivved in the exercise yard Gerry. What's wrong with you? Why did you bring a gun?"

Gerry looks confused. I bring it down to a whisper in case Johnny can hear us through the windows and over the sound of the wiper and what sounds like "Dancing Queen" on the radio. There's snow collecting on Gerry's balaclava. He's looking at me like I'm holding things up for no good reason, he's got an angle on his face like he's waiting for me to say, "Oh right, a gun, okay good, a gun, good thinking Gerry, okay let's go."

"After everything you said to Socks about it you go ahead and bring a gun anyway?"

"All that shit was to stop him from bringing a gun, not to stop me from bringing a gun."

"What's the difference?"

"The difference is I'm not a tampon. I know what's up."

"What's up is some guy's dick up your ass in the fucking shower when you're in for five to ten, what the fuck is wrong with you?"

"What do you want to do?"

"Well I'm not going anywhere with that."

"Fine."

Gerry's pissed, I can tell. Then Johnny turns the radio up. Gerry takes the gun out of the bag and looks around.

"Socks, turn off the fucking radio!" he yells, too loud, "Fuck, I'm gonna shoot him."

He's agitated.

"That's why we shouldn't have a gun. You gotta get rid of that gun right now."

"This is a six-hundred-dollar gun, I'm not just going to throw it in a dumpster."

"Well put it somewhere."

"I'll give it to Socks."

"What?"

"There's no bullets, the worst he can do is put his eye out."

So he gives it to Johnny who receives it in his two hands like it's a birthday present.

"I thought…" he says.

"Fuck you. Don't think. Just be in the front of the store in eight minutes. All right, let's go."

"I thought you quit smoking," I say.

"I did."

"Like ten years ago."

"Yeah."

"You got cigarettes in the bag though."

"I'm tense. I been thinking of starting up again."

"Since when?"

"An hour ago. Be prepared, I say. Look you comin' in or not? You're givin' me the shakes. I might have a smoke right now."

Gerry swings by me with the gym bag and jumps up onto the loading dock platform. We don't need to crowbar the door or anything because Gerry has the key from coming in early all the time. His plan is to break a window on the way out after we turn off the video camera that covers the main part of the store. It was a good plan before the gun. The gun is ruining everything for me. Once we're inside, Gerry hands me a flashlight and we go up the back stairs from the loading dock to Ray's office. Gerry kneels down at the door and I hold the flashlight on the doorknob. This is the only door he doesn't have a key for so he's been studying up about it on the computer. He opens up the gym bag and that's when I see it, when I see them.

"What the fuck is that?"

"What?"

"That."

"Just hold that light steady, I can't see a goddamned thing."

I turn off the flashlight. It's black.

"What the fuck?"

"There's several sticks of what look like dynamite in that bag," I say, "You have a comment about that?"

"My comment is turn the fucking flashlight back on so I can get this fucking door open."

I turn it back on again and shine it in his face.

"Fuck, willya stop with the light? Look, we've only got a certain amount of time before Socks takes off the fuck out of here to get some doughnuts, so let's just do this. Okay?"

I swing the light back to the knob but I'm seriously thinking of just walking out on this.

"Where the fuck did you get dynamite?"

"I can't fucking get this open...a friend of mine works construction okay? I told him I had a beaver dam to get rid of. He helped me out."

He's got tools in both hands now and it doesn't look like anything's budging.

"Fucked you up you mean. What else do you have in there? Heroin? A bazooka? What the fuck else do you have in there Gerry? What the fuck do we need dynamite for? That might draw some attention don't you think?"

"Not if we don't use it. Okay maybe the dynamite wasn't the best idea. Look, if we don't get in here the dynamite's not gonna matter. Look in the bag and get me a Robertson willya?"

I push the dynamite to the side and start digging with the flashlight in my mouth, which makes it difficult to talk.

"Udda bout a connon? Ja bring a connon widju? Ee cud ooze a connon do bow down da door…u godda godmm connon in ere Gevvy?"

There's drool coming down my chin and dripping into the bag and I'm pissed. I'm tired of everything being so fucked up all the time. Why is it? I can't see a Robertson. There's a yellow handle. It's a hammer.

"We've gotta get this open," Gerry is saying.

I stand up and take a cold, solid swing with the hammer. The knob just pops off the door and shoots across the hall barely missing Gerry's head.

"Fuck!"

The knob is still spinning on the floor as I step over Gerry and into Ray's office.

"It's open," I say.

Now we have two flashlights cutting through the little office. We don't turn on the light. The building's empty. I don't know, it just seems unprofessional to turn on the light.

"It's in one of the drawers," Gerry says.

"Which one?"

"I don't know. The locked one."

I try a few.

"Gerry, they're all locked."

"He locks it with this little key he's got attached to his belt."

"They're all locked."

Gerry looks at me. All I can see are his eyes surrounded by orange wool.

"Hit 'em," he says.

So I start with the hammer. The filing cabinet's not so hard but the desk is made of oak or some shit so it takes longer. It's like being in the little room with a wood chipper. Splinters are flying everywhere. We start to rifle though the open drawers.

"Got it," Gerry says.

"Wait."

"Whattya mean wait? I got it."

"Look here a sec."

"What?"

"Russian porn."

"What?"

"He's got a whole drawer full of Russian porn. Look at this."

There's a stack of very shiny magazines in the bottom drawer of the desk on my side. Women and men. Women and women. Women and...things. Women who look like they just got home from shopping for pasta. Men who look like they have to get back to work soon. Men who should really shave more. Men who look like they don't shower. Everybody's pasty white. There are skin conditions. It's all very shiny.

"What's he doing with that stuff?"

I give Gerry a look.

"I mean what's he doing with it here?"

It takes a moment.

"Oh that's nasty."

"That's really what that is. That is nasty."

I close the drawer.

"Let's not speak of this."

"We can't."

"Not even to each other."

"Ever."

"Alright."

"By the way. Shitload of money over here."

The drawer Gerry has opened is full. There's enough money to start a small kingdom. Or to get Otis to Montreal. There's more money in Gerry's drawer than there is porn in my drawer. It's not shiny like porn but it looks really, really good. Like pizza in the oven. Each little stack of it just sitting there like a brick full of "Fuck you I'm goin' to the casino."

"Let's go. You get this into the bag and I'll take care of the video camera."

"You sure there's only one?"

"I was here when he got back from Canadian Tire with it. All I've gotta do is unplug it."

"That's it?"

"That's all."

I think you might not understand the situation about Mel. Red nails, top and bottom. Red nails and ready to go. Always. All the time. Angry about everything.

The situation about Mel is that even in running through

a store I've technically broken into, am about to break out of, with a bag full of money and, technically, in the middle of an armed robbery, I can't get her out of my head. The situation with Mel is that every man who's ever been in the same room with her probably wanted to fuck her. Even the gay ones, doesn't matter what they say. The situation with Mel is that even though we were married, are still married, had a son, son died, we almost killed each other and she's always, always angry like I said, the situation is that I love her. She's always angry and she's always been angry. That's the situation with Mel. If I hadn't made that clear by now, I'm saying. I'll just be up front about that. And she hates me. I guess that's clear enough. I've got video of the two of us together. I mean, together. And I watch it. I'm not proud of this. Never mind. Okay.

Here's what's happening right now: Gerry is running down one aisle and I'm coming down another. He's in the cereal aisle and I'm in the drinks. Everyone walks around like they're in a seizure or a coma. We, however, are alive.

We're stupid.

But we're living.

13.

PERFECT PLACE TO HOLE UP

Let me tell you this: When Mel and I started together we were both in high school and one day I could tell she was sad about something because she stopped being angry for a little while and she asked me if I wanted to see something and I figured she meant something that was usually covered with white cotton or pink satin so I said yes. She took me out of town past the motel on Highway 43. We were seventeen. We walked slowly along the gravel and we didn't talk much. There was nothing much to say. She was wearing shorts and an Adidas jacket. I was watching her walk. I couldn't help it.

"Could you stop looking at my ass please?" she said.

"I'm not."

She stopped and turned and looked at me. It was sunny. She was staring.

"Sorry," I said.

We kept walking. It was getting late.

"Where are we going?" I asked.

She stopped again and she pointed down the road.

"There," she said.

She was pointing at a white wooden cross by the side of the road. I'd seen it lots of times before. It was like lots of others. It sometimes had plastic flowers by it that someone had left and sometimes they were real and it had a name painted on it in blue. Sometimes there were pieces of paper stuck to it that looked like letters. A truck went by. We were right up to where the cross was and Mel was leaning over it and picking some dead petals off some carnations that were there.

Lucy. The cross said.

She sat down on the grass next to it and crossed her legs. She took out a pack of Player's and lit one.

"You want one?" She offered the pack.

I took a cigarette and her lighter and sat down next to her.

"Is that your mom?" I asked.

She just nodded her head.

I lit my cigarette.

A Volkswagen Beetle went by.

I flicked some ashes even though it wasn't time yet and I looked up at the tops of the pine trees across the road. I was pretty sure she was crying and she didn't want me to see. She had her head down on her arms. I put my arm around her.

"I didn't know...she died in a crash?"

"No..."

She was shaking her head and she brought her face up all red.

"No, she just ran off...she just left one day."

She wiped her eyes and took a drag on her cigarette.

"I don't even know why...I just built this here one time because I'd seen others and..."

she sniffed and took a deep breath.

"...and I thought they were nice."

She was looking up at the sky and shaking her head again.

"It's stupid..."

"No," I said.

I held her a little closer.

"I think it's nice," I said.

She put her head on my shoulder.

"Thanks," she said.

I finished my cigarette.

"Sorry," I said. And I meant it.

It wasn't always bad. Somehow the little cross there by itself was sadder than if anyone had really died. I wished I could do something that would help. I knew her mother'd never come home. There was nothing I could do about that. That was the day I got my first blow job from Mel. Somehow it's related now in my mind to her mother leaving her. Probably it was in hers too. Which is unfortunate, but there's nothing I could do about that either. Not gonna say no.

I say my first "real" blowjob because ... well, that's another story ...

"What the fuck is that?"

That's Gerry. He has skidded to a stop and sees the same thing I do: a flashing, blue light flooding the parking lot and leaking though the plate glass windows at the front of the store.

"Fuckity fuckity fuck it! Cops."

Gerry gets down on his knees with his hands on top of his head.

"What are you doing?"

"Get down like this. It's over. Not worth getting shot about."

"But..."

"Just be smart. Slide the bag toward the window where they can see it."

I do what he says. We're kneeling there waiting for the cops, our hands on our heads like on television. I knew it.

"Fuckin' Socks," Gerry says under his breath, "Got us a one-way ticket to an ass fuck."

We watch the plate glass window like it's a movie screen. Nothing happens except for the blue light flashing on the snow. We wait.

Slowly, at the right-hand side of the window, Socks's face appears, his balaclava pulled up to his forehead, his eyes squinted up to peer through the window at us, his hand up like he's blocking the sun. Then he's standing there, full body in front of the window and he's raising his hands in a shrug like he's saying what the fuck are you shitrags doing? That is what he is saying. You can tell.

"What the fuck?" Gerry says back.

Gerry gets up off the floor and walks to the window and I follow him. We both look past Socks to the parking lot where a snow plough runs back and forth, its blue lights flashing. After a couple more runs it takes off down the street and turns the corner.

"Socks what the fuck are you doing out of that car? I told you to stay in that fucking car!" Gerry yells through the glass.

"I thought you needed help, what are you doing?" Socks's muffled voice returns.

"Fucknut." Gerry breathes.

"What?"

"Fucknut," Gerry says again.

"Get in the car, we're coming out!" he says louder so Socks can hear.

Socks nods and slowly pulls his balaclava down over his face. He turns slowly and goes back to the car. But something's changed, you can tell. He's not the village idiot anymore. We are.

Gerry wipes his face.

"Get the crowbar," he says.

As soon as I hand it to him he swings at the window three or four times and then the whole thing shatters out into the snow.

"Stand back," he says, ignoring the fact that it's too late to avoid being hit by the glass now anyway, and the fact that the glass has all gone out into the snow, and not into the store.

"Gerry," I say.

"Yeah."

"Isn't this supposed to be how we got in? Right? I mean make them think we came in this way so they won't think we got in with a key at the back?"

"Yeah."

"But all the glass is on the outside?"

"Yeah."

"Like it was hit from in here?"

"Who the fuck do you think is going to be investigating this, Columbo?"

"I…"

"You think they're going to be going over this with a fine-tooth comb like it's the Zapruder film? It'll be a broken window, and missing fucking money. It'll be they broke the window and they took the fucking money. Case closed let's go for a beer, that's what it'll be."

"I don't know it's just, I'd notice that detail and I'm not a cop, I just think they might, they might think…they might think of that you know?"

We're both aware that Socks is now slowly pulling the car up to the window but neither of us acknowledges it.

"You think they'll notice it?"

"Yes. I do."

"Get out."

"What?"

"Get outside," he says slowly "and I'll fix it."

I step out through what used to be the window and Gerry follows me through with the bag and the crowbar. As soon as we're outside he turns and goes after the next window with the crowbar. One, two, three, four, five, six, seven, eight...seventeen, eighteen, nineteen whacks and nothing's happening.

"What the fuck is this shitty fucking cunty fucking shitty window made of?"

He keeps going after it but you can tell he's tiring. His heart's not in it anymore.

"I don't fucking care, let's go." He hands the crowbar to me and throws the bag into the passenger seat.

"We goin'?" Socks asks, "'Cause I think we should probably go now. I think we better go."

I look at the window and I take one swing. The whole thing shatters and goes down like a waterfall. This time the glass is all on the inside of the store like it should be.

I turn toward the car smiling.

"Are you fistfucking me?" Gerry asks, "How did you do that?"

"I found the sweet spot," I say.

I'm in a good mood now as we're driving down the street. I hit the home run, sank the game-winning putt. We've got the money and Gerry's right. They're gonna say well, somebody broke in here and they took the money, and that's what happened. Probably broke the other window going out for fun. Kids, they're gonna say. They're gonna look at the blank security tape, finish up the potato chips, have a smoke, and call it a day. Things are looking up.

"Where we goin'?" Socks is asking.

"What?"

"We never talked about where to go now. I mean, I say we go to my place because it's isolated. You guys both live in town. There's a place we can push this car right into the river not too far from me. We're losing the car right? That's how we do it. And I got lots of canned beans and frozen pizza and a deck of cards. Perfect."

"I guess so," Gerry says. You can tell he's still pissed off about the window. He's all quiet. Myself, I'm a little uneasy that Socks seems to be in charge now.

"Perfect place to hole up for a while."

"I work on Boxing Day. Door crasher pork sale," Gerry says.

"I gotta see Otis tomorrow. He's got some kind of a problem with his radio. And it's Christmas."

"Well whatever, you guys stay as long as you like."

"Everything's gotta be normal just like it always is Socks."

"You stay tonight, we get rid of the car, we have some beans and play some cards, that's all I'm saying."

"Fine. No Christmas carols and no eggnog."

"No. Some cards is all...that's all."

We drive along for a while with the windshield wiper going crazy and the snowflakes driving toward us like refugees swarming a boat. We're on the lam. I close my eyes and I'm thinking I'm in a Humphrey Bogart movie.

Except I'm the one that goes around the back to hold off the cops and ends up getting shot. Or I'm in a Snoop Dogg video. But I'm still the first in the gang to get shot. Whatever I think about I'm the one getting shot. What is that? Why do I think like that? Then I'm thinking about Lisa. When she…

"What the FUCK is that?"

The rear wheels are slipping out from under us and we're swinging sideways and then we correct hard and stop and we're sitting still and looking out into the snow wall. Windshield wiper is clicking and snowflakes are steaming on the hood.

"Moose," Gerry says.

"Fuckin' what?"

"Fuckin' moose," Gerry says.

"It's in the way," Socks says.

It's true. The moose is taking up the whole of our lane and part of the other. It stares at us.

"Largest species in the deer family," Gerry says.

"No shit."

"Yep. Distinguished by those antlers…palmate antlers, see those? Like a hand," he holds his hand up if front of us "…like the palm of your hand, see, not like a tree branch like a deer, that's how you can tell, well, that and the size of its fucking ass. Look at that mother."

"Yeah. Well. We're stuck. Thing takes up the whole…"

"Hold on."

It's not until I see Gerry out of the car and standing in the headlights that I realize he's got the gun. The headlights make him look more real. Like he's sharply cut out of paper. Like he's one-dimensional. And really clear. And he's raising the gun to the moose's head. Which is about three feet higher than his. The moose is staring him down.

"What…"

Then he drops the gun in the snow and we can hear him swearing and he drops down out of the light.

"He's…"

Then he's up again. The windshield wiper is still going. He puts the gun in his pocket and pulls out a smoke. Lights it up. Steady hands. His lighter isn't working, then he gets it going.

"Is he…"

He's raising the gun again. Then there's a loud pop and the windshield wipers keep beating. The moose goes down like slow motion. Gerry has to do a little shuffle dance to get out of the way. He looks down at what we can't see. He looks like he's deciding and then he shoots again. He throws away the cigarette and gets back into the car.

"It was him or us," he says, "Let's go."

"Well…"

"What?"

"I mean, shouldn't we pull it off the road first?"

"Are you fucking kidding me Socks? Do you know how much that fucking thing weighs? It's like a house. It weighs more than this car. And it's got no wheels on it Socks, so just how the fuck do you propose that we move it?"

"We should try though."

"We can't do it."

"Someone's going to hit it."

For a minute Gerry sits there staring at Socks like he stared at the moose. I think he might shoot Socks too.

"Gerry..." I say.

He pulls out the smokes again and tries to light one but there's nothing coming out of his lighter.

"You want a light Gerry?" Socks asks him.

"Fuck off Socks."

"No, I got a Zippo is all."

"Fuck off."

Gerry is flipping the little wheel on the lighter but he's still only getting sparks.

"It's the best lighter in the world. It's what they use in the army."

"I haven't had a cigarette in eight years Socks, you know that? You're killing me. Okay."

It's true, I haven't seen him have a cigarette in a really long time. Socks takes out the Zippo and lights Gerry's smoke. The flame leaps into the air about six inches.

"Jesus Christ Socks you could cook a steak with that thing."

"See?"

Gerry takes a drag.

"Okay. Good. Now. You want safety?" He's rooting in the bag again, "Here we go."

He grabs the Zippo out of Socks's hand and he's out the door again. We can see him stoop down over the moose, out of the headlights. We watch the wiper. The snow looks like it's letting up a little. Then there's a flash of red and Gerry's getting back in the car. He's batting the snow off his shoulders. He's chewing the cigarette with one side of his face, squinted up against the smoke.

"Fucking moose is all safetied up, now back up, drive around him, and let's fucking go."

Socks does as he's told and we're pulling by the moose slowly. There's a flare sticking out of its ass.

"Why'd you bring flares?" I ask Gerry.

"In case we had to shoot a fucking moose and needed a fucking safety device to shove up its fucking moose ass," Gerry says.

I turn and watch the glowing fire flicker and shrink in the tail lights until it's just a little spark and could be a flare sticking out of the ground or a bucket of sand or anything else instead of a moose's ass. All travellers safe in the night. Canada and all hockey fans in the United States and Newfoundland. And all the ships at sea.

Gerry's still chewing on the cigarette.

"One of these days Socks I'm going to piss in your eggs," he says.

"What eggs?"

"Any eggs you've got Socks, fucking devilled eggs, fucking scrambled eggs, fucking poached eggs, fucking fish eggs — fucking ca-vi-ar Socks, whatever fucking eggs you got planned between now and your last day on the fucking planet, they'll have my piss on them, you take my meaning, Socks? I'll be there and I'll be pants-down pissing on them — your eggs, my piss, that's all, that's it."

I've never seen Gerry this angry without hitting someone. I don't think it's just Socks he's pissed about otherwise Socks'd be holding his nose and spitting out teeth.

"Eight years Socks, and not one smoke," he says, " . . . you're killing me."

"You still got my lighter?"

"Merry fucking Christmas," he says, handing back the Zippo.

"They're expensive, is all."

"Gerry, I thought you said that the gun wasn't loaded," I say.

"Yeah," Gerry says.

14.

CHAMPAGNE AND CAKE

So I do dream that night. Maybe it's because I'm sleeping on the couch at Socks' place with a sheet and no blanket. Maybe it's because we drank a lot of beer while we were dumping the car in the river, but I did a lot of dreaming. The one I remember I was in the kitchen at home. I was just standing there kind of thinking okay here I am in the kitchen, what now? And I couldn't remember why I was there. And Mel walks in and she's wearing nothing but a black T-shirt and she's carrying what looks to me like a submachine gun and she gives me a quick look like she's going to fry an egg or something and then she empties a whole mag into the plywood cupboards and the wood is splintering and flying everywhere like the whole room's being fed through a wood chipper and then she stops. She looks really really good in that T-shirt.

She turns and looks at me and she says, "Don't fucking tell me we're out of fucking peanut butter, mister."

So I don't.

Then she looks down at herself and she says, "Shit my little titties are firm."

She looks at me.

"Like rocks in socks, you know?"

I look down at them again. She's right. Then I notice the letters on her shirt and I read them and they say WAKE UP.

So I do.

Right away I wish I hadn't because I'm freezing and at least in the dream I was warm. And I'm bleeding. You know how some people wake up and they've pissed themselves? I wake up covered in blood. Nosebleed. Happens a few times a year. If it takes me a while to wake up I can look like I've been hit by a train. I don't know if you've ever seen a man hit by a train but I can tell you this: you'll never eat lasagna again. It's cold as nuns in this room. I'm like a blood popsicle. I make it to the bathroom mirror and it looks like I've been dipped in barbecue sauce. I'm a Q-tip. I start washing up. I remember it took us a long time to find a place where we could get close enough to get the car into the river. Most places if you tried you'd end up with half the car in and half out. Which is what ended up happening of course. Makes me feel lonesome, our inability to do anything the right way 'round. So we ended up back at Socks's place which is like a bungalow in the middle of a field near the river and we sat around drinking beer in the cold living room and counting the money. And it's the good life from now on. After we figure out what to do about the car.

"Socks, why is it so fucking cold in here?" Gerry asked finally.

"I don't turn the heat on lately."

"Why not? It's December for Christ's sake."

"I'll show you."

He takes us into one of the bedrooms without turning on the lights and he looks up. We're standing there looking at the night sky through a man-sized hole in the ceiling.

"Who came in through there?"

"Me."

We don't ask why. We go back to counting the money.

"Y'oughtta get that shit fixed," Gerry says.

Johnny doesn't seem to have any towels so I'm drying off my face with toilet paper which is getting stuck to my stubble and it looks now like I've cut myself shaving about twenty times. Sometimes I think my problem is that I think too much about things. But never for very long. That's my problem also. I get distracted. I get stuck. Bright red trickle curving down. Whatever. I could use some toast. Usually I don't care much for breakfast but this morning I'm hungry. Gerry and Socks are at the table.

"It walks," Gerry says.

"You alright?" Socks asks.

"I'm fine. What?"

"Nothing. Just looks like your eyes are bleeding."

"You got any Cap'n Crunch?"

"Just toast."

"Bring it."

Socks gets up and puts some bread in the toaster. Gerry's looking at his coffee like there's something floating in it.

"We've got ourselves a real problem with that car," he says.

"And?"

"And nothing..."

"There's always an and..."

"No. Not this time. But there's a but."

"What's the but?"

"We've got ourselves a real problem with that car, but we've also got some dynamite."

We could tow the car out of the river. But that would leave us with the car and that's what we're trying to get rid of. There's no way to push it in further, we tried that. It's stuck on something, there's a lot of extra shit on the bottom of that river: rocks, dead fish, weeds, shopping carts, condoms, and greeting cards. People have been abandoning things in there for years. Dressmaker's dummies and Javex bottles. One car more or less is not going to make any difference. Like one of those little pirate ships in an aquarium for the fish to swim in and out of. Only Gerry is right, a car halfway into the river is only going to draw attention from all the wrong people. You'd think it would be easy getting rid of a car. Try it.

"How'd you want that toast?" Socks is asking.

"Toasted."

"Right. But with...?"

"Coffee."

"Right."

"How..."

"Black."

Yeah. Dynamite's good. If you can't sink it just blow that shit up. I've always said that. If you can't do something right the first time just do it bigger. The history of the world backs me up on this. George W. Bush. Cheese-in-crust-pizza.

I've disappointed a lot of people. I know that. I have insight. I know what's up.

And I read a lot. I know you wouldn't know it from what I've said except for that part at the start about Bukowski. But I do. I used to. You don't know about it because, well, it's been a while. Nabokov, Bukowski, Ondaatje, Dickens, shit, lots of books. I like all the crazy shit the best. *Buddy Bolden*. I haven't read a book in a while though. I've been busy. For a long while.

"Yeah, dynamite'll work," I say "When do you think?"

"I'd say just the other side of that coffee and toast."

"And a cigarette."

Sometimes I just like the feel of the smoke in my lungs. It frames things.

"Might attract some attention, dynamite."

"Not around here. If anyone comes we'll just say we're fishing. It's Christmas morning, everyone's busy opening shit."

"I'll say this for you," I say, gulping the coffee and lighting up a smoke, " ...you're a thinker."

I guess you could say I'm self-taught. No one else seemed interested in the job.

"You know Adolf Hitler," Gerry starts, " ...he marries his girlfriend, right? The day before the Russians are due in his bunker in Berlin or whatever the fuck, right?"

"Yeah."

"And so he marries her and there's champagne and cake, whatever. They go to bed early. You know. And in the morning he poisons her and then he shoots himself in the fucking head," Gerry points to his temple, "in the fucking head. The gardener burns their bodies ..."

"Yeah."

"I'm saying ...that's a pretty crap honeymoon, right?"

"Heard that joke."

"You heard that?"

"On TV or something."

"Yeah? Well. We're all going to die, heard that?"

"Yeah."

"So I'm saying let's get busy. Morning's half gone. Honeymoon's over."

I'm missing something, I think. Something that other people have. Walking across the field, the crunchy holes our feet make. Nothing works out the right way. The morning has been all mist and it's fallen and frozen on last night's snow. We can see our breath.

Lisa rolls over and smiles at me.

Mel rolls over and smiles at me.

This morning I woke up on a cold couch, my face skinned with dried blood. It's Christmas.

The river is running black. It's hard to breathe. I've still got running shoes on. It's fucking winter. I'm not twenty anymore. I should buy some boots. There's a sculpture of blood cake up my nose. I might vomit. My son is dead. My wife says she wants to kill me. I can't stop drinking and there's a gun in my closet. And now we're going to blow up a fucking car.

I should have that cigarette now.

We're going to blow up the fucking car. Hi-de-ho.

I wipe my nose and my hand comes away red. When I'm fucking Lisa — which, I should be doing right now instead of doing this, is what I'm thinking. I should be doing that. I miss Mel. Jakey.

I miss everything.

"We should go get some real breakfast after this," Gerry says, stopping and throwing down the duffel bag and looking around, "I could use some fucking pancakes."

"Some eggs," Socks says.

They're both looking at me.

"I wouldn't mind some good coffee," I say.

I am barely fucking alive.

"But everything's closed."

"You're bleeding," Gerry says.

"Yeah."

And I don't remember when I stopped. Everything. When I stopped everything. I take out the cigarette. You can say what you like about cigarettes, I know everybody hates them now, because it's the right thing to do, to hate them, and the people who smoke them. Like it's right to hate Nazis. You're supposed to hate the cigarettes the same way now as if they were Nazis. As if the people smoking them were Nazis. They're just nothing but bad. But the thing is when everything else is shit you've still got a smoke. And it's the one thing that's still good, still the same. You can light up a smoke and you're still okay. You can manage. So I do. Fucking lifesavers they are sometimes.

"All right," I say, "Let's blow us up a fucking car."

"Well, I'll tell you the truth," Gerry says, he's got a few sticks of dynamite and he's wrapping duct tape around them, "I'm not really sure how many of these to use..."

Then he's looking at me.

"You're fucking bleeding a lot," he says.

"Bother you?"

He shrugs.

"You do what you want," he says.

"Better add one more stick," I tell him.

"Because?"

"Four's a good round number. I like four."

It takes a while to figure everything out about how

we're going to get the dynamite in the car without getting it wet. Somehow while we're doing that my nose dries up again. The front of my jacket is covered with blood though and I'm feeling a little dizzy but not too bad. I'm actually feeling like a breakfast special would be pretty good. Somewhere must be open.

"Socks, you want to go up and watch the road to see if anyone is slowing down and we'll get this out to the car," Gerry says. He's holding the taped sticks in front of him like a present. You can tell he's pretty happy with what he's made. He's got a pocketful of blasting caps and this orange fuse line. I wouldn't mind some bacon.

"We're gonna have to chop down a tree," Gerry says, "Socks, you got an axe?"

This is a bigger project than I thought. I forget about the bacon.

"Jesus wept, what the fuck do we need to cut down a tree for?" I ask.

"So the fuse doesn't get wet. We need something for it to sit on over the water. Between the land and the car."

"Knock knock," I say.

"What?"

"I said knock knock."

"Who's there?"

"Fuck off."

"No. It'll be easy."

The snow is spitting bright up into my eyes and my head feels like a skid mark. Okay we'll do it. Okay, it'll be easy.

"Johnny," I say.

"What?"

"Get us a fucking axe. And some Advil, Johnny. Bring me some fucking Advil."

"How about a chainsaw?" Johnny says, "And some Percocet?"

"Yeah. Yeah, yeah that's better."

15.

BANG

One time I dream I go for a ride with my son. He's about thirteen, same age as when he died. He's always around twelve or thirteen in the dreams. We just drive and we end up at the ocean, which, of course, makes sense in the dream even though it's thousands of miles away. I'm worried in the dream that he has the wrong shirt on, I don't know why it matters, it just does.

"Have you ever seen the ocean before?"

"No," he says and he's off across the beach.

When I catch up I look at him standing there, his eyes squinting against the grey horizon, his little feet welled down into the wet sand.

"It's not that great," he says.

I look out over the water. He's right, it's not.

"It's just water," he says.

If he'd lived he'd be seventeen now.

The last words of Willy Beaumont of Dayersville, Texas when he was executed in 1953 for killing three people in a liquor store holdup were: "All right, Warden, let's give them what they want."

I read that once and it's always just stuck with me, even the details. I could tell you more. Two of those killed were customers, a fifty-seven-year-old woman and a seventeen-year-old kid. The liquor store owner's name was Triggs. Beaumont had a tattoo that said, "Lucky." He was arrested the next morning in a hay barn and his words then were, "You fellas had your breakfast yet?"

But, "give them what they want." It's not bad advice.

I'm thinking about all this while Gerry's rigging up the dynamite. Thinking about things like this gives my mind something to do when it has nothing else to do, like while I'm waiting for Gerry to tape the dynamite to the inside of the roof of the car. We're both pretty wet and cold from crawling across the tree to the car, most of the actual tree is underwater but Gerry just plans to string the fuse through the branches anyway. Keep it dry. The crusted blood in my nose is making little whistling sounds.

"I've never blown up a car before," Gerry says like a kid about to have his first hot dog or something.

"You ever used dynamite before?"

"You ever had all your teeth knocked out and had to suck meat through a straw?"

"No," I say, Gerry's getting a little testy for my mood, "…why?"

"There's a first time for everything, that's all," he's trying to get the tape to stick to the underside of the roof of the car and it's not working, probably wet, so he's angry. Finally he has it.

"Sorry, just none of this is going the way I thought it out."

He's wiping his hands on his pants. Welcome to the club, I think. This is life.

Now he's back to being the kid with the hot dog.

"This is a time fuse," he says holding up the orange wire, "…we just jam one end into that little package of bang, then to the blasting cap, we get to shore…and we light the other end…"

"Isn't there just a button we can push?"

"Only in the movies."

He wipes his mouth with the back of his hand.

"Guy explained it all to me," he says, "This isn't the movies."

So we slide off the roof of the car and we're back over the tree and soaking wet in the cold. My feet are sticking in the mud at the bottom of the river. Gerry is stringing the wire in the branches. I'm trying to remember what it felt like to be able to feel my fingers and balls.

"I can't feel my balls," I say.

"You feel your balls a lot?"

"I like to be able to if I want."

And we're on the shore and Gerry's standing just as happy as shit with the fuse up in front of his face. Then.

"What the fuck is that happy asshole doing?" Squinting.

"You told him to stay with the bag and watch the highway…"

"Yeah, I didn't tell him to light up a fucking smoke."

"He's fine."

"He must have one hot nut for a smoke. He's a piss stream away from a pile of dynamite."

"He's alright, c'mon…"

"Fuckstick…okay…"

Gerry's focus is back on the fuse. He pulls out his lighter and then looks at me. I just look back at him and nod my head. He nods back and lights the fuse. It doesn't light up like a sparkler like in a Bruce Willis movie but it's burning really good. It's like watching one of those videos of falling dominoes the way it twists up over the trunk and through the branches.

"We better crouch down," Gerry says.

"Really?"

"I don't know. They always crouch down in the movies."

This isn't the movies, I want to remind him, but we crouch down anyway. The fuse is almost out of the branches and into the car.

And then it stops.

Nothing.

"Fuck."

Fucking fizzled out. Dead.

"Fuck."

and,

"What the...fuck...is...Socks...doing?"

I look over at where Socks was standing and now he's looking at the bag on the ground like it's going to attack him.

And there's some smoke coming out of it.

"FOR FUCK SAKE SOCKS WHAT THE FUCK ARE YOU DOING?" Gerry is yelling.

Socks is leaning into the bag.

And I'm yelling now too, "SOCKS! WHAT THE FUCK ARE—"

— and that's when he blows up.

All over the place he goes, he's there and then he's not, and then he's everywhere. He's into the bag after dropping his fucking Zippo is what we figure later, and then suddenly he's not, and then slowly it seems, right after the big sound of the explosion, he's about a hundred-and-sixty pounds of cubed, marinated beef flopping down onto the snow, wet piece by wet piece. That's the only sound: the flopping. Flip. Flop. Like the sound of little fish falling.

I've never heard fish falling but this is what it would sound like.

"He's..."

"He's..."

"FUCK!" Gerry yells and then he's off and running back into the river toward the car.

I start walking slowly toward where Socks was.

"He's..." I think I'm still saying.

I know someone is saying it, and it sounds like me.

"He's..." I'm saying.

But he isn't. He's just not.

He's just little pieces. I'm walking through a little storm of Johnny. That's part of his arm with the jacket still on it. That's...I don't know what that is. There's so many little red, and other little coloured parts of him, just lying around on the snow. I'm expecting them to move. But they don't. He's a gutted fish.

"Gerry?" I say.

I can hear him yelling.

"FUCK!"

He's mad. He doesn't like it when things don't go good. And they're not going particularly well.

Right now.

"OH MY FUCK!"

I don't know what he's doing, but I'm still looking at the tomato snow. I almost bled to death when the Jeep crashed. Nothing like this. That was just a lot of blood, and it was mine. And not mine. This is carnage. I might throw up. No. I'm not going to, but...

"SHE'S GONNA GO NOW!"

Gerry's running towards me out of the river and just

as he gets close the car goes up like a rocket. Well, the roof goes up like a rocket. And then the water's coming down like rain. Gerry is crouching down and covering like we're under enemy fire. The water's coming down just like Socks. I just stand there. It's only water. The roof is slowly falling back down and it hits the river with a wet slap. Gerry stands up from his crouch, brushing the water off his jacket and looking around. You can see it in his face now, what he's seeing.

"Yeah," I say.

The brutal shit people do and have to go through sometimes. No one wants to be the bad guy in their own lives. Sometimes it just happens though and you either fold or you don't.

Gerry's still looking around. Now he's throwing up, bright orange and pieces of toast into the snow.

"Yeah," I say again.

Because I can't think of anything else to say.

And then I think of Mel. And Lisa.

All women want to hear that they're loved. I know that.

Doesn't mean they want to hear it from me though.

And I feel a little like crying. But I won't.

Because I have to clean this shit up.

"Gerry."

He's still throwing up but there's nothing coming out now.

"C'mon."

He stands up, wiping his mouth with the back of his hand. There's a string of spit hanging from his neck.

"We don't have much time," I say.

He's coughing.

There's nobody on the road now but there could be any time, even early on Christmas morning, even on a dead-end road with nothing on it. And there's a lot to get rid of here. I can hear the little waves at the shore.

"It's times like this..." Gerry says, "a man either keeps it together..."

"Or he goes to pieces," I say.

But there's no laughing. There's just the work to do. Things are too true right now to be funny. That's the way it is sometimes and there's nothing you can do about it. It's not a time for laughing. It's time for some real, it's time for this shit. There's too few people in anyone's life for even one of them to go away. I picture what happens next from above like you'd see it in a movie but it isn't from above at all. This is close up. Like Gerry said: this isn't any movie. Gerry's back from driving to the house and he's brought garbage bags and work gloves. It's not good work. Up close it's picking up the bigger pieces with both hands and putting them in garbage bags. It's scooping up the little pieces into fistfuls of snow like trying to catch goldfish. It's trying not to throw up and forgetting what you're really doing. Feeling your heart pound in your forehead every time you bend down. Gerry says he thinks we can get most of it up and then just kick the snow around. Maybe come back with a pump on a generator later and hose the place down. We're lucky that a lot of him just seems to be gone. What we end up collecting probably wouldn't make much more than a torso. And the feet. And there's no head. And that's lucky too. No face. No Johnny, really. When we're finished there's really not much left to see. I find the crowbar next to the river. The roof of the car is floating upside down but otherwise the car's pretty much gone now too. The roof reminds me of a kiddie's pool slowly being filled up by a garden hose. Soon it will sink too. It's lucky Johnny lives so far down this little road away from everything.

Lived.

I could eat something now actually. And I could use a drink. I'm on empty.

There's not too many times I feel like going home, but this is one.

After all, it is Christmas.

Late night phone call:

"Lisa."

"Yeah?"

"What are you doing?"

"Well, Merry fucking Christmas to you too."

"Yeah . . . I know . . . but, what are you doing?"

16.

I'M NOT STUPID

Lisa's asleep and I'm watching her. It's 3:15. 3:15. 3:15. 3:15.
3:16.

I'm watching her because I can't get back to sleep after this
dream I've had. Not that it's as bad as some I have, I just don't
feel like sleeping right now. And she looks like the opposite of the
dream, so I'm just looking at her until I feel like sleeping again.
It's funny how people who are asleep are here and they're not here
at the same time. She looks like everything's okay.

3:17.

Everything's okay wherever she is. She looks really quiet and
okay. Anyway, the dream. In the dream I'm in the backyard of this
school I went to when I was a little kid. Grass, green, blue sky, and
sun — you know the deal. And I'm picking the wings and legs off
of these flies one at a time and then I set the little useless bodies
aside in a row on the concrete. Little pile of legs like a woodpile.
Used wings drifting in the breeze. After a while I've got quite a
crowd watching. I myself am quite focussed. Nothing captivates a
child's attention like cruelty.

Like I say, Lisa looks like the opposite of this. I'm afraid to
touch her.

Well now it's Boxing Day. Ray wants the store open on
Boxing Day because he figures people have run out of food
after a day of stores being closed. I think people have
enough turkey, eggnog and macaroni salad leftover that

they're not going grocery shopping for a while — maybe some milk or bread. Gerry's working because it's time and a half. I'm not working because I didn't get a shift. So I'm back at Johnny's house to clean up again and make sure that everything's really okay. Which it pretty much is now I think. We spent most of yesterday working on it and then we went to my place and got really drunk really early. It snowed a lot so now I'm looking out the windshield of my car and I can't really see any sign of a guy being blown up here. We pretty much cleared everything away and then it snowed a pile last night so...not too much to see. What I'm doing now is going back into the house to make sure we didn't miss anything. You know how it is when you've done an armed robbery, killed a moose and watched a man blow himself up, and then cleaned up all his little pieces like picking sardines up off the kitchen floor. You might miss something, because your mind is distracted and you're not thinking the best right now. I made a list of things in my head for clarity, these are the things I think matter most right now:

The car: it's gone, nobody's looking for it and they're certainly not going to be looking for it where it actually is, even if someone finds it they're not going to trace it back to us so it's Johnny's problem now, and Johnny's not in a position to have problems right now.

Johnny: also gone, this is mostly a problem but also a solution, he's not going to get pie-eyed at the bar and start telling stories; he doesn't really have anyone other than us who give two shits about him anyway so it'll be a while before anyone even notices he's gone. Sorry Johnny, but it's true.

The money: it's in my ceiling, I know this did not work for Paul Bernardo but people were looking harder for those tapes than they are for this money and I think they missed them for a long time until Karla told them where to look. Anyway, we don't have anyone to go all Karla on us, plus we didn't kill anyone. We didn't kill anyone, and that's important to remember. Anyway, Gerry says he knows what to do with the money.

The moose: gone from the highway when I drove by this morning, which I thought was pretty quick for a Christmas morning, but I guess that's the way they do things. A moose shot at point blank range with a handgun on Christmas Eve is going to draw some interest, but there's no reason to tie it in with the robbery, so no reason to think they're related events. What kind of idiot murders a moose after robbing a store? Gerry does, I know that, but the cops don't know that...

I didn't actually write this list down, I'm not stupid. It's in my head with other things like: Gerry has to work today like there's nothing up; we both have to work tomorrow and keep everything regular; we can't tell anybody anything; I have to fine-tooth comb this house until I know that it's so clean you could snort coke off it and I don't have any trouble sleeping, at least not any trouble sleeping caused by what they might find in the house. And nobody can see me here this morning. First I check all the places we weren't because who knows, Socks may have written down little reminders for himself: *robbing the store in three days with the guys, buy some eggs.* I start in the bathroom 'cause I've got to knock out a piss anyway. I feel kind of bad about snooping in a freshly dead man's medicine cabinet but then I feel bad about a lot of things lately: the Jays had a lousy season this year, what's left of a dead man is in two green garbage bags inside a box labelled "Gay Porn" in the rear of the IGA meat freezer (Gerry says: "Trust me, the guys I work with, nobody's touchin' that box."), and the chances of me ever feeling good about anything again, well, let's say that's a long shot. These facts, combined with the fact that the medicine cabinet is filled with more illegal prescription drugs than I have ever seen in one place, conspire to greatly reduce my overall enjoyment of Boxing Day. Other people are acquiring reasonably priced electronic goods. I'm looking at Percocet and OxyContin prescriptions made out to over a dozen different names. Let the bells ring out and the banners fly. Fuck me. Socks we hardly knew ye. I don't want the drugs mind you, I've been a confirmed alcohol man for some time now, but I don't want to leave them here for someone else to find. It's the least I can do for Socks to make them disappear. I'll put them down the sink before I go. Or maybe Gerry wants them. No. Better to wash them away. Give the fish a thrill.

Seems Socks was not a man for the regular toilet brush and disinfectant routine. But I'm not here to judge. I'm here to piss. While I'm doing that I notice a few magazines tucked down beside the toilet against the cabinet. Glossy ones. Porn. It's like being a super hero, you know? It's like a magical sixth sense, your nose twitches, *there's porn in this room!* It's not a useful super power and it's not one I really want. Who needs all that shit, and who needs glossy pictures and folded pages? I use my other super powers just to not pick up the magazines. That little secret I'll leave for the police to find, what the hell? I'm not here to save Johnny or the world. Plus I've given porn up. I just decided. It doesn't look so good down there with the piss stains and the sticky hairs. I flush. I check under the sink and find an empty shampoo bottle and a pile of disposable razors. Cheap-assed bastard. A dead one though, so... never speak ill of the dead. I guess. Cracked, cake-white rubber bathtub plug. Close the cupboard. I'm wearing gloves but I think it's probably stupid to even do that. My fingerprints aren't on file anywhere. We're not going to get caught. We didn't kill anybody. Johnny choked to death on his own big stupid. He was weapons-grade stupid. Plutonium dumb. Who drops a lit Zippo into a bag of dynamite? That's the Nobel Prize of dumbass. Sorry Johnny. But it is. If you hadn't been that stupid I'd be home in bed right now with a glass of eggnog and a hard on and you wouldn't be iced and bagged and boxed. These are facts.

There's two bedrooms: one with a bed and one with an enormous fucking hole in the ceiling. I was thinking about that and he must have been trying to fix the roof or something. Stepped between the, whatever the fuck they're called, studs, rafters. I open the door that we had closed against the cold and I realize in the daylight that the hole doesn't go through the roof after all. Just a big, dark hole in the drywall ceiling and a bunch of pink insulation around the edges and lot of attic black. Like looking up into a big haemorrhoidal butthole. Cheap brass chandelier lying on the floor, yellow nylon rope tied to it. Fuck me.

Cunt.

Not so stupid after all.

Just suicidal.

He dropped that Zippo just because he wanted to, because he saw his chance. And then he left us here to clean it all up for him. Socks you bastard. You fucked us over. You fucked us all up. Used our fucking dynamite to do what you couldn't manage to do yourself. Well that's it. I'm leaving your fucking drugs right where they are and I'm nailing your porn mags to the front door. Son of a bitch. I had to pick you up with tweezers. Like cleaning out a fucking ant farm. You cunt. Wait till I tell Gerry. Gerry's gonna be pissed. You believe what this shitstick did Gerry? He saw his fucking chance and he fucking took it. Hell with you bastards, he said, I'm out. Couldn't do it myself, thanks for the help! Pick up my tab will ya? I'm a little short this week. Things'll fuckin' get better in time. I'm good for it.

Fuckin' Socks. Cheap-ass yellow fucking nylon rope. Leaving us with your fucking tab.

I find my own blood on the couch. Must have missed that yesterday. Gerry, I'm telling you he just was in it for the ending the whole time, you see? Probably never even planned to come out alive. Jesus Gerry, he was just looking for a way. That's why he wanted the fucking guns. If the cops had come he would have been running at them screaming. I get a towel and wet it in the kitchen sink and rub away at the blood on the couch, turning it dark and wet and spreading it further. I'm surprised he didn't just try to shoot himself while he was waiting outside the store. Maybe he did. I wring out the towel in the sink and watch the dark swirl down. Sometimes you just think:

Jesus Christ, it has come to this now? This is it. You are here. This is where you are. Right here. You're doing this? This is what you're doing? This is a dark moment right now. Dark like the inside of a dead puppy.

I look up out of the little window over the sink and see the cop car pulling slowly into the driveway.

When I was about six or seven my mother was out somewhere and Otis was watching me. Like I was someone else's kid and he was the babysitter. Except that he wasn't a very good babysitter. He was a drunk babysitter is what he was. I kept asking him to do stuff and he kept saying no.

"Play guns."

"No."

"Hide and seek."

"No."

"Make me a sandwich."

"Fuck no."

I remember him saying, finally: "Look, you want to play a game? C'mere."

Taking me by my shoulders, all stubble and rough hands and whisky, and standing me out by the road.

"What's this game called?" I asked.

"It's called 'Watch'."

"How do you play it?"

"Well, you stand here, like this see, and you watch, and you see if your real father drives by..."

It's funny the things you think about. When you're fucked.

There's nothing else to do but drop to the floor. So that's what I do. Fast. It hurts. But what can you do? If they open the door, which isn't locked, I'm done. What are you doing here Sir? Just cleaning up some blood off the couch. See? Here's my bloody rag right here in my hand. I don't live here though. If you're looking for Johnny he's in a box behind the chicken fillets down at the supermarket. Well, some of him is. In the box marked "Gay Porn." Just tell them I sent you, will ya? Thanks.

Knock, knock.

Who's there?

It's the cops.

It's the cops who?

It's the cops you're fucked.

There was a morning, a long time ago, Mel wasn't around, I don't know where she was, she hadn't been around for a couple of days, so I get Jakey up out of bed, this was before he was going to school. I get him out of bed and get him his cereal and toast. I drive him to his preschool which is in the basement of this lady's bungalow just a few blocks away. Mel thought he should go there because it would get him used to school before he got there. Pretty good idea. I drop him off. This lady's name was Maureen. She had thick, heavy, dark glasses. Big smile. Some facial hair. Holes in the drywall but you could tell she was good with kids. All the kids were happy there, nobody ever crying. Anyway, I drop him off and I'm driving home, I pull a rolling stop at a stop sign. Cop pulls me over.

"You been drinking at all today, Sir?"

"Actually," I say, "I've had this acid reflux problem, so just lately, I've given it up..."

It was all I could think of at the time.

"Is that a bottle of vodka there by your feet, Sir?"

"I mean not giving it up all at once, you know...in stages..."

"Sir, please step out of the car."

What I mean to say is: police officers do not often have a sense of humour. Not when they're on the job anyway. That's been my own experience. So if this one decides to enter the premises and sees me lying on the kitchen floor with a bloodstained towel in my hands there's not going to be anything I can say to him except to tell him that I have a pocket knife in my back pocket and that I have no intention of using it at this time. I will do this in a calm voice without making any quick movements. I will do this from my fully prone position with both my hands in the air. I will do this having already practiced it in my head. I will do this with wet legs not because I have pissed myself but because Johnny's sink seems to be overflowing now and flooding the floor. I know I didn't put the plug in because I remember the blood swirling down the drain.

"Don't worry officer," I imagine saying, "This is all my own blood..."

I'm just fucked.

Then something funny happens. I become unfucked. The cop knocks once more and then sticks a piece of paper into the screen door and leaves. I wait on the floor just getting wetter until I hear the cruiser start up and pull away over the crunching snow. It's a Boxing Day miracle. I'm still wet. I get up slowly like somebody might be left waiting behind and peeking through a window. I can see the cruiser still pulling away through the trees, too far and too fast to be looking back at the house now. So I stand up straight and I turn off the tap. Something's blocking that drain. I walk over to the door and look out again. I open it just enough to reach for the paper.

Ontario Provincial Police are currently seeking assistance in an investigation in your area. On or about the early morning of December 25 a moose was shot, molested, and killed on County Road 18 near the intersection of Donnelly Road. Anyone with information related to this event should contact . . .

The boys are on the case.

The Case of The Murdered Moose. Case of The Mystery Meat. Case of The Road Killers. Case of The Holy Shit They Don't Even Know Johnny's Dead . . . *molested?* Shit, Gerry's gonna love that. Molested.

Of course they don't know Johnny's dead. Because nobody except for me and Gerry know about that. Socks was a loner. He was underemployed. Nobody liked him. Sorry, Socks, but that's the truth. There'll be no case until someone figures out you're dead. Which might take some time. And there's really no reason for them to link us to you. Unless they find one of us in your house all covered in blood and dishwater. I should stop talking to Johnny as if he's here.

And get the fuck out.

Take a picture of me right now. Wet pants. No shave. Bloody hands. Have not slept. That guy's got the staggers and the jags you'd say. The guy's got the DTs. Guy's got a one-way ticket to Ass Town. Look at him.

Trash.

On the other hand despite appearances I'm rolling elevens right now really. The cops are out looking for moose killers. Trying to solve the big moose crime. And

I've got Lisa. I'm going to fix up Johnny's plugged drain before I go. I like a little plumbing job.

It's too bad Johnny killed himself. I would have liked to beat him purple with this cutting board instead. Just saying. Gerry was right about this guy. I mean, no offense to the dead or anything Johnny, it's just that suddenly being dead doesn't wipe away the stink of the dumbass. Stupid is just stupid. He could've got us killed instead of himself. Guy was a burning bush advertisement for suicide. I should have seen it before it happened. But I'm not sure that I would have stopped it. Sometimes you just can't stop things. Things happen anyway.

Why does my shit always miss the hat?

17.

LOWERED EXPECTATIONS

When I got home I called Lisa. I don't know why I'm telling you this. But I did. She was out. I made some cereal. I was thinking about that story in the Bible, about Lazarus, how Jesus raised him from the dead. I always wonder what it was like for him after that. He was in there four days that's what it says in the Bible and it says there was a stink. So there he is wrapped in the stink of death and they take these linen strips off him. Like paper his skin would be, white, and dusty, linen stuck and tearing at it. He's naked in the sun, squinting. He's walking around. "There goes Lazarus . . ." they say. "Dead."

Can't have been easy on him. Supposed to be dead and then he's not, and now he's out there shuffling around and scaring the kids. Cracking his knees. This was not something he asked for. Then he'd have to die again. I think about these things. I think about Johnny Cash kicking out the footlights at the Grand Ole Opry. I think about a lot of things all at once. All the time.

"Hey Gerry, Ray wants to see you," Ruth the cashier is calling to Gerry over the meat counter.

"See who?"

"You."

"Well, I want new pants. A lot of people want a lot of things. But we don't all fucking get them do we?"

"So you're not going to see him then?"

"Well, let me tell you Ruthie, it's like a hooker with a peg leg, you know, kinda you want to...but also kinda, you don't."

"So that's a no? I just gotta tell him yes or no Gerry."

"What does that hard-on want?"

"He wants to see you."

"Why?"

"Because he wants to see you. A lot of people want a lot of things Gerry."

Oh, I forgot to say, I found Johnny's finger. It was hanging from a little bush down by the lake. I'm not sure what to do with it. Funny thing about a finger on its own; you'd think it would look bigger on its own without a body attached to it anymore, like it's not just an add-on anymore or maybe that it would look smaller than it really is, like a postcard of Niagara Falls, but no — it looks just the same. Only it looks lonely. And the only really disturbing thing about it is the hair. Well, that and the blood. But somehow the hair on a severed finger doesn't look right, it looks out of place, like it shouldn't be there anymore. You're expecting the blood. You're not expecting the hair. I had to carry it back to Johnny's house just in my hand. Which felt like leading a small child, you know, when they reach up and take you by the hand. Cold though. Johnny didn't have the Tupperware container I was hoping for to put it in. So I put it in a condom and then put it into an old hydro envelope. That seemed pretty good. I thought for a minute, wait, that spermicide is going to sting. Then I stopped thinking that. Technically it's probably not that smart, after a messy suicide that you're trying to keep quiet, to carry around a body part in an envelope with the owner's name and address right on it. It can't be helped. I wasn't going to leave it there, and the ground's frozen. And the toilet didn't seem like the right thing to do. Anyway...well, Jesus liked the lepers. But then that was Jesus. He had a lotta help from his dad. I'm just trying to get by.

"What'd he want?" I ask Gerry when he gets back from talking to Ray.

"Fucker's crazed. He wants to know if I'll keep my ears open, you know, maybe someone knows something about the break-in, maybe somebody'll say something the police could use...maybe I could pass it on to him if I hear..."

"What'd you say?"

"What'd I say? I told him I'd wear a fucking wire, what the fuck do you think? Careful what you say, you're live on the air right now."

"All right."

"Fuck it. I've got chops to cut."

"Okay."

I've got milk to rotate in the cooler so I go do that. First thing I do is drop a small carton of chocolate against the wall because as soon as it's dented you can drink it because it's against the rules to sell it dented. Chocolate milk makes me feel more peaceful and less like the back of my head's on fire. Things'll be okay. Everyone walks around like they've had a seizure. Everyone walks around like they've got somewhere to go when really there's only one place we're all going. That's how it looks from inside the dairy case today anyway. It's as clear as a burning bush from in here. I remember that song from the '80s or the

'70s. *Loving yourself is the greatest love of all* or something. Like I said, what a load of horseshit. Really. I'm pretty sure the greatest love of all involves either God or some really great sex. And you can't do either on your own. I've got Johnny's finger in my freezer at home now, right inside an empty lasagna box. And who's going to be touching my Giant Tiger lasagna? Nobody but me. Perfect hiding place. Finger's gotta be kept somewhere for now. I like being in the dairy case. It feels clean in here and the air is fresh. Why did anyone think banana-flavoured milk would be a good idea? It's a thin line between innovative and crazy as fuck.

Women have been kind to me mostly, except for that time Mel set fire to the porch, or when she closed my hand in the door of the car.

"Oh my god what do I do now?" She asks, my fingers turning purple blue.

I say: "Open the *fucking* door!" And she just walks away.

Or the time she fucked me for an hour telling me not to come, *don't you fucking come you prick*, and then she comes and she gets off and she just leaves. *See you later sucker,* she says. Or the time she throws a beer at me, and I don't mean in my face, I mean she rockets one like Cy Young right from across the bar over five tables and banks it off the side of my skull. Five stitches. Doctor in emergency says, "What happened to you?"

I say: "Marriage."

I say: "Lowered expectations."

I say: "The lady at the bar like a burning fucking eighteen wheeler."

And he says: "I hear you."

I hear you, he says.

He says: "Do you want me to freeze this up?" I say: "I don't feel anything."

Lisa hasn't done anything like that. But probably she will eventually.

I need another chocolate milk. Half the people you see on cell phones are playing Candy Crush Saga. We're all going to hell. It's a question of velocity.

You have to move the bags so the new milk is at the bottom and the old milk is at the top. This way Jack and Jill Milk-buyer will choose the day-old milk instead of leaning over to pick up the fresh milk. It's a trick: now you see it, now you don't. It's simple but it works. Because once upon a time we were a people who would walk through the ice and snow at 4:30 in the morning to lean over and actually milk a cow through our own steaming breath and now we are a people too tired or fat to lean over to pick up a plastic bag in a temperature-controlled pleasure dome a thousand miles away from any cow shit.

Let me tell you about Sweaty Betty. Sweaty Betty used to turn tricks out in back of the Canadian Tire. She could have done the same thing at home I suppose but then she'd have these strangers in her house and it could be awkward with the kids, so Canadian Tire was the place. Guys called her "Aisle Thirteen" because there were twelve aisles at Canadian Tire. Aisle Twelve was camping supplies. Then there was Sweaty Betty out through the emergency exit door. In one busy night she earned enough to buy a snowblower. That's a work ethic. You see what I mean? This country used to understand that making a living was hard work. Hewers of wood and drawers of water.

Two-handed fist fuckers. They made this country. Now we eat American potato chips and we watch NASCAR. That's my point. Sweaty Betty works at the bowling alley now. Renting out shoes I mean, not giving rides behind the building. She's earned her rest. Nobody earns anything anymore, that's my point. Myself included. Hell, maybe me at the top of the list. Everything comes plastic wrapped or frozen. I'm just saying that everything now is easier than Betty ever was. Everything used to be as hard as a nail in your forehead and people earned what they got, good or bad, and they did it with frostbitten fingers. I do wonder what made Johnny blow himself all to shit on a foggy Christmas morning and I wonder why nobody even bothers to check the date on the little plastic tags on the milk bags. There's some guy in Tokyo selling apples in the subway. Try getting some of the fuckers around here to do that job. They're too busy playing Employment Insurance *Price is Right*. EI EI Owe. There's too many bastards ready to line up behind a major retailer after closing with their peckers out and not enough Sweaty Bettys, that's what I'm saying. That's why China will win in the end. 'Cause Betty spends a whole night making enough to buy that snowblower and that snowblower was made in China and some fucker over there is rich and he's never even seen snow or had to handjob some greasy shitheel in order to be able to afford to clear it out of his driveway. Anyway, like I said, we're all going to hell. Maybe not Sweaty Betty. Maybe she's earned herself a buy.

But that fat Chinese fuck, I think he's headed for a rotating spit. And he won't be alone.

After work we have a few beers. I explain to Gerry that

Johnny killed himself — death by Zippo. He seems relieved. Then I tell him about the cop.

"So he came right up to the door?"

"I'm saying I almost shit myself Gerry, right there on the floor."

"They're out there looking for a moose killer?"

"They got a broad-daylight suicide, a missing person, and an armed robbery, and they're out looking for the guy who shot Elliot Moose."

I slide him the flyer.

"Molested? It says the moose was *molested*? Holy shit, I get nailed for this I'm going to play the suicide card. I am not going to jail for molesting a moose. Imagine that around the lunchroom table in the big house. 'What are you in for?' 'Molestation?' 'A kid?' 'No, no, a moose.' If it was a kid I wouldn't make it to the next day. A moose I wouldn't make it to the counter to stack my tray."

"Well. People do like animals," I say.

"Yeah."

"Yeah."

"So the house is clean?"

"Except for my panic shit on the kitchen floor, yeah."

"I can't see there being a problem. It'll take a while for anyone to even notice he's not around. It's bad to say, but who's going to miss him?"

"End of the month, bills won't get paid."

"Phone doesn't get answered, services get cut off..."

"Two months before anyone even looks Gerry...and that house is like a poster for suicide."

"They figure he killed himself or he just took off. When they don't find a body they'll figure he took off."

"I found his finger."

"What? Jesus Christ. Where?"

"It was hanging from a bush, looks like a bird had been at it."

"Jesus. What'd you do with it?"

"It's in my freezer in a box of lasagna."

"Jesus Christ."

"Yeah. Well, what else though? You can't just throw it out, people notice shit like that. And the ground is too frozen to bury it."

"We could burn it."

"Yeah…"

"You cannot keep the thing in your fridge like a fucking popsicle." Gerry looks around the bar and lowers his voice. "It's the only thing that links us to him or us to the robbery. Well, besides the gay porn box or the cash in your ceiling. But I have a plan for those too. That finger's gotta go."

Gerry starts to get all intense like when he has a big cut of meat to work on.

"Let's pay up and get it done. I don't want this thing hanging around."

He throws some money on the table.

"It's time for a barbecue," he says.

18.

SKUNK KILL

In high school she was unapproachable. Two rows away and just all kinds of warmsoft under those clothes and no way to get at her. Last night she was riding me backwards. It was a dream mind you, but it was really quite a good dream. This is why I mention it, and she was doing it just like Lisa does it but it wasn't Lisa. No, it was definitely Elaine (come to think of it, not a particularly sexy name but, never mind, she was plenty of sexy in the dream, and in real life). The way she looked back over her shoulder, and her naked back. The side of her breast. The long, straight spine line, the downy down of her (she was quite a slim girl) and her ass just rising up and falling, up and down. And the way she looked back. I'm telling you: that shoulder. It's all in the shoulder, and in the eyes. Just makes you want to. But I didn't. I woke up. So then I'm looking around in the dark in a mixture of hot damn and hard cock and what the fuck? And then the radio alarm goes off and some voice says: "That's a half-side short rack of dripping barbecue hot rib goodness," and I say, "Yessir," and I say, "Why don't ya shut yerself up right about now howzabout?" and I small the snoozer and I take my bobbing throbbing self right into the bathroom. I don't know, it's just dreams. Elaine. Almost forgot about Elaine.

So we go get Johnny's finger from my freezer. Which, you know, is weird when you just say it like that, but that's what we do. And it's not like we're thinking of it like a barbecue. I mean, we don't bring any fucking buns or barbecue sauce or anything. No condiments, no chopped onions, no coleslaw. I'm sitting there in the car with little Johnny in my lap. I've taken him out of the hydro envelope and removed him from his condom wrapper and he's sitting there in the fading sun. And Gerry says: "You sure that's him?"

"What do you mean am I sure?"

"I mean it doesn't look like him."

"Who the fuck else would it be? Besides, it's not him — it's his finger."

"Which one?"

"Which — how do I know which one fuck? What does it matter which fucking one? It's the one that landed in the fucking bush."

"I don't like it. Not like that. Why'd you take it out?"

"I thought we should defrost it."

"Defrost it?"

"Yeah, you know, for the barbecue..."

"You gonna marinate it too?"

"No, but."

"No, but shit."

"Well, what the fuck, I've never barbecued an appendage before...I didn't know there were rules."

We sit there in silence for a while.

"I think it's his middle finger," I say.

"That fucker."

Silence.

"He doesn't mean anything by it."

"What are you his best friend now? Let me tell you, all that suicide shit? That was just his huge middle finger right up our ass."

"Asses."

"Whateverthefuck...he screwed us over."

"I don't think that was his main thought at the time, Gerry."

"You know what my main thought is right now? My main thought is to barbecue the fuck out of what's left of him and then get myself laid. And are we still goin' to Montreal?"

"Yeah."

"Oui oui monsieur...when they see me dance, the ladies in France, remove their pants..."

"You got any propane?"

"Enough."

Gerry's place is in town but almost out. You could throw a rock and hit woodlot. Mostly Gerry throws a rock and hits the side of his neighbour's garage when his neighbour's kid is in there practicing with his band. Gerry's not big on rock music, or kids. Or small animals. Or people. Which explains all the live traps around his property. He's got a thing about racoons and skunks on his property. He doesn't like 'em. He likes country music and no kids and no small animals. And no people. Really he just likes country music and vodka.

"Shit."

We arrive and right away Gerry's out of the car quick and running back to the side of a little shed behind the house.

"I got one!"

But I don't know what he's yelling about or what to do with Johnny's finger.

"Hurry up!" Gerry's yelling now.

So I throw the finger on Gerry's dash and I run over.

Gerry's grabbed a pitchfork and he's advancing on a cage sitting on the snow near the shed.

"Gotta finish the prick off before he sprays."

The skunk in the cage is eyeing us very warily and backing up into the corner. He's right to be suspicious. We are not trustworthy people. We have done bad things and we will probably continue to do them. Nobody will stop us and we are unlikely to stop ourselves. Gerry lunges in with the pitchfork. I can't stop thinking about Johnny's severed finger on the dashboard of the car. How it looked really lonely sitting there like that. Gerry's trying like hell to get at the skunk but the points of the pitchfork won't reach to where it is. The skunk's pissed now and it's only going to be a matter of time.

"Get me something!" Gerry yells at me, "...damn thing's gonna squirt us!"

I open up the shed and grab the first thing I see, which is a chainsaw.

"What the fuck?" Gerry yells, still lunging.

"I know..."

There's nothing else to do now so I start it up. This really sets the skunk off now and it starts to lunge back at the pitchfork which is probably a bad idea since it clips him and now it's hissing and it's back into his corner. The chainsaw is really loud and leaking smoke pretty bad so I shut it down. Gerry's into some kind of martial arts style attack now with his legs far apart and one foot really forward and one arm up but the pitchfork is still not reaching. I run and get the garbage can and the garden hose from the side of the house.

"What?"

"We'll drown him, he'll be dead and the water will soak up the spray..."

"Too late."

He's right, the smell is everywhere and at this range it is strong. It sucks up all the oxygen in the yard. This is skunk ground zero.

"Bastard!" Gerry's shouting and he's stripping off his clothes and running around in small circles in the snow like he's on fire.

"I hate fucking skunks! I fucking hate fucking skunks!" He's yelling.

He's like Chef in *Apocalypse Now*. "Fucking Tiger Man!"

I am just calmly filling up the can with the water. I'm going to stink for days now so there's no reason to get too excited or hurry. Gerry runs past me towards the house. A very angry naked bald white man in the gathering dusk. This is the difference between me and a lot of people. I've seen hell. And this is not it. So relax. It could be so much worse than this and one day, it will be again. This is my peace. I can hear Gerry slamming around in the house to turn on the water. He has the lights on now and he yells to go ahead. When the water finally reaches the top of the can I pick up the cage and I lower it in.

Only the cage is a little bigger than I thought. Or the can is smaller. Either way the skunk is able to climb the wires and hold his head above the surface of the water, the poor bastard. He's clinging there looking at me like Leonardo DiCaprio in *Titanic*. I reach into the can and try to push the cage further down but it's wedged on the sides and it won't move. The skunk takes swipes at my hands with its claws and I have to let go. Nothing is the way you think it's going to be. Ever.

"Get out of the way!"

I turn around and Gerry's back, still naked, still angry, still bald. This time though he has a handgun and he's pointing it at the skunk.

"Don't," I say really calm.

"That little fucker's goin' down, move aside."

"Gerry. Too many people," I say, real quiet, my hands up.

It's true. Even here there are lots of people to hear a gunshot in the cold air and come over asking questions and this is not a really good time for us to have any questions asked. I can see this knowledge pass across Gerry's face. He lowers the gun.

"We'll just start a fire," I tell him, "We'll start a bonfire and we'll put the cage on it. Then we can get the barbecue going and we'll say goodbye to Johnny."

It's like I'm explaining things to a child like you do when something goes wrong. *Look, we'll just pick the cake up and we'll put it back together. It'll be as good as new. C'mon, you'll see. Wipe away those tears, Champ.*

"Wipe away those tears, Champ."

"What?"

"Sorry, that wasn't supposed to be out loud. C'mon, just let's get things going. We'll cook up some live skunk and a human finger and it'll be great. It'll be great."

For a minute I believe it.

"Hey guys."

It's Lisa. Which is not that great. Gerry's naked in the snow, we're about to do some live animal cooking and fuckingshitfucker there's a human appendage on the dash of the car right next to where she's standing right fucking now. All the lights from the house are shining on it. Right there. Don't look. No. Don't.

"Gerry's naked, come and see," I shout.

"What?" she yells back.

"What?" Gerry hisses.

Well, it's all I could think of in a hurry.

"It's all right, she's a nurse..." I tell him.

"So?"

"So...she's got low expectations. Look, she's standing right next to Johnny, we've got to get her moving."

"Lisa, come over here!" Gerry yells. "I'm naked! Hey, look at this!"

After we explain that Gerry thought he was having an allergic reaction to skunk spray so he took off his clothes; and after we get him wrapped in a blanket and then into some new clothes and she checks him out and I drag the cage to the back of the property for a humane release, we start the fire and I drive out to get some marshmallows and we sit there under the stars and toast them up, everything seems pretty normal except for the finger wrapped in tinfoil at the centre of the coals.

Except for that.

And the skunk smell.

Lisa stares into the fire and leans her head on my shoulder.

I don't know. Life's funny I guess.

It's two in the afternoon and Otis is asleep with that look that he has of being completely untouched by the world and all of its dirt. He only has this look when he's sleeping though. I guess he'll have it when he's dead too. I've never seen it on him in the daylight. The room has the lightness of a very sunny January afternoon. Everything is white. Everything is peaceful. It's like heaven. But it's not heaven. It's here. Otis wakes up. It is 2:08.

"You bring me some porn?"

"I brought you some Beer Nuts."

"Fuck you."

My Poppa. My Daddyo. Pappy Mine. Quite a lot of him kind of washed down the drain now. Swirling. He's worn away at the edges.

"That you?" he asks squinting.

"It's me."

"Close them drapes up tight."

Otis doesn't like the sun. He says it hurts him. He says that when he's gone it's just going to go on spitting bright regardless and fuck it for that. *Fuck it for that,* he says. *Pissing its yellow at everyone* he says. Otis has not pissed yellow for a long time. *Straw,* he says, *I'm pissing straw. There's no colour in my piss he says because there's no colour in my food.* He's forgotten all of his friends. He remembers all his enemies. But they're all dead. Now he has no one left to fight.

"Your mother once poured all my rye down the toilet," he says.

Hands like he's tapping out a cigarette.

"I drank it anyway," he says.

He looks at the drapes.

"Rye and water. Right out of the bowl."

Like father, like son. After ninety, people's eyes are more open than before they were ninety. They're wider.

"I used to run with the bingo hall chicks and she didn't like that much I guess."

They're rimmed with pink and water.

My grand old man. He picks up a pill from the floor.

"I just got a straw and drank it right from the bowl. Is this yours?"

"No."

So he pops it. Looks around for water.

"Wait," I say and I look around for a glass.

"Never mind. It's down."

"What's it for?"

"Fucked if I know. Not sure it's even one of mine. Maybe it's for the herpes. Maybe the clap. Maybe it cures painful rectal swelling. I was really hoping you might bring me some Jimmy Dean Jerky..."

"Next time."

Otis likes a lot of salt, says it's the only thing he can still taste; that and pussy. Not that he's tasted any of that in the last twenty years, but the man has dreams and aspirations. So he likes his Jimmy Dean Jerky and he likes his Beer Nuts. But not the fucking sun.

Fuck the sun, he says.

19.

SUCKER PUNCH

There's lots of times I don't want to leave the house. Because I know nothing good will happen if I do leave the house but at the same time I have to eat. I have to go and line up with the other Mc-Fucks. More and more I eat peanut butter on bread. Sometimes it's just the peanut butter I eat. I eat apples. I'm trying to get better. I get up in the morning and I don't have a drink and a smoke and I have a shower and I make some toast. I simply make some toast. I put jam on it.

That's not a dream. It's something I wish.

"Okay Fucko, you got no beef jerky, and no Beer Nuts for me, and Gerry tells me that weird cunt you knew in high school, that Socks guy, he blew his ass off with your dynamite."

"More than his ass, and it was Gerry's dynamite, not mine. He told you that? When?"

"I called him on Boxing Day to find out if the beer store was open. He's my secondary emergency contact remember? You didn't seem to be around much this Christmas... and I ran out of beer."

"That's not an emergency."

"It is around here, Sugar."

"They told me not to bring you any more beer. It makes you cranky. And I was a little busy picking pieces of my pal's ass out of the trees on Christmas. Did you call my place?"

"Sure I called your place."

"Well. I'll bring you some stuff tomorrow."

Otis is rubbing his face.

"I remember that kid. I always thought he had a little hitch in his giddyup. Well, everybody dies. And everybody dies alone."

"That's cheery."

"Well, you got time to think of that shit when you're sitting here not drinking the beer that you don't have."

"You won't die alone."

"How do you know?"

"'Cause I'm gonna get you a couple of hookers, and I'll have 'em on standby."

"Good. I feel like I could fuck the jam out of a doughnut. Are they clean?"

"Sure, they're clean."

"Last thing I need is a dose of crabs just before I die."

"You'd die before you even knew you had the crabs."

"How do you know?"

"You haven't seen these girls. They'll kill ya."

"Good deal. Bring 'em on. You know I took a bullet once right to the mouth."

"I know."

He's got two fingers jammed into the empty space he's got up top there on the roof of his mouth.

"I spat that bullet right back out," he's wiping his fingers on his sweater, "and I threw it at him."

"How'd he like that?"

Otis looks at me as if he's never told this story before, his eyes lit up like last call.

"Not much!" He says.

"No?"

"No, not much!"

He's laughing now.

"And I'll tell you what else."

He falters.

"...I'll tell you what else..."

It's slipped away on him. He's not sure what's happening. He looks down at the things in front of him. Cup of water. Newspaper.

"We used to trap foxes..."

"I know."

"Sometimes we'd catch these feral cats, we'd have to kill those too...traps fucked 'em up too bad, but nobody wanted them pelts..."

He touches the buttons on his sweater. Looks up quickly.

"What're you lookin' at me for ya gapeface?"

Nothing.

He picks up the cup and throws it across the room.

When I was a kid they had these guys who came around and they'd do assemblies in the gym and we'd all be trooped in and we'd sit down in rows on the floor and we'd be pissed off if we were missing gym and pleased as shit if we were missing math and one of these guys would hot step it up to the stage and start yammering about something that happened to him when he was young and stupid and how we should never try to make that same mistake because we should be smarter than he was. Like we weren't allowed to be stupid. We had one guy tell us about his adventures with heroin. We had this one guy who looked at the solar eclipse without using a pinhole camera thing, you know, so you can look at it on a piece of cardboard instead of direct in the sky because that can blind you as any simple fuckleton knows except apparently this one didn't or he didn't listen. I guess that was the point and he has to be helped up onto the stage and shown where the microphone is. I guess there was an eclipse coming up and they wanted us to be smart and not the slack-jawed yokels we appeared to be most of the time. He told us all about how he thought he was being cool until he smelt something burning and then he couldn't see anything and I guess his eyes were on fire or something, his retinas sizzling up like eggs on a hot grill, and how he couldn't see since that day and now he can't get any work except for coming around to schools and providing us with his inspirational message. Like we didn't already know. I was guessing he didn't have a job before he fried up his eyeballs either. On the way out of the gym I turned to my friend and I said: *I'm tired of these smack shooting pinhole camera motherfuckers coming around and bitching up my gym time, it's fucking depressing.*

So the teacher was standing right behind me. I got suspended for that. Otis just said: *Talking back to the teacher, eh?*

No.

Well, I guess that's a pig you won't be riding in any parade again anytime soon.

I…

So whyn't you go get me a beer?

Some things don't change. We talk about Montreal. He really wants to go and I can't see any reason not to take him, aside from the fact that he's not allowed to leave the Manor. For a while he talks about being in Montreal in the '40s and the bars and the gangsters. I picture the big old black Fords and Chevys and the rain-wet streets and the neon signs. He wants to go to Schwartz's Deli and die there with a mouthful of smoked meat and pickle. That's all he wants.

"Maybe some fries," he says, "or maybe not. I just want a mouthful of smoked meat and then I can die happy. If I can't die fucking, then I'll just take the pastrami. And a pickle. They dole the salt out around here like it's fucking heroin."

We talk for a while but eventually his eyes drift to the side and they become grey. They're like Christmas lights, sometimes they're on and sometimes not. He can't keep himself plugged in. His eyes become glazed and rimmed with red like the eyes of a fish lying one side up on the surface. You can poke him with an oar, but he's not moving on his own. He's heavy in the water. He watches John Wayne take off his hat and jump from a horse.

"Who's that?" he asks.

"That's John Wayne."

He nods. No memory at all. He wants to say, "Who are you?" But his eyes go back to the screen.

A fish. Just floating.

So I head home.

"You know, guys like us..."

Gerry's in my head.

"...we're not made to win anything, you know? We're not ever going to win like other people win. New car. Great wife. Million dollars. White teeth. But we don't have to lose either, you know? Not all the time."

He's got his points maybe.

"Besides, Johnny didn't have the common sense God gave a peanut shell, right? So maybe he deserves to have his internal organs hanging from the trees. Why not? It's what he wanted. Look, no one's ever gonna be in our corner but us. Don't kid yourself."

That feeling like you want to roll down the window for some air. But there's no window there.

Who's in my driveway? Lisa's in my driveway.

She's in her car and she's got some Neil Young playing really loud. Maybe that's a good sign. I come up from behind and tap on the window. She turns like she's surprised someone would interrupt Neil. She cracks the window open.

"What?" Neil gets louder. So do we.

"Good morning," I say.

"Where ya been?"

"There was a sale on at Bed Bath & Beyond."

"No," She turns down the music.

"I was just visiting Otis."

"I think we should twalk."

"We should what?"

"You know, talk and walk. Twalk."

"Okay."

Twalk. Sometimes she's sixteen and sometimes she's forty. Never. Never okay when they tell you that talking will be a good thing. It's never good. *We should talk more.* No, I don't think we should. I think we should be quiet more. It's particularly bad when you have to walk to do the talking. That means something's broken, and the chances that you're going to have whatever it takes to fix it sticking out of your back pocket are very slim. It's either something you can talk your way out of or it's not, but it's never good. I wish I was driving down the coast of California. The Pacific Coast Highway. In an Eldorado. Maybe with Jesus there. Or even Neil. I always liked them both. We'd, all three of us, have the wind blowing through our long hair. We'd have those big reflective sunglasses on. We'd stop and get Jesus a burger. Or whatever else he wanted.

"What do you want Jesus?" Neil would ask.

"Treat each other as you would wish yourself treated," Jesus would say.

"No. I mean to eat."

So we'd get some bread and some wine. Something He likes.

It takes a lot of time to get people to give up on you. They don't want to do it at all at first. It rattles them. It goes against their picture of who they are. Who they've been taught to be from the movies and TV shows they've watched. A lot of time and a concerted effort is what it takes and eventually they'll give up. This is what makes me a high-octane highfructosehightestosteronemotherfucker. I give up first. I don't give them the time of day to do it to me. It's already been done. Rabbit out of the hat and you didn't see it coming. At times like this I amuse myself by playing "Down On The Corner" by Credence in my head. So I'm clearer. *Down on the corner, out in the street.* It clears my mind so I'm ready for anything. So I'm not thinking that Lisa's going to blindside me with...

"This isn't working out the way I thought it would..." or...

"You know, you're great, it's just that..."

or...

"Why don't you just stop touching me. I hate it when you touch me..."

So I lead off with: "I love you."

Start with the best shot you've got in case you don't get another one. Didn't see that coming? Neither did she. Blindsided. I guess we're all surprised a little here. So now I'm either on the bar floor sucking up stale, dirty beer or I'm the champ. Right? Okay. Fine.

Fine.

"I mean that's it. Things are good I think, but I don't have much else to...we have great sex and, I have a handgun if you ever need one, or if you need to borrow a toaster, or the car...I think things are pretty good. Great. I like them."

Hopefully I'm not scaring her with this machine gun fire because I don't know what the fuck I'm talking about. This is one of the problems about talking, especially to women and especially when you're trying to walk at the same time. So we're walking down the snow sidewalk and I'm looking at her boots. I should really shave, it's been days, since before Christmas for sure. They're those ones the young girls wear that look like bedroom slippers covered with that soft stuff they cover sofas with. And salt stains. And she's talking a lot and really fast. Like young girls do. So I start to listen.

"...and I know you're going through a tough time and I, I respect that, so if you're still going to take Otis to Montreal, you know you're not allowed to do that, but if you are going to do it then you'll need someone like me to come too because there's more to looking after him than you think there is and, well, I know what to do and I'm coming and that's all there is to it, and, so…"

She's saying this all at once so I stop walking and this stops her walking and it shuts her up too, then…

"…so yeah, yeah…uhm…me too." she says.

Fuck.

So that's it then.

Jakey brought a riddle home from school once: "What did the rude interrupting frog say?"

"I don't know, what did…"

"FUCK OFF!"

Mel and I thought that was hysterical. We told him not to say "Fuck Off." But we told each other the joke for weeks.

20.

GRINDING AHEAD EVER MORE QUICKLY TOWARD OUR OWN DEMISE

Dad?

Dad?

I don't think about what happened to Jakey often.

But I do think about what won't happen to him, I think about that all the time. No eighteenth birthday. No getting caught with a cigarette. No first time touching a girl. No driver's license. No hunch over the toilet on a first drunk. No everything else. Everything else that would have happened but now won't. None of it.

Dad?

He didn't die right away. There were moments. They trickled by. We could see what was coming. I could. The sky was empty. There was so much blood. A piece of the plastic Jeep roof had gone through the side of his neck. I held it closed with my hand. I was afraid to take my hand off even though I could see it wasn't doing any good. It was hot, the blood. Everything was wet with it. Red syrup. Pumping. Then cold. There was nothing else to do. It was daylight. Everything was ending.

"Dad?"

"It will be okay."

No way.

His eyes were so big, but I don't think they were seeing anything at all. I was trying to put the blood back in. He went like water from a glass. You could see it leave him. Whatever it is. An empty house. And then.

I started scrambling around the Jeep thinking that I could do something. If I could get the door open. It wouldn't be too late to do something. There was still something to do in those seconds. There was snow blocking the place where the roof had sliced away. If I could get some of this stuff out of the way. Sweater. Ratchet. Coffee cup. If I could roll the Jeep back over. Everything had come loose and rolled around everywhere. Stuff I couldn't even recognize. I started kicking at the window. Then hitting it with the ratchet. There was still time. I saw the blue flashing lights moving.

There was no time.

And I wake up in the middle of the night now and often I'm crying and I don't know why I am and then I do.

I have the clothes he was wearing because they gave them to me. They're in a black plastic bag at the back of the closet. I have the book he had out from the school library. They never called about it. That was probably on purpose. The Black Diamond Mystery. *He was on page fifty-seven. His name on the card in pencil and the due date stamped. When you pick up the bag of clothes you can tell they've all gone hard with the dried blood like they'd been covered with plaster.*

I had everything fixed up on the Jeep to put it back to the way it was before. It was all covered on insurance because it wasn't my fault. So I got everything done the right way but I probably would have done that even if I'd had to pay for it. And now I drive it carefully and I get the oil changes done and I keep the tire pressure up. And I believe that's where he is. And so sometimes I sleep in it too. I look after it.

It wasn't my fault.

In the back of the closet. Where the fuck else am I supposed to put them?

Jakey. Death steals everything.

"Your dad's here at the beer store."

"What?"

"Otis… he's here at the beer store, can you just come down and get him? Now? Please?"

"Come and get him?"

"He's scaring people."

Takes me a while to shake everything off and it's still stuck on me as I pull into the parking lot. I pull up to a stop and sit there for a minute watching. Otis is wearing brown pants and a belt. And nothing else. His white arms are waving in the cold. Tufts of white hair. Veins standing out like blue extension cords. People are avoiding him, veering around him with their empties. One woman stops and tries to talk to him. He takes a swing at her. It's starting to snow. I throw open the door and yell out:

"Hey! Otis! What are you doing?"

But he doesn't know. And I don't think he knows me. He peers across at me like I'm offering him something and he doesn't know if he really wants it. What do you mean you're giving me a horse? A *real* horse? What horse? Do I want a horse? Where is it? That's what he looks like.

"What?" he yells, his face tightening up around his eyes.

"Get in the car."

"What for?"

"Because it's cold."

"Cold? You're cold? You pussy."

"Yeah I'm cold. Now get in the goddamned car."

He looks around like *Yeah, what other offers do I have?* and then he crosses the parking lot. He leans into the window with his arms on the roof.

"Where you goin?" he asks.

"Somewhere where there's shirts."

He's peering around the inside of the Jeep.

"Do you even know who the fuck I am?" I ask him. "Otis. Otis, do you know who the fuck I am?"

"Fuck you."

"That's not a definitive answer. Just get in. How'd you get out of the Manor?"

"I killed a man."

Hopefully he's lying. If he's not then the Montreal trip will be off for sure. He gets in and slams the door.

"You know, Otis, January's not a good month for tanning."

"Fuck you."

I'm backing up out of the parking lot to the road.

"Hey, what about my beer?" he asks.

"I got beer at home."

"What?"

"I said I've got beer at home. And shirts. We'll get you a beer and a shirt."

"Three beers."

"Okay, three beers."

"And you can keep your shirt."

"You're not sitting on my couch without a shirt."

"All right Nancy, I'll wear a shirt. You never used to be so formal."

"You know who I am?"

"Yeah. You're the fucking guy with the beer and the shirts."

"I'm the guy."

He drifts in and out quick when he's drifting but he also pretends sometimes. This time he was faking it. Nobody wakes up in January in someone else's car with no shirt on and just takes it easy. Not even Otis.

"Three tall boys. None of those short-ass beers."

"Do I look like a guy who drinks short-ass beers?"

"You look like a guy with a hat full of stupid. Leafs are playin' tonight, we better hurry up. Speed up."

"Did you really kill someone?"

"Not today."

I get him set up with a beer and the radio. Otis prefers to hear the game. He gets distracted when he can see it. We sit at the kitchen table waiting for it to start.

"Last summer I was working at the fair," I tell him.

"Yeah? Which one?"

"South Mountain."

"Yeah?"

"I finish up and I get into the Jeep to come home. Fair's over, wrapping up. People heading home."

"Yeah?"

He takes a long pull on his beer.

"So the headlights are on and I'm just sitting there. I'm tired, you know?"

"Sure. You know this is a hell of a story so far."

"Just wait. And I see this girl coming through the field where a lot of the cars are parked. She's looking around you know, like she's worried someone will see her..."

"Yeah? You nail her?"

"It's not like that. She's just looking everywhere, you know, and she ducks behind this pickup, only I'm sitting there and the headlights are right on her. She rips her pants down and takes a piss. Right there."

"Standing up?"

"Squatting. I'm saying she looks everywhere and she doesn't even notice my lights are right on her."

"High beams?"

"Of course. I got her lit up like a billboard."

"Nice ass?"

"Sure."

I get up and pull out a bag of chips.

"You didn't nail her though?"

"She was just taking a piss."

"Some girls like that. You know this'd be a much better story if you nailed her."

"Would that make you happy?"

"'S not really about me is it?"

"Not really. I wasn't up to nailing anyone at the time."

"You better now?"

"In that department, yeah."

"So what's the point of that story?"

"I don't know. It's just something that happened."

I open up the chips.

"The point is I don't understand women."

"Who said you were supposed to?"

He takes the bag and takes a handful.

"That's a fair point."

"And you sure didn't hear that shit from me. Not supposed to understand 'em. Supposed to nail 'em. Never mind. Listen up...game on."

But he's asleep by the second period, just sitting in his chair, so I get him into bed and I turn off all the lights. I'm sitting at the kitchen table in the dark and the phone rings.

"Yeah?"

"I'm coming over."

"Okay."

"You've got him there right?"

"He's sleeping."

"I'll be there in ten minutes."

"Okay."

"Is he alright?"

"He's fine. Yeah."

"Okay."

Her voice sounds nice. Sounds like she cares what happens. That's nice. I open another beer and look out into the backyard lights of the houses around me and now it's starting to snow. Red tail lights flash down the street. I sit and read the Keith's can: *Alexander Keith's India Pale Ale continues to be Nova Scotia's most popular beer and the number one specialty beer in markets across Canada. Return for refund where applicable. Veritas Vincit.*

21.

ALL THE KIDS FORGOT ABOUT DUTCH

I'll tell you what I want, what I really really want. What I like. A Cobb salad. A nice steamed hot dog and a bun loaded with sauer-kraut. Some Lay's potato chips. You can't eat just one. Nice big hunk of ham on rye bread with lots and lots of mustard. Key lime pie. Good spaghetti. Cold beer. Salted peanuts. Steak. A fudgesi-cle. Pork chops and corn relish. Mashed potatoes. I read this book once when I was a kid, Bath House Sue. *You can guess how that went. Lots of dog-eared pages on that one. Haven't had any dreams lately. I haven't got anything left.*

And I don't know why I'm crying. And kind of I do.

There's a dog barking across the yards when she knocks on the door. Dogs have a limited range of interests but they pursue them with no small amount of passion. So I like dogs. And I like Lisa. I wipe my eyes. What the fuck? Anyway, she's wearing her hood up with the fake fur around it like she's looking down the barrel of a furry gun. Her eyes are white in the porch light. That dog is really going at it now.

"You oughts to get this porch fixed up a little bit, Mister."

"I know it."

Then there's this pause like she wants to say something, and I want to say something but I have no idea what the fuck to say.

Options:
You look nice.
I have been crying. Probably you can tell.
Glad to see you.
C'mon in.

She probably would like to hear any of these. But I keep quiet. Women know all about crying. I don't get it really. It's unpleasant. It hurts and you can't breathe.

"I've got to say something to you," she says.

"Okay."

"Then I won't say anything else."

"Okay."

"If we're going to keep at this I'm going to need more from you than great sex and a handgun."

"Okay."

"Okay?"

"Well, like what though, exactly?"

The dog has finally shut up. Someone turned all the sound off everywhere.

Breathe.

"I don't know what. Exactly. Yet."

"Okay."

There's a train.

"But there'll be something. And I'll let you know."

"Okay."

I'll do it. Whatever it is. I know this more than I know most things now. I like her more than I like dogs. More than dogs like bones. More than I like Cobb salad. I like her more than I liked *Bath House Sue*. And I liked *Bath House Sue* a lot. On the inside of my head there's a billboard that says, "Yes." It's nighttime and there's a spotlight on it. *Yes*, it says. I pull the car over to the side of the road and just look at it. It's a big summer night and there are crickets in the trees like somebody is winding up a huge watch. The billboard looks nice. Just the word "Yes" in big sticky yellow letters. Like somebody just spent an afternoon pasting it up there for fun or maybe it's a new advertising campaign and you're supposed to think, *Yes what*? It doesn't really matter. I know what it means. It means I'm fucked, really. It means I'm Liston on the mat and Ali is standing over me in those white satin trunks and he's looking like he just shit out the world and it's solid gold. But I don't mind. I'll just lie here for a while. It feels okay. Down here. It feels nice.

So she comes in and I take her coat and I hang it up. It looks good in there with my beat up stuff. It's beat up a little too but next to my stuff it doesn't look it.

"Why are you here?" I hear myself saying.

"You know, Otis."

"No..."

She knows I mean in general.

"Oh."

She looks around the room like there's something to say lying on the couch or the floor, like she could pick up a piece of paper off the floor and read it out loud. Or like there'll be something on TV she can change the subject with. She shrugs.

"You look at me really hard sometimes. Like you're really looking. Right now that's good enough."

"Okay."

"My life kind of sucks. I know I don't show it."

"Nope."

Not at all, I'm thinking.

"How come I'm the one answering questions? Mother of Fuck I thought I just got finished saying I need more than a handgun and great sex."

"Don't you need those too?"

"I don't need a handgun."

Jakey was about four when we lost the rabbit. We didn't really lose him. It would have been better if we'd lost him though. The beagle we had at the time made a bathroom carpet lasagna out of him. By the time I got there he was a little tapestry of sinew and fur. He was like one of those fuzzy urine mats people sometimes have around their toilets only made with blood and fur and brain matter. I was in bed downstairs having one of those dreams you have over and over and can never quite remember no matter how hard you try. Nothing will keep it in there and you just have to wait for it to come back and then you forget it again. Mel never woke up at night, even when Jakey was really little. *It's nothing that can't wait until I've had some coffee and a piss.* It didn't sound human at first, the sound he was making. I thought it was still part of my dream.

"Hey. Wake up."

"Fuck off."

One of us was always telling the other to fuck off. It was usually her, but it was a two-way street. Fuck Street. That was where we lived. 123 Fuck Street. Holy holy holy holy holy fuck how did I marry her and end up here? I'm just asking the question. The sun there on that street doesn't go down until 3:00 a.m., and it never really comes up. Blinds were always down. You try filling out "Fuck Street" on a school registration form and see how far you get with that. I decided to grow a beard mostly because she didn't like beards. You come into the world on your own and you go out that way too. Everything else in between is a bonus, or a kick in the balls. I didn't know that then. Forgive me. When you're no good for her and she's no good for you, sometimes you just go on anyway because it seems easier. You make toast. You make decisions. You think you do anyway. Mostly you make toast. And you don't unplug when you stick the fork in because you really don't care anymore. Fuck electricity, you think, waiting for the jolt and the last cold spasm on the floor and the pissing out onto the linoleum. I digress. It wasn't a marriage they make cards for. Nobody vacuumed.

What is it?

How the fuck do I know? I'm going to see, fucking okay? You just stay put there.

All right.

Fuck.

It was Jakey. He was in a little ball just inside his bedroom door. I guess he'd opened up the bathroom door and then found his way back to his room. The bathroom door was still open and the light was on and slanting across the carpet to his door. He'd brought the classroom rabbit home for the weekend. All the kids took it for a weekend. It was his turn. We weren't set up for rabbits or house guests of any kind. We weren't a family that did grocery shopping. Or laundry. Or dishes. We were getting better. Then Jakey died. But first the rabbit. I have to finish the story about the rabbit. I put my arm around Jakey and asked what was wrong but he couldn't stop crying.

So I pushed the bathroom door all the way open. It was still shocking even though it was just a rabbit. A lot to see all at once especially if you're four and you're not expecting your life to suddenly throw up right in front of you. It was nothing new to me, but seeing it through his eyes, it hurt. Kindergarten gives you no frame of reference for it.

"It's okay Jakey, I'll fix it."

Good luck with that, Champ. It was like someone had been making furry sausages in there. I grabbed a garbage bag and a towel and started scooping. My plan was to drag everything to the centre of the floor where I could make a little mound of rabbit and then scoop that up and into the bag. It worked okay. Then I grabbed a wet towel and the roll of toilet paper and succeeded in making a little lake out of what was left: blood and brain matter and water with fur floating in it. His name was Dutch. I don't know why. I left the little lake to dry up and went back to Jakey.

"Is he okay now?"

Not really.

"He'll be okay Jakey, he's just not around here anymore."

"Where is he?"

Mostly in the bag, some on the floor, and some inside the beagle. Why can't I ever remember that dog's name?

"He'll be okay."

"Can I see him?"

"No."

I told him to get into bed and I'd finish up what I had to do and come see him. Fucking dog had made it back into the bathroom and was pawing at the bag.

"Fuck you, Rover."

I'll call him Rover because I still can't remember his name. I edged Rover out with the side of my foot and finished cleaning everything. It looked pretty good now. The rabbit in the bag was already starting to stiffen up. I threw everything out on the back porch and went back to see Jakey. He was still sniffling and doing those breathing gasps that kids do when they've been crying too much and they can't stop.

"What's going to happen?"

"I don't know. It'll be okay."

"I have to take him back to school on Monday."

"Yeah."

"Can I?"

"No."

"I have to."

"I'll explain everything to your teacher."

Listen. The rabbit's dead. Dog killed the rabbit. No more Dutch. Yeah, fuck, I know, right? It's a bitch…

"Is Dutch going to be okay?"

He knew Dutch was not going to be okay, even at four years old he must have noticed Dutch's head was not attached to his body, it's just what kids do, they ask questions to get the answers they want. It was normal. I just held him for a while on the bed until his breath stopped catching inside him.

"It's gonna be okay," I told him.

A couple of hours later he crawled into bed with me.

"Do you think maybe he could still be alive in that bag out there?"

"No."

"Okay."

And that was it. The next day was Sunday and I went out to buy a replacement rabbit. Like somebody invites you over and you bring them a bottle of wine. You break somebody's window with a baseball you offer to fix it. Go after someone's car with a pry bar... but the pet store had no rabbits. Apparently they were on back order. I bought a fucking parrot instead. Cage on a stand and the whole works. Big fucking feathers and it could say, "Hello" and "You're nice" and it really kinda sounded like somebody talking. All the kids forgot about Dutch right away. Except for Jakey of course. I didn't fix that. Teacher gave me the hairy eyeball when I brought it in and explained what happened but it all worked out okay. I know what she was thinking: *You're the guy with the burned down porch.* It wasn't burned down back then but if it had been burned down she would have been thinking that. I'm sure she is now. That was that guy whose porch is all burned down now. The two things go together in her mind: people who let rabbits get butchered in their bathrooms burn down their own porches. That's what she thinks. They have recycling boxes full of empties. It's simple for her because she doesn't see how it works, how one thing leads to another and nothing starts out good in the first place and sometimes the connections just get broken. And when those connections get broken then things in the real world get broken. You can't stop it. It's not as simple as brushing your teeth every morning or lining things up so they're in a nice straight row. Those things are excuses. They're just things you do so you don't have to think about how broken everything really is. The row's never going to stay straight or really be straight anyway. It'll just look that way. Your teeth have already fallen out. And it's okay. But she doesn't want to think about how her porch is really just waiting for a match and the flowers she plants by it are never going to stop the fire from happening. So she didn't want the parrot. But mostly she didn't want the parrot just because it wasn't a rabbit. She was expecting a rabbit. More than that, it wasn't the rabbit that left her class on Friday. She was blind to the parrot. The rabbit that got smeared across my bathroom linoleum prevented her from even seeing the parrot. Polly want a cracker? Polly wolly doodle all day. Pollyanna. It was like I was a magician pulling a rabbit out of my sleeve and she couldn't even see it.

"Look at this, it's a fucking rabbit!"

Nope. Nothing.

"I don't know that we can really accept a parrot," she said.

"What's to accept? It's already here," I said.

People like that drive me crazy. They're the same ones who don't understand why there are so many empty bottles in front of my house on recycling Tuesday. *Why are there so many?* Because there are. Oh, and fuck you. He probably pisses in the kitchen sink, that's what she was probably thinking. And so what if I do?

I only do it when the bathroom seems too far to go. She's the type who worries about getting a cold, and forgets that we're all just going to die anyway. The kind who says I don't care what you show me, if it's shit — I'm not going to call it ice cream. But she was wrong, she couldn't even see that bird and it was creamy milky sugary fun. It was a creamy bird. People who are against pissing in the sink forget that there's fifty billion bacteria on every inch of human skin. That's a real number. Wash your hands as much as you want, they're not going anywhere. You can flood them out if you want to but they'll claim insurance and rebuild. Most toilet bowls are actually freer of bacteria than most kitchen sinks. That's a fact. But people think they can fix that.

"We'll clear them out like the Viet Cong!"

No. You won't. The Viet Cong stayed put.

Ever wonder why there are hand sanitizers everywhere these days? It's because the hand sanitizer companies want them there. It's good marketing. Nothing more. Has the death rate gone down since they started putting them up? Nothing sells like fear.

So Lisa goes to check on Otis and she says his pills can wait till the morning since he's already asleep and so we just go to bed. I have this string of little Christmas lights I'd plugged in back before Christmas thinking I'd hang them up but I just left them on the floor. While she's up on top of me she reaches down and she starts draping them around herself.

"Make a wish…" she says, her voice slow and gravelly, her hands winding them around "…and blow me…out …"

Jesus Christ. She's like fucking a Christmas tree but, I guess, a whole lot better. I get this feeling like things are going to be better now maybe. Nothing comes from nothing. That's a law of the universe. You put nothing in and you get nothing out. That's the way that it works.

"I like you," I tell her.

"Well," she says, "I guess so. But what can you do about it?" She rises up. "Mister?" Down. "Huh?" Up.

Then she reaches down and pulls the Christmas light plug out of the wall.

"Ow. Man, these little fuckers get hot."

Freckles.

That was that beagle's name. We weren't very imaginative.

22.

A SOFT DRINK IN A HARD PLACE

I think I might write a book called Death for Beginners. *It would give people an idea about what it's like to watch someone die, or what it might be like to almost die yourself. It just wouldn't say what it's actually like to die because that's the one I don't know anything about yet. No one can write about that anyway. But a lot of people don't know what the others are like and I think it would be a handy thing to have a book that would tell you about them. What it's like to watch most of your blood come out of you in the middle of the afternoon. Or someone else's. Or have that cold metal circle against the skin of the back of your head. Your temple. Your lips. Or to touch a cold leg under a stiff sheet as if there's still someone there. Lots of people know that stuff already, but lots don't. That's my book-buying public, the ones who don't know. But then people mostly don't want to know anyway. That's why we hide all that stuff away all the time. Body bags. Sheets pulled over. Yellow police tape. We only like to look at it when it's not real. Which is weird too. Or when it's got nothing to do with us. We have this huge appetite for fake death, for people pretending to die, pretending to be dead. We have no stomach for the real thing. Unless it's someone we don't know. It wasn't always that way. It used to happen in the living room and the bedroom instead of in the hospital. And when somebody died suddenly and unex-pectedly it wasn't such a tragedy. Uncle Johnny got stuck in the combine. I mean, sure, it was sad, people cried, but it was also just the way that things were. People got stuck in combines. It wasn't, "How could this happen?" It was just what happened. And nobody called the lawyer. Nobody sued the combine company or blamed the government for a lack of regulations about combines. Just recently we've cleaned it all up and put it all away in a drawer. Now death is like the shrink-wrapped flesh in Gerry's display case at the store. It's clean. But it is nothing at all like that. Ever been to a slaughterhouse? Or a chicken farm on de-beaking day? Or a car accident? Or a suicide? Death doesn't look good from close up, it's ugly. It's a very cool title I think. But nobody would read it. Because they don't want to know. Which is the whole reason we put the bodies into the boxes and hide them underground in the first place. Well, that, and the stink.*

It hurt me.

I'm driving the Jeep down to the store to tell Ray not to book me any shifts for the next week so I can take Otis to Montreal and this woman comes out of nowhere at an intersection and she sideswipes me like she's in a smash-up derby and I'm the last thing between her and the trophy. Did you ever notice how the wrecked pieces of a car look like a human injury? The fender torn and the shreds and mangled wedges of plastic signal lights and quarter panels lying in the road. It brought everything back, which is why they found me sitting in the middle of the street holding one of the off-road lights from the front bumper in my hands like a puppy. I was talking to it, they said. Shock, is what they said at the hospital. I knew better. I don't like it when anything's wrong with the Jeep, a little change in the steering makes me jumpy, I like to keep the tire pressure right. I like for it to be the way that it should be. I like to take care of the rust spots. I'd rather have something go wrong with me than anything wrong with it. So now there's something wrong with both of us and I don't like it at all. I tried to start it up after the crash and the dash lit up like fucking Carnival night in Rio. So I'm sitting on an examining table and a doctor's got a light in my ear and I think, *Fuck it*. I think we're taking the train to Montreal now. We got a pile of money. Why not? We'll take it out of Johnny's share. Jeep won't be going anywhere for a while and neither will Johnny and Gerry's car is always fucked, needs brakes, and a suspension. And a door. I cried when I saw that Jeep hooked up to the tow truck. I wanted to take it home and make it better right away.

It hurt me. The hell with it all then, we're taking the train. I like trains.

So we're on the train. We're on our way bright and early in the squinty morning. Me, Gerry, Otis, and Lisa.

"I hate trains," Otis says.

"What's wrong with you?"

"I don't know. Lotsa stuff. Ask my nurse here. I took seven extra strength whateverthefucks before we left but they ain't helpin'. My head feels like period cramps and my nuts are sore and I hate fucking trains."

"Why is that exactly?"

"My nuts? How the hell should I know?"

"The trains."

"Why exactly? It's because your grandfather got his arm tore off by a train, that's why. Exactly."

"Is that right?"

Otis looks out the window.

"Of course that's right. You think I don't know?"

"I didn't say that. He had it out the window did he?"

"No." He looks back. "He was layin' passed out on the track. Damn train woke him up pretty good though."

"I bet."

"Lucky thing for his wife he was left-handed."

"Oh, for shit's sake Otis."

"What? He didn't lose none of his sexual artistry, that's all I'm saying."

"I woulda been okay with you saying a lot less. And that's your mother you're talking about right?"

"My stepmother. For Chrisake not my mother. Grab some class. She was his first wife, this one. She had the rickets."

"So?"

"So nothing. She had 'em is all. Had a walk on her like a nutcracker, one leg, the other leg, the other leg, like she had no knees, nothing bent on her."

"And him with just one arm."

"Oh you could see 'em comin' from a mile away. It was like a circus sideshow. Small children ran at the sight of them."

"It's funny, I remember meeting him when I was little. Seemed to me like he had two arms."

"You don't know fuck. Little kids don't know fuck. You didn't have a two-armed grandfather to compare him to. It's just he had a way of holdin' his sleeve like there was something in it."

"Like a rabbit."

"Fuck a rabbit, no, I'm talkin' about makin' it look like

he had an arm in it. Why the fuck do you bring rabbits into it for?"

"You know, like a magician, like a rabbit up his sleeve."

"That's hats. Magicians have rabbits in their hats," Gerry says.

"No. They got rabbits in their sleeves and then they jam them into their hats so they can pull them out of their hats. That's the trick."

"You sure?"

"That's why they say, 'There's nothing up my sleeve,' you get it?"

"Why?"

"Cause they got a fuckin' rabbit up there, that's why."

"So why don't they just pull 'em out of their sleeves then? The fuck with the hats."

"I don't know. People like to see 'em come out of hats is all."

"Why?"

"I don't know. People are crazy for rabbits in fucking hats. Why do people do anything? It's a fucking mystery to me."

"They gonna come around with beer or what?"

"It's eight-thirty in the morning."

"So...no?"

"So no, I don't think so."

"What's the point of first class then?"

"They'll bring peanuts maybe. Coffee."

"People don't wear hats anymore. You know that? They wear baseball caps. Toques. Not real hats."

"So what?"

"So what do these magicians do now? You know what?

I see a fucker comin' at me with a real hat these days I say here comes a fuckin' magician. I bet he's gonna pull a rabbit out of that fucker."

"Shitty job."

"Being a magician?"

"No, being a rabbit. Of course being a fucking magician...kids parties, little pukes pullin' at your shiny pants with their snotty little piss hands...mister...mister..."

"Lookin' for rabbits..."

"Anyway," Otis interrupts, "...hadn't been for that train he woulda had two arms. That's all."

"You didn't really take seven pills did you, Otis?" Lisa asks.

"Guess you'll know I did when I kick it."

"Otis, I know how many pills there are in each one of those bottles," she says.

"Fuck you do." He's staring at her.

"It's my job." She's staring right back.

There's nothing else to say then so we all just sit quiet and wait for the steward to come with bags of peanuts and shit.

"I don't like being in this situation," Gerry says.

Which one, I'm wondering. The situation where you've committed a felony? The one where you've witnessed a secret ritualistic suicide that you supplied the equipment for? The one where your wife left you for a sixteen-year-old box boy? The burning of a body part? Taking an old man to Montreal so he can die with a mouth full of pastrami? Being a general nuisance to the community? Or the moose you shot?

I'm pretty sure it's not the moose.

"In a few minutes there's going to be a pretty young girl smiling at me and offering me nuts."

He looks out the window at the ass ends of the farms we're passing.

"I don't know what people expect me to do in that situation."

Nobody says anything to help him. Barns go by.

"This is your biggest worry?" I ask him.

"One thing you could do would be to say, 'Yes please,'" Lisa says, "Another could be 'No, thank you.'"

"Yeah. Thanks. There's five-hundred answers to that question that go through my head. And none of them are 'Yes, please' or 'No, thank you.'"

"And how do you know it'll be the girl?" Lisa asks. "Maybe it'll be the guy."

"There's a guy? Good. Maybe it'll be the guy then."

"Cause you wouldn't say anything to him? When he says 'Nuts, Sir?'"

"I'd say 'Thanks, pal.'"

"You wouldn't thank him for offering you his nut package and ask him if it was salty?"

"No. I wouldn't."

"But you would brighten her day with 'I got my own right here thanks for noticing.'"

"Some girls like that shit."

"Which girls?"

"My ex-wife for one. First time I met her she was wearing this low-cut top. I pointed to her tits and said, 'Looks like two bald-headed men having an argument.'"

"And she fell right into bed with you?"

"We got married."

"How'd that go for you?"

"Super-duper. I'll introduce you sometime. You two'd get along great."

I'm not sure why Gerry and Lisa are at each other this morning. I don't think they agree on Otis's treatment plan. Hers involves medication and rest and Gerry's is mostly beer and porn. He thinks the home should provide computers and Wi-Fi so the old guys don't have to hold on to magazines with their gnarly, papery hands when they go about their business. He's got a point. I also think they should have the facilities for making a little homebrew if they want but there's gonna be some guy in a cheap suit who says that's not possible according to regulations and he's gonna spend money setting them up to make birdhouses and shit. Count how many ninety-year-old men you know who would rather make a shitty, plywood birdhouse than make their own beer? If you can come up with any names at all then you need to associate yourself with a better class of people. Fuck the birds and pass the opener, that's what I say.

"Would you folks care for some cheese crackers?"

Damn. Now we'll never know what Gerry would have said about the nuts.

I'll never own nice furniture, the kind of furniture that doesn't smell like dog piss and beer. Some things are just true no matter what you do. Pizza boxes in the corner. Unpaid phone bills. They just are. Pretty girl though, that can make it all worthwhile for a bit. There's something about a woman in a uniform that just makes me want to see her without it. I don't know if that's a sexist thing to think. Maybe it is. But it's true. So fuck it. Otis is asleep.

He sleeps like a dog these days, meaning mostly all the time. Gerry's stuffing his jacket between Otis's head and the window like a pillow. I picture Gerry dancing at the bar and yelling over the music, "How's it look when I lift my leg like this? Good, right?" pointing at his dance partner and nodding like he's got a chance in hell. Maybe he does. He's a good man. Most of the time.

So Otis is asleep and Gerry is now into his crackers and coffee. Apparently he's not feeling the nut stress anymore. No longer feeling the societal pressure to conform.

"How the fucking fuck do you fucking open these fucking fucking crackers?" he says, louder than most people probably would and he rips the little foil bag with his teeth so the little orange crackers explode like birds taking flight and come in for a landing on Otis's lap.

Cars line up on the snow road at the crossing we're passing. Otis doesn't wake up.

I'm thinking that there's lots of room in a train washroom for two people who are close to each other and in a physical relationship and there's probably one of those little tables that fold down to change a baby in there. At just about the right height. This is what I'm thinking.

Apparently it's easier to get thrown off of a VIA train in the middle of nowhere for "public sexual misconduct" than you might think. Easier than I had thought anyway.

Once I wanted to know if Jakey had been taught what to do in a fire, if they had taught him to stop, drop, and roll.

"What would you do if your clothes were on fire?" I asked him.

He thought for a minute.

"I wouldn't put them on," he said.

I pictured him opening up his closet to a wall of fire and standing there, looking at it, then just closing the door and walking away.

He was smarter than I am. Was.

Am.

23.

COLD AS FUCK

No matter how many times you hit a wall it's not gonna turn it into a door.

Feeling sorry for yourself isn't going to get you any further down the tracks. Not when you're shin deep in snow in street shoes and it's January and you're watching the train pull away from you. This is the time to just hike up the ball sack and get something done. But:

"I'm a fuckup," I say.

"Yeah," Lisa agrees, "You are. But c'mon, let's go."

And she starts picking her way through the snow with her arms out for balance looking like a girl holding her high heels up and trying not to step on the broken glass after a party. I don't know if you've ever had the experience of following a pretty, young girl crunching through an empty field somewhere outside of Alexandria halfway to Montreal in the middle of the morning with just a suitcase and a little bag of crackers but I find it to be a sobering one. And cold. And then I realize: Lisa thinks she can fix me. Well, fuck that.

We're not really dressed for the deep snow and Lisa's not complaining but she's wearing leggings that don't come all the way down her legs and I can see her skin turning pink like a little kid's cheeks do when they've been outside playing too long. I feel like Billy the Kid, thrown from the train...on the run. Wish I had a gun. I mean not to shoot anyone or anything, just for fun. Just like a kid playing cowboy. Something you probably don't know about Billy the Kid: his first crime was stealing a few pounds of butter. Also that photograph of him is the most recognized historical photograph in the world, according to some poll. More people recognize Billy than anyone else. Also there was a famous midget wrestler named Billy the Kid. Anyway, I'm feeling like an outlaw. Lisa probably is not feeling like this. She is probably just feeling cold. And pissed. If it was Mel she'd be pissed. Not that it was my fault. I mean, yeah, I was the one who suggested going to the bathroom in the first place but I was not the one yelling and kicking at the thin, metal walls. Not that there's anything wrong with that, at all. And I don't mind getting thrown off a train and feeling like Billy the Kid for a few minutes. At all. Especially under the circumstances. But I hope Gerry takes good care of Otis until we catch up. Not that I think he won't, it's just that Gerry's not always the clearest thinker all of the time and it's going to take a while for us to make it to Montreal on foot. But I guess we'll just get the next train, or a bus, so it's just however long it will take us to get into Alexandria. There's a Dairy Queen there, I know that. I could really go for a banana split or a shake. The fact that some shitwipe in a VIA uniform is totally against any multiple orgasming in his steel shithouse might work out okay for us after all.

But by the time we make it to the road, Lisa's calves are the colour of pink popsicles and we are both shivering and our shoes are full of ice and I've lost interest in having any ice cream treats at all, but not in the idea of nailing Lisa right here in this snowbank next to the frozen windswept pavement, of being on her like a jackhammer with the tractor trailers honking by and the cars of wide-eyed families and curious dogs.

Noses pressed to the windows. Is there something wrong with me? I don't think so. Maybe.

But I need an old priest and a young priest, this I know as clearly as I know my own name. That's the kind of fixing I'm in need of.

And anyway, there are no trucks or cars. There's nothing but salted, grey road with brown-hipped snow humps on either side. Down the road on the right there's a weathered looking farm. Doesn't look like a place where I want to be at all. Not that I want to be someplace pretty. I'm thinking of being in a greasy Montreal motel room with cum-stained walls and pizza box carpets. And Lisa. And not Mel. And maybe just watching TV or listening to music or something. Even if she wants to fix me. Let her try. Then going out to a bar. Sleeping. Listening to the crappy heater thumping. Weird. This feeling about her that's not in any way about fucking her, or only partly about that. More about just being with her and what it would be like in a perfect world. In a perfect world we'd all love our wives forever and we'd all stay strong. Not be near death and with our knees out from under the blanket in the cold air. Grey and thin. Hey, you look like a million bucks, yeah, you know what I mean: *folded up and wrinkled.* I was in love with a woman before Mel. I thought I was going to marry her. She didn't think anything of the sort though so that was that. Thing is it hurt so bad that I just made myself stop thinking about her at all. I just stopped, like giving up smokes. No more. And I haven't been able to do that since. These are just the thoughts I'm having walking down the road beside Lisa and trying not to feel the cold. But thoughts become things. We all know that. That's some true shit for you right there. Thoughts become things. That's true like the bass guitar in a good song is true or like a string of Christmas lights in the night dark is true. Thoughts become things. Thoughts are dangerous. Sometimes it's better not to think anything at all and sometimes you just can't help it no matter how hard you try. What we need are thought condoms. Something to keep the thoughts from getting out into the world and becoming the truth.

We are walking toward Jerusalem like two sad pilgrims. I told you I read, you remember? Maybe you didn't believe me back then. Maybe you don't now. I can't remember where I read that about walking towards Jerusalem. Maybe it wasn't Jerusalem. Maybe I made it up. Maybe I should write it down. See, if I picture Mel in twenty years she's outside a bar putting the boot to some guy on the ground and if I picture Lisa in five years she's holding a baby and the thing about me is I can't tell which of those things I really want. You could just wear the condom over the top of your head like a beanie and the thoughts would stay trapped as thoughts and not get out and become the world the way that they have the tendency to do. You know. The habit. I want to be at the bar with Gerry. I want to be completely white-girl wasted and weaving across the floor to the bathroom and coming back for another beer. I want some fresh-faced freckle-headed fuck to walk up and start making some trouble or to say something stupid. I want a fight to start. And then I want bacon and eggs and home fries and beans and a Dr. Pepper in the morning and a head that feels like it's got a big hole in it. Wanting things is how you get things. I should want bigger. But I don't want bigger and I never have. I know they're just simple things but these are the things that I want. Right now. And maybe a better coat. One thing about cigarettes is you can always have one when you can't have anything else. Unless you don't have any cigarettes. Which is the worst. I don't know. I don't really need a fist fight right now. No fires. Nothing to scare those horses over there. Maybe we could steal a horse.

But just a smoke. Would be fine.

They say things happen for a reason. Some people say this I mean. The dumbass ones. Young woman dies in a head-on collision with a transport and the next day someone who loved her a lot says well everything happens for a reason, I guess. But the reason is that the driver of the transport was up late the night before watching motel porn and he fell asleep and knocked her Kia off the road like a golf ball. That's the reason. I'm not saying there's no God. I'm really not in a position to say anything about that. I just know that if there is one then He, She, or It wasn't responsible for that fat fuck deciding to cue up *Riding Miss Daisy* on the pay-per-view when he should have been banking eight hours of solid sleep time. I'm saying that people make the mistakes and if there's a God then God's business is the clean up afterwards. God provides the road. If you choose to use it to smear some young girl across it like a June bug because you stayed up late to watch *Chitty Chitty Gang Bang* that's your call. You gotta live with that because God didn't make that shit happen. You did.

And time, you've got me going now, time doesn't really even exist, now did you know about that shit? I read that too, and it got me thinking. The idea is that time is just an idea that people made up and if we'd never been here to make it up, it wouldn't even exist. It's a convincing illusion that we conjure up collectively. It only exists because we think it does, and we only think it does because we thought it up in the first place and now we let it ride over us like it's a four-hundred-pound lifer and we're the punk ass newbies in the cell block. And some Japanese guy had this idea that really everything is time. That tree is time. That mountain is time. And they're like clocks all running at different speeds. Then physics says we're all made up of the same stuff. Only nobody listens to physics. Jesus said we're all one. Nobody much is listening to that either. People like me are too busy wishing for bar fights. Everything is time though, that's a hell of an idea. This snow is time. The sky is time. Lisa's ass is time. This road is time. Otis is time. Time gentlemen please. Otis is definitely time. Mouthful of pastrami, swig of beer, and down he goes like a plank. Time's up. Clockwork. Here's the thinking on the no such thing as time idea, at least the way I understand it: a seed becomes a tree and it sprouts though the ground and it gets bigger and bigger and it stops getting bigger and it falls over and then it turns into dirt. And we say it took a hundred years for that to happen but that's just an idea we put over top of the reality to make it manageable so we can think that we understand something and all we're really doing is making things smaller than they really are and we put this idea inside a little machine and we wear it around on our wrist like we know some shit. Like we're the masters of everything. We know nothing. All we do is make things smaller than they really are. We do this all the time and we do it every day. We put the dumb onto everything with our greasy, pudgy fingers. That thing that fell over isn't even a tree. We just call it a tree so we'll get this idea across to each other about what a tree is or so that we can own it or feel that we made it up in the first place. It knows it's not a tree. It's just what it is. It just is. Calling it a tree is stupid. The tree doesn't care. Otis is going to die soon. But that's not going to be time's fault. Or God's. Or Otis's. Or Schwartz's Deli's for that matter. I could use a sandwich. Anyway, for a ninety-year-old guy Otis is pretty tough. Tough enough to crack an egg while it's still in the chicken. So they say. Damned tough anyway. So who knows how long he's got left? Sandwich and a pickle. And I could use a beer.

"How cold do you think it is out here?" Lisa asks.

"Once you can't feel anything it really doesn't matter," I say.

"I've lost all feeling from my vagina to my toes."

I stop walking and peer down both ends of the highway. Nothing.

"We're going to have to start drinking our own urine," I say.

Lisa crouches down in a squat and at first I think she's having a pee to get started but she just sits there and starts rocking back and forth. Her knees through her leggings have the look of stretched balloons. She's crying. Midget wrestler Billy the Kid probably would have seen this coming and maybe he'd have done something to prevent it. Some encouraging words. A gesture, like giving her his coat. Well maybe not his coat. It would be too small probably. But you know what I mean.

"Hey," I say. I kneel down next to her and take my jacket off to wrap around her shoulders. It strikes me how small her shoulders are. "Hey," I say again.

"I fucking hate crying," she says. "It's the fucking stupidest thing in the fucking world, a woman crying when there's nothing worth crying about."

"Hey. Happens."

"I hate fucking girls who cry when they just really need to butch up."

"You don't need to butch up. This is kind of a tough spot."

I wrap the jacket around her more tightly and start rubbing her back.

"Sex and funerals," she says, "Those are the only times you should cry."

She wipes her nose.

"Good times to laugh too," she says, "…sex and funerals…"

There's a little string left hanging from her nose so I wipe it away.

"That's sweet," she says, "…wiping a girl's snot string, I mean."

"Just trying to get you to sleep with me."

"Figures."

"I've got a real thing for snotty girls crying on highways. It's actually a real fetish. There's websites for it. You can look it up."

There's a moment, after really good sex, where you think: *this is it. Right here. Now.* This moment right here, this one, you're lying there and it's this moment and you're in it and there's nothing wrong and there's nothing outside of it and you're never going to be exactly here again. It's a few seconds of perfect. Doesn't happen when your pants are around your ankles and some guy in a VIA Rail tie is screaming at you and pounding on the little metal door of the john. There's lots of times it doesn't happen. But the times when it does... I don't go to church as often as I used to. I used to try to get Jakey to go to church and he kind of liked it at first but then Mel got into making pancakes every Sunday morning which kind of got in the way. She usually just got up, made the pancakes, and then went right back to bed but she timed it just right so that they were coming out of the pan just when it was time for Mass. Hard for Jesus to compete with hot syrup and melted butter. Meek and mild against warm and sweet. The carbs always win. We could use some carbs about now.

What we could really use is a car.

Like that one right there.

Which is actually a Jeep.

"Look."

Even better.

"I see it."

Maybe.

When we're in the Jeep I can't stop thinking. It's a day for thinking. Not for fucking on the train or for being warm, this is apparently not a day made for those things.

There's this new subdivision being built by the side of

the highway, you know, one of those subdivisions that comes up out of nothing by the side of the highway far out from town just because somebody sold some land and somebody bought some land and now they want to sell it again only this time with houses on it. We pass by slowly. Big sign with "Dream House" written on it and this picture of a man and woman like they've just had sex in their new house and then put on their sweaters and gone for a walk in the autumn leaves. They're selling more than land here. They're selling barbecued steaks and white wine and high speed internet. And sweaters. They're selling peace.

Only somebody else owns a graveyard right next to the new houses and so the houses are putting up this expensive, new wooden fence about ten-feet tall and it looks like it would cost more than any of the houses. And they're doing this to keep out the dead of course. Nobody likes the dead in their new neighbourhood, walking the streets with sightless eyes, knocking on doors, grinding their muddy feet in the hallways. The dead bring down property values. But what I think is really funny is that they are putting this fence up at all. Like you can stop death, or block it out. Which is what we try to do all the time. Don't look at it, it's not there. Like a kid hiding behind their own hands. But just the thought that you could do it with supplies from the lumber yard strikes me as funnier than the ways we usually try. This can't go on much longer. I remember thinking that standing under the ice-cold shower of a woman I'd just up-assed in her basement family room over the back of her sofa with the home shopping channel on the TV and thinking all the time her husband could come home; she says he's out of town but she's also said he's a pretty big guy and not in the Doritos sense of the word, big more like throw-me-through-the-window sense of the word. Enormous ass all there for me over the back of this, settee, I guess it would have been. Enormous in a nice way I mean. In the best possible way. Creamy white handfuls of her and red elastic marks still at her waist. Grabbing tight. This has to stop soon I thought. In the shower afterwards I mean is when I think this with an empty Head and Shoulders Shampoo bottle and a man's disposable razor in the little plastic basket hanging from the shower head. These things can't go on much longer is what I'm thinking. It's four o'clock in the afternoon. It's Wednesday. I'm drunk. She doesn't want me in her house. Her ass yes, but not her house. She wants me out but she kisses me first in the hall by the door.

"I'll see you," she says like it's not a question.

It was, and I didn't answer. And I never did. See her again I mean. I didn't matter to her, I don't think, and I know it didn't matter to either one of us. It was this shitty little thing we did. That type of thing wouldn't always be shitty. Lots of times it's great. This wasn't though somehow. I mean everybody enjoyed it. At the time. But it didn't matter. Something mattered as I walked away from the house looking for a corner store to buy some chocolate milk, but it wasn't that. It didn't matter if I ever saw her again. It didn't even matter if I found the chocolate milk. But something mattered. I just didn't know what it was at the time. Maybe I still don't. Couple of weeks later I was pissing out yogurt. Well.

She was a redhead.

"You know what they say," she said, "a rusty roof means a damp cellar..."

Which is how we ended up over the back of the settee. I found the chocolate milk and I bought it along with one of those little packages of Advil they keep behind the counter.

You wake up in the morning. You're at a cabin by a lake. You look at yourself in the mirror. Wipe away what you see. Shave. The blade's a little dull so you switch it. The new one cuts. The bleeding stops. You're ready to piss so you do. Then you throw on some shorts and head through the screen door and down to the lake. The little cedar seed cones stick to the bottoms of your feet. You walk out to the end of the dock, you test the cold first, and you jump in.

Only you don't swim.

You never learned how.

You suddenly remember that you can't swim.

But it's too late, it's all over.

The driver of the Jeep is an off-duty OPP Officer.

Well then.

24.

MAYBE I'LL STOP

You set fire to one house and right away people start to judge. Lots of people judged Mel, before and after. You judged her too, I bet. I judged her too but I'm married to her and it was my house so you know what?

Fuck you.

A different life might be simpler. But I'm not having a different life. I'm having this one. In this one things like this happen: people blow themselves up right in front of you, your ex-wife tries to burn down your house, your son dies in your arms, and an off-fucking-duty fucking OPP fucking officer picks you up off the fucking highway against all the fucking odds. I mean how many fucking people are driving their fucking cars around the Montreal area today and we get this fucking hump. You know I'm looking for something. But Columbus, he was looking for something too. And he didn't find it, what he found was Cuba and, nice as that is, it's not what he thought it was and anyway he right away started fucking it over. Right now I'm looking for a cigarette or a drink and right now what I've found is an off-duty OPP officer. Maybe I'm looking for more than a smoke and a drink. Doesn't matter, what I've found, what we've found, what has found us is this shrub who, he's a happy enough fuck I'll give you that, but he's way too much of an adult, if you know what I mean. He's wearing a tie. I've never been good news-ed by anybody wearing a tie; nobody wearing a tie has ever done me any good. This guy seems very grown up. I've never met that many adults that I could call really grown up. And the ones I have met I wish I hadn't. This guy seems very serious, but happy too. A little too happy for this time of the morning for my liking. I don't get him, but I do know an OPP officer is not our best bet for a chauffeur at the moment. I could use a better breakfast than cheese crackers and I could use a drink. I feel like a Caesar with celery and horseradish and ...I don't know what else right now but, not this guy. I don't want this guy. He's got a too-trim mustache and cheek skin that looks like bubble gum and ham but he's got the Jeep right now and we don't, not us, so...

"Where you folks headed?"

Fuck off.

"Montreal."

"Got business there?"

Fuck off.

"Meeting my dad."

"Oh yeah?"

Fuck off.

He's eyeing Lisa in the back now where she's crunched up like an accordion, there's not a lot of room in the back of a Jeep. She has her legs right up and her tights are stretched to the breaking point. At least she's warmer now.

"You okay back there? Look a little crowded."

"Oh, I'm fine."

Fuck off.

Fuck off Fuck off Fuck off Fuck off Fuck off Fuck off

Fuck off Fuck off Fuck off Fuck off you and your moustache just both of you Fuck right off.

"You on your way into work, are you, officer?"

And that's when things got a little weird. And they stayed weird for a while.

"Did you know the driver was a police officer, Sir?"

"Does that make a difference?"

"For the purposes of this inquiry, yes Sir, it does."

"How long is this going to take?"

"Would you like a coffee?"

"Can I take it to go?"

"Well, technically, you're not actually being held."

"So I can go?"

"Just a few more questions. Were you aware he was a police officer?"

"Well, the uniform, yeah."

"Just a few more questions."

All my life nothing but nine-inch nails and me with no hammer.

"Would one of those questions aim to settle why your boy had his hand on my girlfriend's ass?"

"Yes Sir, that, and why his service weapon was discharged, yes Sir."

"Well, those two things are related."

"Yes?"

"How about that coffee?"

"Yes Sir."

"And you can stop calling me sir. It's making me jumpy."

"Okay."

"I'm not going to sue you and I'm not going to the media, I just want to get to Schwartz's Deli."

"Why?"

"I'm hungry."

"I don't believe anyone mentioned the possibility of a lawsuit."

"I did. I did just now. That was me."

"We could get some sandwiches...some doughnuts?"

"Kinda wanted some Montreal smoked meat."

"We could perhaps..."

"In Montreal."

"Oh."

"And a pickle."

"Right."

This guy folds too easy. I'm feeling like Popeye. He's in a position to show some sack, mostly due to his uniform, and the private room, but he's all oatmeal south of the belt and I'm all spinach and anchor tattoos. If I was him I'd turn out these fluorescents and take my face to blood town against this table but I guess that wouldn't be a good career move for him. And it seems to me this is not your Wednesday morning day-shift report writer. This is some guy called in special to make problems go away. After all it was his man all cracked up or tequilla'd up first thing in the morning and picked up some shitheel and his girl by the side of the road because he wanted to play some grab-ass. When my fist explained to him that he couldn't just do that I guess he lost control of the Jeep on some black ice and when both hands slipped from the wheel to form a cup for everything that was suddenly spitting out of his head from his nose that's when we jumped the ditch. I'm not sure what happened with him next, I lost track of him while I was trying to get to the back seat to Lisa because, well, you know. Really. I didn't need to lose anyone else. Only you can't move the way you want to or the way you think you can when every thing's sliding away under you, especially in a Jeep, and that's when the world stops making any fucking sense. Not going to happen again, I was thinking. I did seem to break her fall maybe, I got in her way I guess, anyway, and she was okay. Which is more than I can say for Officer Fuck who kicked open his door and left us there and staggered into the snow field and started shooting his sidearm into the sky.

"FuckFuckFuck," he was saying.

And he'd shoot a round on each syllable.

Fuck Bang Fuck Bang...I'm guessing that there were some pent-up issues there which the old home office knew all about because they certainly didn't give me the hard time I was expecting from them given the fact that I had no valid photo ID and I'd just cherry tomatoed the nose of one of their finest. When I knew Lisa was okay and after I'd counted off what I thought was four rounds I clotheslined the fucker with my right arm as he ran back past the Jeep toward the highway. If he had two rounds left I wasn't giving him time to squeeze them off into us. My life has not turned out the way I thought it would. But it wasn't going to finish in a snow bank outside Alexandria. If I'm going to be honest, it was Lisa's life that wasn't going to end there. I still didn't care all that much about mine. Not right then.

"Did you notice anything unusual about him?"

"Aside from the broken nose?"

"Yes."

"And the crazy?"

"Yes."

"No."

No. He was just your average zooed-out, coked-up copper on a rampage. Well. Off a rampage now that he was unconscious. Lisa climbed out of the Jeep and stood next to me looking down at him. He looked quite rested with the snow all around his head, now that he'd stopped improperly discharging his sidearm. He looked very peaceful. Even though his moustache and mouth were caked with red. He looked like he felt better about things. Lisa took my hand.

"My hero," she said.

"Now, now."

Well, so, big temptation to flee the scene right then and there. But there's a big difference between cold-cocking a police officer who may have been trying to murder you and your lady friend and leaving him there in the snow to die. Evidence in our favour: four shots fired, blood alcohol test, he drove the fucking Jeep into a field, he grabbed my lady friend's ass. Evidence against: in spite of the fact that we might present as an almost perfectly respectable couple, we were just thrown off a VIA train for almost-public copulation, pretty public if you count the sounds. And the recent armed robbery and then the death-by-explosive misadventure. When you added it up it didn't sound so good for anyone really. However, there was no link to Johnny being in pieces and the cops didn't even know about that, or any connection to the robbery or even speculation that the robbery was an inside job so no connection to me at all. Really, they wouldn't even know about the train-fucking so...on balance it looked much worse for Officer Fuckshow than it did for us. Me: an innocent bystander. But we definitely couldn't leave him to freeze, though surely someone would arrive soon to check the vehicle. You don't just drive by something like that. Of course by the time someone found Fuckshow in the snow we'd still be walking down the side of the road. Excuse me you two, were you aware there was a police officer dying back there? Where did you say you were going?

Well fuck it, none of that mattered anyway because by the time I got finished thinking it there was already a car and a pickup pulled over and two guys picking their way through the snow towards us.

"Anybody hurt?"

"You better call it in," I said.

"Officer down," I added, mostly because I had always wanted to say that. And how often are you going to get the chance?

"Did he at any point say anything regarding active cases?"

"No."

"Or evidence of any kind?"

Enough.

"Look, I'm sorry Officer Shit the Bed is having a bad day, week, month, life, and I guess I'm even sorry about his nose but my lady friend and I have to be in Montreal before dinner and it's really quite important and you're going to get us there pronto or this is going right from my girl's cell phone to YouTube and that tweeting thing, capiche?"

Well, when will I ever get the chance to say pronto or capiche again? Capiche is the kind of thing you can say only in a bad movie or a small, white room smelling of pit sweat and bad coffee. And I don't plan to find myself in either one for the foreseeable future.

"That can be arranged."

"Okay then, Schwartz's on St. Laurent, and make it snappy."

Again, when else? Snappy's not a word you can throw around anytime you want. The time has to be right.

"And my friend and I need some coffee for the trip, and not from any of the shitpot crapcookers you've got boiling around here."

Octane it up. Time is passing and so is Otis if he has anything to say about it. If he's going down in a hail of pastrami I plan to be there. Giddyup. I'm off like a fuck.

St. Laurent is busy in the middle of the day and there's no parking anywhere so it helps if you're dropped off by a police car with its lights on that can just stop anywhere in traffic. Everyone in the line for Schwartz's looks up to see who's getting arrested and they look disappointed when all that happens is that me and Lisa get out of the back of the cruiser. It started snowing heavy on the way and everyone in line looks like they're thinking, *All I want is some fucking pastrami and what do I get? More snow.* I have to get better at life. Maybe I'll stop drinking. But then who would Gerry drink with? Things aren't so bad. Bastard is not just going to just die after polishing off a pastrami on rye and a cherry Coke. You can't just decide to die when you want to unless you've got a gun. And that's when it occurs to me that maybe he does. Then I think of that scene in *The Godfather* when Pacino shoots that guy in the head in that little Italian restaurant after he gets the gun

Clemenza hid for him in the bathroom. But I've got Otis's gun at home. He's not going to shoot himself in a deli. He's not that kind of guy. Maybe I'll just get rid of the gun. Hand it in or something. Pacino shoots Sollozzo first, then shoots the cop in the throat and the forehead. It's a pretty grim scene. I've seen *The Godfather* a lot of times. *Leave the gun. Take the cannoli.* It's a good movie. Pacino's really nervous before the hit and there's this sound of the elevated train, it gets louder and louder and blocks out everything like it's going through his own head. You oughtta see it if you haven't. I'm not saying I'll get rid of the gun for sure, who knows? But it's weird to be thinking I might. I like it.

That feeling of I just can't do this anymore, I forgot to have it at some point. And things matter. Again. Think back to when it hurt too much to get out of bed. Or to stay in bed. There was no way to go away from it. And now I'm looking forward to lunch. So I know I said I didn't care that much about my own life, but a nice crispy kosher dill pickle. That would be good. And I'm looking forward to it. The snow is really coming down now.

The little boy walks into the bedroom. It's morning. It's hot already though, hot enough that he's just wearing underwear. The bedroom is all yellow light and shade. His parents are asleep in the bed. He barely looks at them, knows they won't be awake for hours yet. He pushes his hands against the cool mirror of the sliding closet door and slides it open, careful not to make too much noise even though he knows it would take a considerable amount to make any difference here. He kneels down carefully as if at an altar. Looks behind himself to the bed. Looks back to the closet floor, moves some clothes aside and pulls out a paper bag. He sits with the bag in his lap in the sun for a moment, just looking, his hands resting on the paper. Eventually he reaches into the bag and slowly pulls out the heavy handle of a handgun.

"Jake?"

I woke up right then and I quietly said his name. So maybe I saved him that time. Something could have happened, you hear about that shit all the time.

Yeah, though I walk.

But you can't talk your way out of a burning house. That was one time I got lucky and that's all it is. And when he died I didn't. And that matters and that's why I couldn't get out of bed for such a long time. But I just feel pretty good right now. Just right now I like these big flakes of snow falling as if little girls are cutting them out from white paper with safety scissors and letting them drop. I like the feel of Lisa's hand and her leg touching mine as we stand in line. But. Sometimes when you feel like you're walking on water it's just because somebody pissed in your shoes. Do you know what I mean? There's a guy in a blue toque throwing up in the alley. I didn't always stock shelves at the grocery store. I didn't always do a lot of things, but I do them now. Gerry got me the job. It was obvious I was never going back to the old job. Stacking up cans with the labels to the front was good for me. Is good for me. I like it.

That guy throwing up is pushin' it up like a sailor after shore leave.

"He's been at that a while," Lisa says.

"He's gonna crack a rib," I say.

Though I can appreciate that pastrami and fries with a cherry Coke is one of the best ways to cure a hangover it looks like it's too late for this guy. Puke is hanging in shining snakes from his lips to the snow and slush below and he's into the dry heaves now with the odd spit and wipe and he leans over with his hands on his knees for one more grim try, kind of like he's praying. It's kind of like watching porn, a mix of excitement and disgust. Only without the excitement part. If this guy keeps losing his breakfast I'm going to lose my appetite although it's pretty strong after having had just some cheese crackers all day. Big stack of creamy pork fat would still do me some good.

"There they are," Lisa says.

25.

I LOVE YOU HONEY BUT SOMETIMES YOU GOTTA SHUT UP

Baby races.

There's two of us couples. There's me and Mel, there's Steve and I think his wife's name was Sherri and that's why we called her Cherry, anyway, we called her Cherry, and there was Candice and she didn't have anyone but she had a baby so she was there, and we had this thing, we'd get together every Friday and have a few drinks and we'd race our babies across the kitchen floor. Bottles or baby food or plastic clowns at one end of the room. Played it as a drinking game mostly. Jakey was usually first across the line and everybody else had to drink. We drank too. He loved those clowns.

No. That never happened. Except the drinking part. I saw the game in a movie once. It could have though, except we didn't know any other couples. Something that did happen was this:

Mel and I are downtown, and we're drinking. We're walking from the bar after it closes and we end up down this alley and my hands are down her pants and this big guy is there with us and I'm like, what the hell buddy can I help you with something? I got my hands down my girl's pants here. And he's just staring and he's got these grey looking eyes staring down at us and he just says, "You got some money, Mister?" This is a big guy now, he's at least six four maybe more and he's gotta be two-fifty and change and nor-

mally I'd just give him the Big Wall of Fuck, you know like, "I'd really like to help you buddy but the sad fucking thing is I really just don't give a fucking fuck about you, I don't fucking care if you're fucking hungry, I fucking don't fucking care if you've got no fucking money, I fucking don't fucking care if you've fucking got no fucking place to fucking sleep and I fucking sure as fuck don't fucking care if you fucking had a fucking sad fucking childhood and your fucking mom didn't fucking love you e-fucking-nough to fucking suit you the fucking thing is none of your fucking fucking fucked up fuck of a fucking life is any of my fucking con-fucking-cern so fuck yourself off you fucker," except before I start in with it he takes a gun out of his pocket and he's pointing it at us. That many fucks in a sentence usually just wears people down and they get confused and they don't know what to do anymore. I saw one guy start to cry when he got the Wall of Fuck thrown at him. No kidding. But he didn't have a fucking gun. So I hold my fucks and I move Mel behind me slowly with one hand and I just stare him down. I stare him down like a Grade 5 stare contest at recess behind the soccer nets. Only with a gun. I give him a good old dose of the old eye-to-eye right there. The stink eye. I don't blink and I slowly reach into my pocket and I pull it back out slowly just like they do in the movies so he can see it's not a knife or a gun or anything and I hold up the twenty and I say, "Take this and go away" and I don't stop staring him down and he doesn't stop either and then he licks his lips and that's when I know I've got him and he takes the twenty and he lowers the gun and then he looks at the twenty and the gun starts coming back up and I say, "No. That's all there is. Now listen to me, you're going to walk away with the twenty and I'm going to take my girl home." And he looks at me and he just nods and he shuffles off down the alley. Sometimes everyone wins.

But then it doesn't last.

"My girlfriend's going to jail," Lisa says, putting away her cell phone.

Otis is trying to get the attention of the waiter. He wants some ketchup.

"These boys eat mayonnaise and vinegar with their fries," he says. "There's no goddamn ketchup on the table. And that ain't right. Hey, *Garçon!*"

"I don't think they like to be called garçon Otis," Gerry says, which is an unusually sensitive observation for Gerry.

"What?" I ask.

"It's a French thing, I'm just guessing, but I don't think they're gonna go for any of that garçon *merde*."

"No, I mean 'My girlfriend's going to jail,' what?"

"Her boyfriend was killed," Lisa explains.

"How?"

"Waffles."

"What?"

Otis will not be distracted. "I just want some ketchup. Hey! *La sauce tomate! Bonjour!*"

"I don't think they have waffles here."

"No. He was killed by waffles."

"Food poisoning?"

"*Hey!*"

"No. Well, actually it was the wanting the waffles, is what killed him."

"*Garçon!*"

"I don't think he's gonna come over here if you keep yelling that at him *en Française* Otie."

"I'll yell any goddamn *mot* I want to. *Ici!*"

"See, he really wanted some waffles."

"So?"

"Or he might come over here Otie but it won't be for the purpose of bringing you any ketchup."

"So she didn't want to make him any waffles, so she told him 'I ain't making you any fucking waffles,' that's what she told him."

"Fair enough."

"He didn't think so though, so he says 'I want waffles you stupid bitch,' and she didn't like that."

"Sure."

"I gotta get my own fucking ketchup *ici*? Is that it?"

"Plus the night before he gave her a black eye."

"Why?"

"Why? Because he was a fucking asshole, aren't you listening?"

"Hey! *Mon ami!*"

"Otis."

"What?"

"Don't try to talk French."

"Don't you get it? He called her a bitch because she wouldn't make him any waffles...but that was after he hit her."

"I get that."

"So?"

"So how did he die?"

"He was in the bathtub. He's calling into the kitchen *'Where's my waffles?'* So she plugs the waffle iron into an extension cord and she walks it into the bathroom. She stands there in the door and she says *'You want some waffles?'* He says, *'Yeah, I want some fucking waffles!'* So she throws the waffle iron into the tub and she says *'Make your own.'*"

"And that killed him?"

"No."

"No?"

"*S'il vous plait? Monsieur?*"

"No. But I guess it should have. But shit like that only works in movies. It fried him a little though. The waffle iron just shorted out and he came roaring out of the bathtub with some pretty bad burns."

"So then what happened?"

"He chases her back into the kitchen and he's naked and wet and he slips on the linoleum and he goes down hard."

"And that's what killed him?"

"No. That just knocked him cold. It was the butcher knife in his throat that killed him."

"So she's going to jail? But wasn't she just defending herself?"

"It went into his throat thirty-seven times."

"That's a hell of a defense."

"Well, I guess she was pissed."

"*Merde.* These crap wagons are ignoring me. How'm I supposed to eat my fries with no ketchup?"

"You want some ketchup Otis?" I ask him.

"What the hell have I been saying?"

So I get up and walk over to the main counter and I say to the guy standing there in the oily T-shirt.

"My father...he would like some ketchup..."

Only I give him the eyeball that says *I will go after both your kneecaps with a ball-peen hammer out in the alley if it's not on the table on this side of two minutes,* and says it in both official languages.

"*Bien sûr, Monsieur,*" Jimmy says and he carries a bottle of Heinz over to the table.

"Now how'd you get that loser boat to do that?" Otis asks.

"He knew I might actually punch him in the throat. It's as simple as that."

People, mostly, the ones who haven't died, or come close, or been next door to it, don't have this all-the-time feeling that it's right down the street waiting, that it's right in the car next to you, in the next bastard you meet, or around the next corner you turn, in the middle of the night or in the too bright of the day. It's always just waiting. Always there right next to you when you're just busy being alive. You're making your peanut butter sandwich and there's a blood clot bullet heading right for your brain. Driving down the road and there's a drunken axe flying at you behind the wheel of another car. Everywhereallthetimeeverywhereandallofthetime. A lot of people don't let that in. Or they haven't been reminded lately, or at all yet. Happens to all of us and lots of people don't see it lurching towards them ever, until there it is. Oh hi, it's you. Everyone you know, everyone you love, everyone you've ever met, everyone on the fucking planet will be dead in a hundred years. Most of them in a lot less than that. Nobody who's here now will be left then. There's a regular turnover around here. Time to look snappy. Be about your business. That's what I say. At least today. Right now I do, I say it now. Everyone you can see right now in this restaurant is going to die. But by all means have another nap. Watch some television. Play some Bejewelled Blitz on your goddamn fucking cellular phone.

Tick tick tick tick toc. We all know it on some level. Otis seems pretty damned certain about it in his own case. And now that he's got his order of fries and his little cardboard boat of ketchup he almost seems smug about it. Finish off this pickle. Die. That's his plan.

"You still planning on kicking out when this meal is done?" I ask him. "I mean, you're looking pretty healthy right now..."

Otis dips a fry into the little mountain of ketchup he has created.

"Don't you think," Otis says, popping the fry into his mouth, "...that the soaking wet bastard Lisa was just talking about looked perfectly healthy before he had his kitchen floor bleed out?"

He wipes his mouth with a paper napkin.

"I mean healthy looking don't mean shit," he says.

He reaches for his cherry Coke.

"Before I go though," he says, "I do have one last piece of advice for you..."

He draws it out like he's polishing up a jewel. He lets the straw pop out of his mouth with a smack and he wipes his hands on his knees.

"Never fight in a basement," he says.

"That's it?"

"Whaddya mean? That's some good fucking advice. There's no doors in a basement. Nowhere to go when the tables turn. You end up on the ass end of a fight, you do not want to be climbing up a set of stairs on your knees followed by some bastard with your name tattooed on his kill switch, believe you me."

And that being said he wipes his mouth again, crosses

his hands over his chest, and leans his head back with his eyes closed.

I look at Lisa. Lisa looks at Gerry. Gerry looks at me.

"Otis?"

It's hard to tell.

"Otis, you gonna finish those fries?" Gerry asks.

Nothing.

"Ever?"

We're waiting to find out if he's dead. It's unbelievable. Not that someone would die. This is just one big fucking waiting room after all. At the moment it's all dressed up to look like a Jewish deli with red-and-white paper place-mats and hand-painted signs on the walls. "Kosher Dills." But it's still a place to wait like everywhere else on the planet. When I was a kid there was this kid down the street I'd play street hockey and soccer with. His name was Bill and his dad's name was Bill. Bill Junior and Big Bill. In the garage attached to the Bills' house was a sign that had been hand-painted by Big Bill on a small sheet of tin. "LIFE IS TOO LONG TO LIVE LIKE THIS", it said. Right there next to the Texaco calendar. You can't go to a Texaco anymore because they don't have them. A lot of the people who worked for Texaco are now dead, like Big Bill, who lived up to the ambition in his sign. Bill Junior works as a forest ranger in British Columbia. Which is really just a waiting room made of trees. Once in a while I think of that sign and what made him take out some paint and a small brush one day and paint it. Was he a desperate man? Had he read it in a magazine somewhere and just liked the sound of it? Did he hate his wife? Did he cringe each time she walked into the garage to bother him? Did she serve him tuna fish sandwiches in red plastic baskets not knowing that he hated them and that he hated her? Did he look up into the sun breaking the leaves on a July day and think *God I just want out of here?* Or was it just a sign? Painted one day on a whim and left up there for someone to take down and sell in a garage sale one day when he was dead.

"How much for the sign?"

"That sign? What do you think?"

"A dollar?"

"Sure."

Time can be nasty. I wish we didn't have to do everything in order. Time is a bastard. While it's true there's no such thing as the past or the future, just the right now, it still seems like we're stuck with everything going along in a straight line. Hard to get unstuck. Time is a bitch.

"Otis?"

He opens his eyes and looks out of them at us.

When Otis does die I think I'll get drunk. It'd just be a reason to get drunk then though. But there's always been some reason. That's what addiction is. Or habit. Habit. Like I say, maybe I'll stop. Otis is ready to say something.

"I think that fucking smoked meat is givin' me the fuckin' heartburn," Otis says, rubbing at his chest, "...what're you all looking at?"

"We thought you were dead," I say.

"No." Otis looks around, "Anybody havin' dessert?"

Maybe some cheesecake would be good.

"I could use a shave," Otis says, rubbing the white stubble around his mouth, "...or a blow job."

I signal for the waiter.

"I think we could use some cheesecake or some pie maybe," I tell him.

"We have only coffee or tea," he says, "...and they're not very good really..."

"Just the blow job then," Otis says.

"You'd have better luck with coffee down the street — there's a Starbucks somewhere close..."

"Which way?"

"Either way."

"They have blow jobs over there?" Otis asks.

"They have lattes, Monsieur, and Frappuccinos as well as ketchup I imagine...and I'm sure blow jobs would not be a problem."

"Okay, let's go," Otis says, "These fucking skinbags can't even make cheesecake."

When I was about five my parents took me to the beach. I don't know what beach. There was sand. I've never been able to figure where it was, we didn't do things like going to the beach very often. Ever. At school my friends would talk about going to hockey games or to the drive-in. I'm not saying that I wasn't happy eating Swanson dinners and getting beers from the cooler for Otis and watching my mother smoke. I was. But I remember going to the beach because it was different from what we normally did. My mother made sandwiches and we stopped on the way and I could pick any flavour of chips I wanted which was salt and vinegar. After we had the sandwiches and chips my mother fell asleep on a towel with her sun hat over her eyes. I remember holding that hat up to my face and looking though all the little holes, each one a different small picture of the river and the trees. Otis started talking to some guys who had a fishing rod and were trying to catch bass by casting out from the beach. They had a case of beer and I knew I would have some time to myself so I went swimming.

I guess I was losing consciousness by the time I was aware of an arm around my chest and the feeling of rising. I had been staring down a long blue-and-black tunnel and now I was being torn back into the light and I was coughing and crying with the sun in my eyes and being pulled face up back into the world. I remember the warmth of the towel in the sun and Otis looking down at me blocking the blare of the sky and then moving back, falling onto his ass in the sand and crossing his arms on his knees. Pulling out a wet cigarette and trying to light it. Then giving up.

"Otis, what the hell are you doing?" My mother waking up.

"Nothing. I'm not doing anything."

Pulling out another cigarette and getting it lit.

My father has an old blue tattoo on his forearm. "RAGE." For years I thought it just represented his approach to the world, it just seemed to fit him. When I was in my twenties I found out it was a late-night drunk tattoo, I don't mean he was drunk when he got it, I mean the guy doing the tattoo was drunk, well, probably they both were. Anyway. I asked him about it one time and why he got it and he said the guy owed him some money and he decided to take it in ink instead. Because of the lettering the guy started colouring at the end of the word first but then passed out before he finished. It was supposed to say "COURAGE," but he passed out after the R.

I asked Otis why he never bothered to get it finished off.

"Never got around to it," he said, "Then over time…it just seemed to fit better this way."

Once when Jakey was about the same age as I was the day I almost drowned we were going to a movie in Ottawa with a friend of mine and his son. We took the highway into the city and it was February and someone had the idea of the boys riding in the back of the pickup. I'd look back once in a while and they seemed fine. Eventually they climbed under an old tarp that was back there. We had some beers up front and the radio on. Well by the time we got there they were blue and couldn't feel their arms or legs. We took them into a McDonald's bathroom and ran warm water on them. We had to block the door and we stayed in there doing that until the manager threatened to call the police. We couldn't take them back out in the cold until the truck warmed up so we just kept ordering hot chocolate while most of the people there stared at us. I remember the other kid threw up all over the back seat on the way home and that stain never came out. I can't say that I was the best dad.

I got by, for the most part.

You don't have to get me a fucking Father's Day card.

Relax.

26.

YOU'RE NOT GOING TO TELL ME I DON'T LOVE YA

"Listen, I'll tell you one thing about women. Maybe a couple of things about women. I was out at this bar once with your mother. It was us and some other couples, there was this crowd of people. This is before you were born, before we were married even. And there's this one guy he's got something goin' on in his pants for her and he knows she came in with me, right? And I go up to the bar and this corncob gets her cornered in a booth and he's gettin' all gropey with her, you know? And it wouldn't matter even if she even wanted him to get all gropey because she came in there with me. It's the principle. Anyway she doesn't want his paws anywhere near her and I get back with these two drinks in my hands and he's got his two hands on her legs and he's gettin' all gropey with her knees, like I said. She favoured short skirts at that time. And her eyes tell me that she'd like something done about this situation and like I say I'm gonna do something about it regardless, so I put the two drinks on the table and I say, 'Stand up,' and he says, 'Why?' and I say, 'Because I'm going to put you down' and I do. Now he's lying on the floor with fewer teeth than he came in with. Bastard probably couldn't have got it up without two chopsticks and some electrical tape, you know what I mean? But there was no part of him getting' up now. That's it. You hold on to what you want with your own two hands. They're gonna make you fight for it. And I'll tell you something else for nothin': no woman was ever the worse for knowing me. Some men yes. Maybe, I guess so, some of them. Him, for one. But no women."

I guess I learned all that I know about women from a man that learned all that he knew about women from Popeye. But he tells me this story and he just keeps looking at me to see if I got it. I got it. Those same eyes that watched everything I ever did just to see if I got it right.

"This girl she had her period, it was like raw liver coming out of her, you know? Like chocolate pudding and barbecue sauce mixed together..."

"Oh my God Otis, could you possibly somehow just fucking shut fucking up?"

"Don't be lippy."

"Lippy? Me? Nobody wants to hear their father talk like that. Nobody wants to hear their boyfriend's father talk like that either. Nobody wants to hear anybody talk like that...what the hell is wrong with you?"

"Me? What's wrong with them?"

"*Boyfriend?*" Lisa asks.

"Actually, I don't mind it at all..." Gerry says.

"Whaddya mean *boyfriend*? Like, what? Are we going steady or something?"

"Well I doubt the other people on the train want to hear it."

"Aah, they don't care. They've got their own little shitty lives to worry about."

"I find it pretty interesting actually, go on Otis..."

"I mean, if you're going to ask me to the prom or something...I'm going to have to buy a fucking dress."

She's pissed. I don't know why she's pissed and I'm not interested right now.

"It smelled like vinegar."

"Fuck. If you don't keep quiet I'm going to set you on fire."

"Listen, you never mind, if you two crap wagons don't get your asses kicked off the train this time maybe we can just have a nice meal and a glass of wine, you know?"

"Yeah, because you're all about the fine dining."

"I'm sorry about the crap wagons remark Lisa…I really just meant him, not you."

"S'alright."

"Fuck."

"You need to relax some son. When they bring around the hot towels you should just lay yours across the bridge of your nose…"

"What?"

"It's very relaxing. You should try it."

"Who the fuck are you all of a sudden? I don't know who the fuck you are. Fine dining and relaxation techniques? I'd rather have the liver and barbecue story back."

"Whatever you want crow bark."

"Fuck."

Gerry can't stop laughing, he's shaking his head and looking out the window.

"You having a good time?" I ask him.

"I mean I can play it however you want," Otis keeps on, "I'll just play it as it lays…"

"How about if you just don't play it at all for once? Eh? Otis? Fuck. How about for once if you just go back to the fucking clubhouse and put the clubs away for the first time in your fucking life? And don't play it. How about that?"

"I don't see that happening," he says.

Then he says: "She was something though. When I was

around her I was like a one-eyed dog in a meat factory. I mean when she wasn't on the bleed-out."

"Fine."

"Fine what?"

"Fine, go ahead, tell your whole shitty story, just get it out of ya. Go ahead."

"Listen Sonny, you and I come out of the same Easter basket, don't forget that."

"Yeah."

"Yeah what?"

"Just...yeah. I thought you were going to die after you had the pastrami Otis, I thought that was the deal."

"Guess I changed my mind."

"Yeah?"

"Yeah."

"I mean are we engaged or something because no one ever told me anything about it," Lisa says.

Fuck.

I was standing outside a bar once having a smoke. Some little town. Middle of the day. Bright sun. Gerry comes running out.

"There's a guy in there..." he says like it's the second coming of Jesus or something.

"So?"

"Just nutsacked another guy and he's running around nutsacking everybody..."

"What'd you say to him?"

"Nothing. I didn't say anything. He's just crazy."

"You better get back in there then."

"Yeah."

And he does. He goes running back in, eyes all lit up.

Because he hates to miss shit like that. He just needed me to remind him of that. Who knows what makes you remember stuff at certain times?

And then Otis dies. Just like that. Well, not just yet, first we finish our dinners and Lisa's not pissed off at me anymore. I don't know why she was at first, and I don't know why she isn't anymore.

During dinner she stops chewing and she says, "A one-eyed dog in a meat factory...that's really sweet..."

And after dinner Lisa is asleep with her head on my shoulder and Otis is asleep with his head next to the window. And then he's dead. Just like that. And it's too late.

"What do you mean he's dead?"

"I mean, he's dead, like, as in, the opposite of alive," I say, trying to recline Otis's seat to make him look more natural.

"How do you know?" Gerry says, edging away from Otis.

"Lack of breathing mostly. Lisa?" I shake Lisa awake and she looks at me and then at Otis.

She kneels in front of Otis right away and she feels his neck and then his wrist. Then she looks at me again.

"Do you want me to try and..."

"No."

"You..."

"No."

She nods her head and sits back down.

"So what do we do?" Gerry asks.

In practical terms what do you do with a dead man on a train? I mean, there's the grieving process and everything but what do you actually do with him? Naturally you think of throwing him off the train but then you remember that you don't have to. You didn't kill him.

"We have to tell them," Lisa says.

"Why?"

"Because he's dead. You have to report a death. If he's dead we have to report it. It's just one of those things."

"One of what things?"

"One of the things that you have to do. I'm almost a nurse. I know what you have to do."

"You have to fix his head," Gerry says.

"What?"

"Fix his head, it's falling over. They're gonna know he's dead whether you tell them or not if you don't fix his head."

Gerry seems a little on edge like he doesn't like sitting next to a dead man. He's sliding as far away as he can. I reach over and slide Otis's head back to centre. He's already colder than a real person.

"Give me your sunglasses," I tell Lisa.

"These?"

"Those."

They're big with red frames but they cover his eyes, which is the point.

"That doesn't look right," Gerry says.

"It looks righter than empty staring eyes."

"I guess."

Otis is looking up at the ceiling through the red glasses. It looks okay. Maybe an aging flamboyantly gay man on holiday. And sleeping. Open mouth. And not dead.

"Still," Lisa says, " . . . we have to tell them."

"Why? It's not like they're doctors or the police, what

are they gonna do? Get him a napkin? Take him away in the food cart?"

"Well what are you going to do when we get to the station? Walk him out between you like *My Weekend at Bernie's*? Just tell them, it's not like you killed him or anything."

I look at Gerry. Gerry looks at me. We're both thinking the same thing. Armed robbery, explosive suicides, and the burning of human remains don't go together well with reporting a dead guy in a public place. At least I think he's thinking that, it's hard to tell with Gerry. He could be thinking about yogurt for all I know. I guess when your dad dies you're on your own in a way. People give advice. But you have to make the calls yourself.

"Poor Otis," Lisa says.

"Excuse me…miss?" I call out.

I'm trying to get the steward's attention. She's helping someone with their window curtain.

"Miss?"

"Just a minute sir…"

I'm five. I'm five years old and I'm on a train and I'm all alone. My dad's dead.

"My dad's dead…"

And I'm sad. But what the hell. The shit still goes on.

"…so I think there may be some paperwork or something. Maybe we have to move him? I don't know miss, I'm just telling you what happened."

She comes over and leans into our area.

"Are you saying…what are you saying?"

"I'm saying that guy, over there, that guy there next to the bald guy…"

Gerry smiles at her.

"…I'm saying that he's dead. He's just now passed away."

Gerry points toward Otis helpfully. Otis's head drifts to one side.

"He has died?" she says, kind of like she's confirming a food order. *You want the steak, not the fish?*

"That's it exactly."

She nods.

"We didn't bring him on this way." I point out, "It just happened."

"It's an ongoing situation," Gerry adds.

"It just happened. Just happened now."

It's like we're sitting there with our laps full of guns and knives and ropes, at least that's how it feels. Like we've got an open safe and a crowbar. I can feel the sweat starting. There's no reason for it. Well, there is, but it has nothing to do with Otis. Like Lisa says it's not like we killed him, unless he had a heart attack due to the pastrami, which, now that I think about it, could probably be true. But this is pretty much the way he wanted it, so, there's just no reason to be sweating it out.

"Are you sure, um, that he's…"

"I'm almost a nurse," Lisa says, "and…yeah, yeah he's dead."

"Okay."

This whole reporting to the steward thing is not going that well. She doesn't seem to have any idea what to do next. I don't blame her. I mean it's not like someone lost a suitcase or needs some water.

"Okay. I'll take care of it," she says and she moves off down the aisle.

"I was going to ask her for a drink," Gerry says. "I'm sorry about Otis," he adds, "He was a good guy. But I could really use a drink."

"Yeah."

"Yeah. I'm gonna miss him."

I don't know how you're supposed to feel. It was different with Jakey. This is different than that. Lisa holds my hand. I look out the window and then I look back at Otis.

"It's alright," I say, more like I'm telling Otis than anyone else, like I'm telling Otis, "...it's okay."

Okay.

It's what he wanted. This is what he wanted to happen. He wanted this. We just let the dead guy sleep. My old man.

27.

HOW MUCH IS THAT DOGGY?

*help help help help help help help help help help help help help help
help help help help help help help help help help help help help help
help help help help help help help help help help help help help help
help help help help help help help help help help help help help help
help help help help help help help help help help help help help help
help help help help help help help help help help help help help help
help help help help help help help help help help help help help help
help help help help help help help help help help help help help help
help help me, can you please?*

Help me?

I guess I never did.

But now is not the time for recrimination. Gerry's hands
are drumming on the steering wheel.

"It's simple," he says, "...we just go in there, well, I go
in there, and I pick up the package. It's just like it's any
other day. It could be a car part, it could be a cookbook,
could be a pair of fucking oven mitts, it could be anything."

He stops drumming.

"Sure," I say, trying to be helpful.

"There's no reason for them to think it's a box full of
stolen money...no reason at all."

"No."

We're parked outside the post office. It's three weeks since Otis died. Twenty-six days since Gerry mailed the money to himself. The post office holds packages for thirty days since the day they receive them so there's lots of time but we also thought it would be good just to get the pickup out of the way. Everyone seems to have lost interest in the robbery now. There's still word that a Wal-Mart is coming to town and there's even a billboard up on the highway so everyone's talking about that now instead. Everyone's forgotten. Ray's having kittens that the Wal-Mart is going to end up shutting him down, which it probably will.

The three of us went to see the burial. It wasn't really a funeral because Otis didn't want a funeral, just wanted "to be planted" so we just went to see him put in the ground and make sure that it got done. Lisa brought egg salad sandwiches and we ate them in the car after with some beers, watching the freezing rain come down over the fresh dirt.

"Think he knows we're here?" Gerry asked.

I turned on the windshield wipers.

Lisa raised her beer toward the grave, touched the windshield with it.

"I knew this guy," Otis told me once, "...was in the Vietnam War. American guy. Saw a lot of shit. That was a brutal fucking war. I mean, they all are I guess...he saw a buddy of his skinned alive, no shit, and he said at one point, after he was almost home free but he was still fighting, you know, still up at the front, he was a week or two away from getting on the plane home I guess, and he said he started to get this feeling like maybe he'd make it, maybe make it all the way back home alive. Only problem he says, every other fucker felt that same way, and most of them got bullets."

"Yeah," I said.

"That guy had a cock like a fucking baguette."

You never knew where you were going with my father. But it was always somewhere and here in the car is where we ended up. Well, me in the car, him in the ground.

"Did we bring any pickles?" Gerry asked.

"I didn't bring any pickles," Lisa said.

"No?"

"No. So unless one of you boys brought pickles, then no, we didn't bring any fucking pickles."

"I just felt like a pickle."

"Guess you're outta luck then, Corncob."

Lisa rolled down her window and spit at the ground. And this is really why I love her. If she drowned in a swimming pool I'd really miss her. I might ask her to marry me. Because that's always gone well before.

But I might do it anyway.

"Let's go," Gerry says, "I'll go to the counter, you pretend that you're looking at some stamps or something."

"Why would I be looking at stamps?"

"Maybe you have a collection."

"There's no way I have a collection."

"To me you look like a guy who could have a collection."

"Well, if I have a collection how come I'm looking at new stamps?"

"I don't know, maybe there's some new releases you want to pick up."

"Stamp collections are about old stamps, not new ones. I want to be convincing. If I'm going to do this I want to look good."

"My fist is something around which your face would look good."

"You're an angry man."

"Crawl back into your fucking hole."

"And tense, you're a tense man."

"I mailed stolen funds to myself through a branch of the federal government and now I'm picking them up. Yeah, I'm a little tense."

"Why'd you do that again?"

Gerry squints, peering into the window of the post office.

"Seemed like a good idea."

"As opposed to hiding it under your bed?"

"That's a lousy place to put it."

"The federal government being better?"

"Anybody'd look under the bed."

"Under the floorboards then. In the ceiling. Bury it in the backyard."

"Decision had to be made. I made it. You know God's going to judge you someday for all your negative shit."

"Probably."

"He's gonna go through you like a canon."

"Maybe."

"It'll be like a building falling on you."

"Wouldn't be surprised."

"Let's go."

One time Mel was sick, hungover and sick and she had a broken ankle, so she said, "get me a glass of water could you, just a glass of water?" and I made like I couldn't hear her and I went out.

We walk up to the post office together like it's in slow motion, like there's a camera moving slow with us.

I remember being drunk once and watching Jakey and watching golf on television and falling asleep and then finding him out on the lawn near the road.

We're tilting into the camera like it's a bank robbery we're on, both of us in lockstep. Gerry opens the door, the sun glints off the glass and into the lens.

I kicked at her once. It was the only time I hit her in any way and she was unconscious just like I would be soon and the kick didn't really connect. But there she was on the kitchen floor. And there was my foot, swinging towards her ass. Then I fell.

I have my sunglasses on. My hands in my pockets. We couldn't look more suspicious really.

I remember her screaming at me from across the room another time, everything I could see flipping like film that's stuck in the projector, up and again, up and again. "I'm not going on living like this." "I cannot go on like this." She's screaming. Monster trucks on the TV. Passing out.

Gerry's at the counter. I'm looking at the posters on the wall. "What kind of postal service will *YOU NEED* in the future? We're looking for *YOUR FEEDBACK*."

I'm face down on the couch. Jakey wants to go outside and play. I can't move, the rough of the fabric against my lips. "Daddy you want to play outside? Go outside?"

Cartoon mailbox there with a smile and raised eyebrows. "We're looking for *YOUR FEEDBACK*." At first Gerry's voice is low and soft, polite. Then it gets a little edge to it, then it's louder.

I can't get up off the couch. Nothing will be able to get me up off this couch.

"WHAT DO YOU MEAN YOU CAN'T FIND THE FUCKING PACKAGE?"

And then Jakey's dead. And then he's dead.

"There's no need to take that tone sir."

"THERE MOST CERTAINLY FUCKING IS."

And I'm right there at Gerry's shoulder.

"My friend here...he's a little on edge Ma'am. He's just ...well, he just lost his dog."

"I do *not* have to listen to that abusive language and I *will* ask you to leave."

"I understand. That's very understandable. They were very close. The dog. And him. They were very close."

The post office lady looks from Gerry to me and then back to Gerry again. Gerry's like a figure in a wax museum, he's frozen in place and leaning slightly over the counter with his hands flat, his face and neck red. It's like the movie he's in has stopped and the movie the postal lady and I are in is still going.

"The dog was run over," I say.

She's still looking at Gerry.

"By a train," I add.

She looks back at me.

"What was the dog doing on the tracks?" She asks.

Right.

"It was tied there. Somebody tied his dog to the train tracks."

"What?"

"This is it. This is what has him so upset. He's normally a very nice man."

"Someone tied his dog to the train tracks?"

"That's right. There are sick, sick people sometimes, around...you just don't know what they'll do."

Gerry has turned to look at me but he's still not saying anything and he's still a little red, it's like he's stuck. He's like a tape cassette that's stuck. For a moment I think he's trying to remember if he really has a dog and whether someone tied it to the tracks.

"But who would do something like that?" The lady asks.

"This is it. This is the thing. The police are making their investigations."

"This happened around here?"

"They're questioning people. Yes, Ma'am. Around here. They're trying to keep it quiet. So as not to alarm people..."

"Well people should know..."

"And not to, you know, jeopardize the investigation."

She's looking at Gerry now like she's going to cry. Like she understands and how would she feel if someone had tied her dog to the tracks and left it there to be turned into a crêpe.

"They're real close," I say, "...to catching the guy, I mean. So they don't want to, you know, jeopardize anything. Like I say."

She puts her hand over Gerry's on the counter.

"Or girl," I say "...if it's a girl..."

"No woman would ever do something like that."

"No. No, it's probably a guy. Just like you say."

She keeps looking at Gerry like she wants to take him home and wrap him in a blanket.

"I'll have another look for your package, Sir."

She goes into the back room again and Gerry starts to relax. His fingers come loose from the counter. He looks back at me. I just look back at him and I put my finger to my lips.

"Here we are..." she sings out in a little musical voice and she comes back in waving the box like it's the prize turkey in the Thanksgiving Day Parade.

"It was sorted in 'Current' instead of in 'Hold'," she says like that explains everything that's ever gone wrong in the world and she takes the little claim card from the counter and hands Gerry the package.

"Thanks," Gerry says.

"Thanks," I say.

And we head for the door.

"What was your poor dog's name?" The lady asks just as we're about to step out.

"Ma'am?"

"Well, what was your little dog's name?"

"Socks."

We both say it at the same time.

The woman smiles.

28.

RAY CHARLES

Otis looked like a marine. He had a head that looked like it was shaped by hammering and burning. And polished like a nut. He never understood that he intimidated people just by being in the same room.

"What are these fuckers so nervous about?"

"You."

I had this dream where I brought the Jeep into this garage and the guy there offered to teach me how to spot weld. I never knew how to spot weld so I said sure, why not? So we were spot welding away and smoking and I saw my father walking down the street past the garage door in the sun. His bald head and his white NASCAR jacket that he got for free in some bar one time. I didn't call to him to say, "Hey! Look, I'm spot welding!" I just picked up my smoke and watched him keep walking down the street.

Bright, white and beautiful.

Always amazes me who women fall for. In my previous life as an almost successful writer of advertising copy (I don't think I mentioned that. Yeah. All in all though I prefer the grocery business. It relaxes me in a way that advertising never did. *"Jack Edwards Used Cars — When Only the Best Will Do."* That was mine. Also: *"Mary's Diner — Be$t Burger in a Country Mile,"* that dollar sign was my idea too. I had just started working on something on spec for Toyota Canada when Jakey died: *Toyota, ya oughta!* I wasn't done with that one, but after Jakey, I lost track of most things for, well, quite a while.) There was a woman at the office where I used to work with an amazing look to her and she left a husband and a six-month-old child for a cheese eater. I mean the kind of guy who'd eat grated cheese in bed. Amazing. Who knows why people do what they do?

I'm certainly not one to talk any kind of shit about wise choices in any aspect of my life or in anyone else's. But as a guy you could see this Piñata Pete coming from a mile off and it amazed me that she couldn't do that, couldn't see what would happen next. He's going to use you up and spit you out like a burnt sunflower seed I tell her in my head from across the office, but she listens to him talk his game and her panties are wet and hanging around her knees before the first down. They don't even make it away from the water cooler before his hands are down her pants. Heard her tell one of the other women, *I can't help it, he's my soul mate.* At the time she didn't know he was jamming it into quite a few other souls in that office. And everyone else knew about it. But she couldn't see any of that, she was busy frosting the wedding cake and picking out their living room curtains.

Sometimes I think of myself as lucky, but I know I'm not. Sometimes I think of myself as fucked up and fucked over, but I'm not really that either. What I am, and I know it may not seem like it, what I am is, and I know this for a fact, what I am is I'm naïve. I'm a bit of a ten-year-old kid and I always have been. Well, since I was ten anyway. Some women like that though. A ten-year-old boy who's good in bed. Wow, that sounds really wrong. A thirty-six-year-old man who's halfway good in bed and has a ten-year-old's appreciation and wonder about women. And a few little dark edges too. Some women like that. More of them seem to prefer the cheese eaters for some reason but there's no accounting for taste. Lisa likes me, this is what I'm talking about here, this is what has me kind of licked. I didn't think there was much left of me for some-one else to use. So this book is a love story, is what it is. This is a . . . no, that's not what this is at all. I don't know.

This is a story about two guys who end up in the same bar they started out in. Maybe they're slightly better off than they were at the start. Or maybe not. One has a girl-friend though. They both have a little extra cash, enough to order nachos whenever they want to without going through their pockets first. They're not dead, and that's something right there. And they're not arrested which is the quite surprising part.

"We're going to tear the burnt porch off the front of the house and rebuild it Gerry," I tell Gerry.

"We are?"

"Yep."

"Tonight?"

"No, not tonight."

"When?"

"Doesn't matter when Gerry, just, we're gonna do it and it's gonna be cathartic."

"How do you know?"

"Because it involves climbing up on the roof and rip-ping off burnt shingles with a claw hammer, how could something like that not be cathartic?"

"So what does that even mean?"

"What?"

"Cathartic."

"Relieving, cleansing..."

"Oh."

"What did you think it meant?"

"Cathartic. Like when they put a tube up your dick at the hospital."

"That's catheter."

"Oh."

"That's different."

"I'm glad we're not doing that."

Once I was driving to Smiths Falls and I saw this boat for sale by the side of the road, an older outboard, three wooden seats and an old Evinrude motor. They'd just set it there on the gravel and I guess there was no trailer for it and someone had tied it to the telephone pole. Why? Why would they do that? So it wouldn't get stolen? It's a rope. So it wouldn't float away? If I do manage to put this stuff into a book, I'm putting that in there somewhere. Little things like that. It's important to notice them. I'll fit it in somewhere. A boat tied to the telephone pole like it's a post in the middle of the fucking ocean. Like maybe there'll be a flood and if there is this fucking boat will be ready for it. There'll be room for everything in this book of mine. I'll call it *Shit House* because that's where my character spends most of his time, in the shithouse, in trouble, in this whirl of shit that he just about gets lost in. Then he ends up with the hot girl at the end. People like happy endings so I'll make it go that way in the end. They fucking love that shit. I'll make them get married, maybe. He just out and asks her and she says yes. It'll be great. I'll have to change a bit about the robbery and about Socks so people won't find out about that shit. So I'll change his name. Make him kill himself instead of what really happened. Or maybe I'll just publish the whole thing under another name, not my own. Nobody I know reads books much anyway. I'll find some writer down on his luck, or maybe one who's had a little success, who knows what he's doing, won some awards or something and I'll just give him the book and then he can publish the thing under his name and we'll split the profits.

Skin House. I'll call it *Skin House* maybe and people will buy it because they'll think it's about sex. I'll put some real sex in it too so they won't get disappointed. You gotta please the customer, that's what it's all about, whether you're cutting meat or writing ads or filling the milk case or writing books. I'll use real sex but the names and everything will be different so people won't get pissed off about it. I'll put something in it about the title meaning that all of this is temporary, that we're all just in these houses we've been given for a while. These ones made out of skin. Our bodies I mean, you see? I'll write it down much better for the book though, better than it sounds when I'm describing it now. I'm going to leave Gerry's name the same maybe, I can't think of a better name for him. I'll make him a butcher instead of what he is so no one will be sure for certain if it's really him or not. I don't know if it'll be a good book. I don't really care. It'll have sex and violence, people like a lot of that. I'll put in some of the funny stuff that Gerry says. People like a laugh. I won't say too much about myself so people won't recognize me as the author.

They'll think it's the other guy. Or maybe I will. I don't know. I can see myself sitting at home after we get the porch fixed up and writing it out on pads of paper. Or I'll have that writer over and we'll have sandwiches and coffee and we'll write like motherfuckers together. I'll be able to focus on it and I won't drink so much then. That'll be good for me, and Lisa will be happy about it too. Maybe they'll want to make a movie out of it. I'll write it in a way so that it would make a good movie just in case. Maybe I should get an agent. Big writers have agents. I'll get the biggest agent in the country. It'll be published by the best publisher too. Somebody who publishes edgy shit. Maybe I'll get a computer with my share of the money, I can't see writing all those words out by hand.

I looked it up, the basic first novel is around ninety thousand words. That seems like a lot. I don't know if I can write that many. Maybe I can. I will.

"Call Lisa," Gerry says, "...and get her ass down here. I want to talk to her about Ray Charles again. And let's get some more drinks."

So we do. I look around the bar. It feels like home. I watch the girl pouring the drafts out and walking toward the table. I call Lisa. So things are simple now and we're not going to get caught. We're fine. Things aren't as bad as they were before. Lisa sounds sleepy like I woke her up, but she says she's coming down anyway. And she says Gerry can fuck right off if he wants to argue about Ray Whoever the Fuck and all that old-timey music shit. She sounds good, she sounds like she's happy I called her, even though she was sleeping.

And the way the girl sets the drinks down on the table now feels like the beginning of something, and also now, somehow, like the end.

EPILOGUE

I looked it up on the new computer and this is what it said:

"An epilogue or epilog is a piece of writing at the end of a work of literature, usually used to bring closure to the work. It is presented from the perspective of within the story; when the author steps in and speaks indirectly to the reader, that is more properly considered an afterword. The opposite is a prologue — a piece of writing at the beginning of a work of literature or drama, usually used to open the story and capture interest. An epilogue is a final chapter at the end of a story that often serves to reveal the fates of the characters. Some epilogues may feature scenes only tangentially related to the subject of the story. They can be used to hint at a sequel or wrap up all the loose ends. They can occur at a significant period of time after the main plot has ended. In some cases, the epilogue has been used to allow the main character a chance to 'speak freely' and often to provide the basis for a sequel."

I looked up how to do an epilogue because I wanted to tell you about the M1911 and what happened with it and I forgot to put it in the book. After we got back from Montreal, and after we buried Otis and fixed the house, Gerry and I were watching TV and there was this guy on *Dr. Phil* talking about how people keep falling into the same patterns of behaviour even when they know it's bad for them to do that. He said this type of thing was often "generational" and that it was very hard to "get out of the loop."

I went to the closet and I took out the M1911 and I shot the hell out of the TV.

I remember coming around the corner from the hallway.

"Look out," I told Gerry and when he saw the gun he ducked.

The shots were really loud in the little room where I keep — where I kept — the TV.

There was smoke everywhere and what was left of the TV was sputtering sparks and there was like a little plastic bonfire there.

"What the hell did you do that for?" Gerry yelled, still ducking down and covering his ears.

"Well, no point in having a gun if you never use it." I said."

I ended up getting a big screen TV with my share of the money, one of those new ones where you can see every little hair and pore on some guy's face and every blade of grass when you watch golf. It's pretty nice.

Anyway. I just didn't want to leave you thinking that I used the gun any other way because I made such a big deal about it earlier on. Seventy-five thousand words. Close enough.

I'm still here. And I'm not going anywhere, for now.
And I'm thinking of maybe writing another book.
After they make the movie out of this one.
I'll call it *Skin House Two*.
It'll be big.

It'll be 31 flavours of fuck the fuck off.